Unhinged

JOY FOR DARKNESS

Unhinged, an Australian Beauty and the Beast

Published by Rhiza Connect,
An imprint of Rhiza Press
PO BOX 1519
Capalaba QLD 4157
Australia

Cover Design by Production Works
Layout by Rhiza Press

ISBN: 978-1-925563-24-5

National Library of Australia Cataloguing-in-Publication entry is available

AMANDA DEED

JOY FOR DARKNESS

rhiza connect

Dedication

To my very own "beast." Always and forever.

Acknowledgements

The journey to write Unhinged has been a long and challenging one and as such, recognition needs to be given to all my friends, family and church community who have supported me through the highs and lows of life over the past few years. No matter where I'm at, you always support and encourage me, keeping me pointed in the right direction. There are too many of you to mention, but you know who you are. Thank you!

Thanks also Rochelle and the team at Rhiza Press for helping make Unhinged the best it can be. I love the way you believe in and get behind us Aussie authors.

Lastly, but most importantly, thanks to Jesus, my strength in weakness, my inspiration in the desert, your mercy and grace never end. You are the air I breathe.

1

Serena tugged the curtains away from the window for the hundredth time that afternoon and peeked toward the street. Where was Papa? He should have been home by now. This voyage had only been a short trip up the coast, delivering a load of coal, unlike his usual lengthy visits to India.

Serena's stomach churned with worry. A heavy storm had rolled in from the bay, its thunder shaking foundations and rattling window panes. Had the ferocious weather delayed him? Was the schooner capsized somewhere, or smashed on the rocks? It was hard not to assume the worst.

'Where is he?'

She should focus on sweeping floors and scrubbing the stonework, but anxiety kept drawing her back to the front window. Serena dropped the curtain and turned away as Julianne strode into the small parlour. Her sisters had caught her watching for Papa several times already.

'Are you worried about Papa, Serena? Do you believe he is in trouble?'

Julianne's chin began trembling and Serena needed to halt her sister's fears, even though she suspected the same. 'Papa knows how to take care of himself. *Fate Lucinda* was likely blown off course. It's happened before. I surely needn't remind you how experienced he is both as a sailor and a merchantman?'

'I know. I know. I just cannot help but think. What if he were lost …?'

What if he were lost, indeed? Serena shook her head. 'No, Julianne. He'll be fine. He always is.'

Serena should take her own advice. And yet, in this case, a sense of foreboding filled her, as though her sixth sense wanted to tell her something, but Serena refused to speak that aloud.

'Where is Rachel?'

Her sister stared at her momentarily. 'I think she is experimenting with a new hairstyle. I can see what you're trying to do.'

Serena lowered her gaze to where the bristles of the broom met the wooden floor. How could Julianne not fret? They only had Papa left. If she were ever to have a life and family of her own, oh, the thought was too dreadful. He must come home. What if they soon found themselves orphans? As the oldest, Serena would become her sisters' sole carer. It had fallen on her to raise them both, since Mama had passed. At sixteen and fourteen, they were too young to marry. If Papa didn't return…

Serena shuddered, and she shook her head to free it of her growing concern. A better question to ask was why she allowed her imagination to carry her so far into an unknown future? She should trust that Providence had it in hand. Serena let out a deep sigh. 'I'm sorry, Julianne, but worrying will get us nowhere.'

'Then stop peeking out the window. You're making me nervous.'

True enough. Her constant checking held no magic to make Papa appear. 'Well, let's get this house cleaned before he comes home then, shall we?'

Julianne nodded, her eyes still wide with anxiety. 'I'm not sure what help I will be. My stomach is quivering.'

Serena held back a frustrated sigh. 'Why don't you dust the furniture and then come and help me with dinner.'

'Do you remember what happened last time I tried to cook?' Julianne twisted her hands together, drawing Serena's eyes to the burn scars that marked them.

'Can you at least peel the potatoes then?'

Julianne nodded again, with a shrug. 'All right. I'm not sure I can eat though. Not until Papa comes home.'

Dinner had long gone cold before Papa's shuffling steps were heard on the front porch. With great relief, Serena rushed to the front door, her sisters close on her heels, and flung it wide. 'Papa, we were so worried!' She threw herself into his arms.

Without a word, he wrapped his thick arms around her waist and held tight. 'Serena. My girl.'

Serena buried her face into his coat, his familiar smell of salty brine bringing relief. Finally, he released her to embrace Julianne and Rachel, but although he seemed happy to be home, fear creased his brow.

'What is it, Papa? What happened?'

'Yes, Papa, do tell us.' Rachel echoed, clinging to one of his arms.

Papa's gaze briefly landed on her before shifting over his shoulder. It was only then that Serena noticed another man standing in the shadows behind him. Papa fumbled with the hessian bag slung over his arm. 'You'd better come in.'

Serena gestured to her sisters to back away from the door. They stared in silence as the stranger stepped inside. Papa and the stranger both bore the signs of being caught in the storm—damp and bedraggled. The other man wore a dark scowl and grunted a greeting to them. Papa showed him into the parlour and asked the younger girls to prepare some tea.

'Serena, come with me.' Papa led her to his bedroom and dropped the hessian bag on his bed.

Usually when Papa returned from a trade journey he brought home a bag bulging with goods and gifts for his girls. Today the sack was limp and empty.

'What is all this about, Papa? And who is that gentleman in the parlour?'

The weary man sighed and sat heavily upon the bed. 'The storm blew us off course. We made it inside the heads and I thought we had escaped trouble, but we ran aground on a reef. I feared the schooner would break up and I called to abandon ship. We lowered the small boat and all eleven of us escaped. But the waves were so rough that some of us were thrown overboard.'

Serena clutched the fabric at her throat.

'How did you get to shore?'

'We weren't far from land to begin with. The waves carried me and dumped me on a beach. I knew not where I was precisely, and I was so very tired from trying to stay afloat. I still don't know if the other men made it safely. Neither do I know how badly damaged *Fate Lucinda* is.' Papa ran a hand through his sand-matted hair.

'You're safe now, that's all that matters.' Serena reached out and squeezed his rough and calloused hand. 'And never mind about the ship. We'll manage.'

Serena mentally counted the provisions remaining in the larder, knowing supplies were low, but she refused to allow him to see her doubt.

'Are you sure?' Papa pressed his lips into a grim line.

She nodded at her father, hoping she looked convincing.

Serena studied her father's face. The deep etches of angst still lined his forehead. 'There's more, isn't there, Papa? The man in the parlour is not one of your crew, is he?'

He kept his eyes downcast, and patted the bed beside him. 'You'd better sit, lass.'

Swallowing back a sudden urge to panic, Serena did as he suggested. What more could there be?

Papa cleared his throat and opened his mouth several times before he spoke. 'I've been very foolish, my dear. You may never forgive me.'

'Surely not too foolish Papa?' she offered a weak smile. But the shadow on his countenance demanded seriousness. 'Papa? What have you done?'

'I don't know where to start.' Whatever had happened, it obviously grieved Papa.

'At the beginning, Papa. That is always best.'

With a heavy sigh, her father launched into his tale.

'As I said, I was washed ashore somewhere inside South Head. I rested briefly before heading inland through thick brush. The rain was so heavy.

'At last I pushed into a clearing. More than a clearing, actually. It was the grounds of a large property, in the midst of which stood a huge house. Naturally, I saw it as shelter. As I approached, I saw that the front door stood wide open. I called at the doorway but there was no answer. The noise of the storm no doubt drowned out any sound I made.

'After waiting a few minutes, I decided that the residents could not take offence if I took shelter from the storm inside their entryway. I was soaked through, so I found the nearest fire and tried to warm myself. The storm continued to pound against the roof and after a while I became curious and ventured further into the house. I discovered a dining room with a fresh meal laid out. Still, not a soul appeared, even when I called.

'At least fifteen minutes passed while I stood there, my stomach reminding me I had not eaten since early in the morning. I succumbed to my hunger. Do you blame me?'

Papa stopped there and dropped his head into his hands, rubbing his face.

Serena gaped at him. Although shocked that he had helped himself to a stranger's table, she supposed it was understandable. 'Don't be so hard on yourself, Papa. The owners must be very ungracious if they are so heartless as to turn away a half-starved victim of a shipwreck.'

'But that's not all,' he mumbled through his hands.

There was more? Serena swallowed, becoming uneasy.

Papa lifted his head, his face filled with shame. 'After eating, I continued to explore the house since the storm still raged outside with thunder and lightning. I found a display of beautiful miniature paintings. Not portraits of people, mind you, they were roses.'

He paused and his Adam's apple convulsed as he swallowed hard. Papa rushed on, blurting out his confession. 'I remembered that you asked me to bring you a rose. You never ask for much and I wanted to give you something special. There were so many of them and I foolishly thought they wouldn't miss one. Surely not one tiny rose among so many. I was tucking it into my coat pocket when there he was.'

Papa's face paled and his eyes widened as he looked at her.

'Who, Papa?'

'The owner of the house. Edward King.'

Serena sucked in a deep breath, aghast. 'Edward King, the architect? You stole from *him*?'

'I didn't realise it was him. Or his house. And he was unrecognisable when I saw him. He'd obviously been caught out in the storm, too. Water dripped from every part of him, leaving puddles in his wake. He was enraged, Serena. I can't tell you ...'

'What happened, Papa?' She slipped off the chair to kneel before him and placed her hands on his knees, the coarse weave of his trousers rough beneath her fingers.

He shook his head, his face contorted with grief. 'He threatened to haul me before the magistrate and have me imprisoned at the penal settlement.'

'No, Papa.' The blood drained from Serena's face and a wave of dizziness engulfed her. 'They can't take you away from us. We need you.'

'I begged and pleaded with him, but he refused to hear me.'

Serena's hands fell from Papa's knees as he stood. Her mind filled with questions that stampeded one over another in their haste for an answer. She couldn't move. What would become of them?

Papa leaned on the mantel over the fire, his back to her, and rested his head on his forearm. 'I'm only here because he allowed me one small mercy—to say goodbye.'

The words were muffled, or mumbled. Serena wasn't sure she'd heard correctly. Was that him in their parlour—Edward King? 'Goodbye?'

Her father did not speak for a long while and she wondered if she had mistaken him. Again, the questions crowded in her mind, competing with the crackle and spit of the fire in the grate.

'He is taking me to the magistrate tonight.' Papa raised sad eyes to meet hers. 'His charges will likely keep me in prison for several months.'

'No! But, Papa. We need you here. Who will provide for us?' Serena searched her mind for solutions. 'I might be able to obtain work, but surely it will not be enough. Julianne and Rachel are still so young ...'

Papa's shoulders fell. 'There is no other way. I have tried to reason with Mr King, but he is unbending.'

Desperation gripped Serena's heart. Without Papa, they would be destitute within a very short time. All their dreams and hopes, gone. Why, oh, why did he have to steal from Edward King, of all people?

She thought back over her nineteen years. Papa had always been good to them. He had always provided for them and loved them. Even in those months of desperate grief after Mama died, his love for them hadn't wavered. Papa was a good man and had done his best. And having made this one, small mistake, he now faced the cruellest of fates. Did he not deserve grace? Did not everyone need grace in their life? It was a pity that Edward King did not offer that mercy to her father. But if Mr King couldn't, perhaps she could.

'You said Mr King has a large house?'

Papa lifted his head in a sluggish nod. 'But—'

'I have an idea.' Serena squeezed his hand as she moved to leave the room. This must be done now, or she might lose her nerve.

She stormed into the parlour, pinning her eyes on the stranger whose very presence meant upheaval. Without waiting for the man to turn from where he stood, facing the mantel, she launched at him.

'How can you be so merciless as to take a man from his family like this? Do you have no heart?'

With one arm leaning on the mantel, he only half-turned

towards her, showing a stern profile against the firelight.

'My heart has naught to do with it. Your father broke the law, and violation of the law leads to consequences.'

'His ship was stranded! Have you no compassion? Can you offer no grace?'

He turned fully then, a deep frown marring what would otherwise be rather appealing features.

'I am here, am I not? I might have taken him straight to the authorities, leaving you to wonder what became of your father.'

His casual dismissal drove Serena to angry tears. 'It should be you who is put in prison. You are a monster.'

'Serena, what is happening?' Rachel appeared at the doorway, colour draining from her face, Julianne hovering at her shoulder.

Narrowing her eyes at Mr King, she answered, 'This *gentleman*,' she ground out as though the word was poison on her tongue, 'is taking our father away to prison.'

Their gasps shook her from her rage and she turned to face them. 'I am sorry, my dears. I ought not to have scared you so. But it is true. Papa must go to gaol, it seems.'

'But, what are we to do?'

Her sister's plaintive wail shook Serena to her core. She couldn't let this happen.

Papa shuffled into the parlour behind them, his head still hung low.

'It is time to go.' Mr King straightened from the fireplace and walked toward Papa, taking him by the arm.

'No!' Serena dropped to her knees and blindly clutched at his sleeve. 'Please don't take him. I beg of you.'

Julianne and Rachel's cries increased.

Mr King looked at her hand on his coat as though it were

a slug and shook her loose. 'Your begging changes nothing. He committed a crime and must be punished.'

Serena scrambled to her feet and grabbed at his sleeve again. 'No. Please. Take me instead.'

Silence swelled to fill the room, punctuated only by the odd sniffle from her sisters and a log shifting in the grate.

'What?' Several voices questioned in unison.

Serena gazed at each in turn, at last landing on Mr King. She swallowed 'Papa … Papa says you have a large house. Surely you need a maid somewhere. I will work off my father's debt, for however many months he should be imprisoned. Just let him go in peace.'

'Serena, no.'

Mr King raised a hand to silence Papa's protest, but kept his eyes on her.

'You would do that? You would take his place?' For a moment the frown was gone, replaced by an indefinable expression.

'If it means he can remain here with my sisters, then yes.'

Edward King stared at her again, his gaze only briefly shifting to her father before settling on her face. 'Let it be done.'

2

Today began like any other day. From my bed, I could see the giant fig through the glass doors of my balcony. All day long it called to me, its branches beckoning like bony fingers, but I could not summon the strength to shift my feet from beneath the blankets. Why does my quilt seem weighed with lead? It presses on me with the heaviness of sleep.

But the sleep never lasts long enough to bring true rest. Too soon I was gazing at the relentless fig again. Why did I never cut it down? Now it torments me day and night.

I admire its mighty limbs. Would those branches hold my weight? I daresay they might.

The fig tree's long arms beckon in the moonlight. It is an embrace I must consider.

3

Serena woke on a sofa in a strange room. She struggled to shake the heaviness of sleep, knowing her body still needed more, but the reality of where she sat forced her to keep her eyes open. *He left me here all night?*

She raked back through her memories of the previous evening. The heartless man had remained sullen for the drive home, aside from a warning. 'If you attempt to run away,' he'd said, a sneer curling his lips, 'I will return and take your father to the authorities.' He'd barely given her the time to pack a few small belongings into a bag, and bid her sisters a quick, tearful, farewell.

Her sisters.

Who would care for Julianne and Rachel? Papa would soon be gone again, sailing on his next voyage. Until now, the girls had not shown any success when left to fend for themselves. How would they manage? Perhaps it was time they grew up, after all.

How would Papa get on? He relied on her to keep things in order at home—so much so, he had denied her marriage to an eligible suitor some two years earlier. The only thing she'd ever wanted—her own home and family. She shut the memory down even as it surfaced, bringing fresh pain.

Serena stood and paced the intricately woven carpet.

They had arrived last night in darkness that shrouded her surroundings, but now she gazed about her at the high ceilings and ornate wood panelling. Heavy velvet drapes hung beside pointed windows, and elaborate artworks decorated the walls. Saints above, it was just as she'd imagined Pemberley, or even Rosings Park to be when she'd read Miss Austen's novels. One could not deny Mr King's excellent taste in decor.

This image of a gentleman versed in the arts belied his rude and callous behaviour. Serena gritted her teeth. Heavens, he'd left her in this room with a curt 'wait here' and never returned. She'd waited and waited. The fire in the grate had long since died out, leaving her shivering with cold. Thankfully it was not yet the dead of winter.

Serena went to the window to better see the property. All she'd managed to discern last night was that they'd driven away from the city. Manicured lawns spread before her, dotted at precise intervals with trees and shrubs, or carefully placed flower gardens, and even the occasional statue. There was order and symmetry everywhere she looked—it spoke of fastidious design. Was Mr King a man who commanded detail in every area?

Serena scanned her memory for everything she'd heard of Mr King. As far as she knew, he'd been in the colony for at least ten years—from England, or was it France? There was talk that he was a genius, his brilliance recognised from childhood, but people also called him eccentric. The newspapers often reported on his strange ways, his flamboyant appearances at social gatherings, and then his practical disappearance for months on end. Well, however society labelled him, Serena decided he was naught but a churlish, rude ogre. Her days within these walls might well become a severe trial.

Serena became aware of footsteps in the hallway. It was not

the heavy tread of a man, but the quick, light tap of a woman's shoe.

As the door creaked open, Serena held her breath, her fingers gripping the folds of her skirt.

A lean woman entered, and Serena was surprised not to be greeted. The woman was obviously unaware of Serena standing there and moved to collect something from a card table in the corner. Serena studied the face and guessed her to be in her late thirties. She had a pleasant face. Serena discreetly cleared her throat causing the woman to jump. She swivelled to face her.

'Who are you? And how did you get in here?'

Clearly, the lady had not been informed of her presence, and seemed rather alarmed. Serena gulped back her nerves and tried to breathe normally, belatedly offering a small curtsey. 'I'm here to work for Mr King. He brought me here last night.'

The lady's eyebrows shot up in surprise and confusion, but then her eyes narrowed. She measured Serena with suspicion. 'New help? Last night? What a bizarre tale.'

'Though bizarre, I agree, it is true. My name is Serena Bellingham.'

The woman scanned her from nose to toe once again. 'Well, Miss Bellingham, I really don't know why Edward hired you. We have no need for more staff. Wait here while I go and speak with him.'

With that she swept out of the room. Abrupt and curt as Mr King, and leaving her with more questions than answers. But what was Serena's occupation to be? Why had Mr King agreed she come and work for him when he had no use of her? Surely the housekeeper knew the staffing needs of the house, assuming that's whom she'd just met? But then, the woman's bearing and attitude spoke of good breeding. A family member, perhaps. Either way, the lady had been resolute.

So, how might Serena occupy herself in a house requiring no additional workers? Sit and stare at the paintings on the walls? She bit on her lip as her thoughts led her to a frightening possibility. Surely not! Serena scanned her memory for any snippet of information she'd heard of Edward King.

Oh my. Saints in heaven. She recalled reading rumours he'd been seen on various women's arms in the past several years. Was she to be his new plaything? Was he of such a high opinion of himself that he believed she'd agree to such a thing? Never. Not in a thousand years of hot Australian Christmases. How dare he? Indignation coursed through her.

No, Serena. Once again, she had let her imagination run away with her. Mr King had shown no signs of interest in her, quite the opposite, in fact. And as soon as the woman returned, they would correct any uncertainty. If he did have no use for her, perhaps she would soon be on her way home, back to her sisters who certainly did need her.

Jerking to her feet, she explored the large ornate room, looking for housekeeping that might remain undone. Serena dragged a finger across the smooth top of an oak table and then inspected it in the light from the arched window. No dust. In fact, her finger had left a smudge against the perfectly polished surface.

She checked lamps and candles, but the wicks were trimmed, oil topped up, ready for the next use. Several items of silver shone in the morning light, a sign of recent polishing. She moved to the hearth where there was little overspill of ash in the grate and a fresh supply of logs filled the wood box, their earthy fragrance pervading the room. Even the fire utensils were cleaned.

Serena sighed. Nothing appeared undone. Not in this room at any rate. Spotless and neat in every detail. Did every room hold such perfection in this house? She glanced at the door through which the lady had departed. Still closed.

Since there was no one to see her, Serena knelt on the floor, spreading her skirt around her. She lifted the edge of the large rug that covered the stone floor, checking for dust beneath it. Not a crumb. Determined to succeed in her search, Serena crawled over to the luxurious sofa and bent to peer beneath it. *Aha.* Yes. A small raised shadow against the pile of the rug. She stretched her hand as far as possible, but had to lay flat and half submerge her head beneath the couch before she reached the item.

'Find anything interesting?'

Serena jumped with fright, banging her head on the wooden frame of the sofa. With rapid heat rising in her face, and wincing at the pain on the back of her head, she scrambled to her feet. 'I'm so sorry, I was ...'

Her words vanished as her eyes settled on the man in front of her. Why had she thought Mr King was an older man? In the morning light, the gentleman before her seemed less than thirty. And handsome, in the manner of handsomeness that set her heart fluttering and made her face even hotter. Well, if it weren't for that perpetual scowl anyway. And why should she even notice—he'd abandoned her in the drawing room all night?

He stood there, a little dishevelled, unshaven by the shadow on his chin, but otherwise attired to exquisite perfection. Mr King stared at her with his hands thrust in pockets. Was he still angry? Or did he laugh at her behind his stony face? She couldn't tell.

Serena dropped her gaze and remembered the object in her

hand. 'I found this.' She held out a key.

'You may leave it on the card table there,' he gestured with a jerk of his chin.

The clink of the brass key on the wooden surface echoed through the spacious room.

'The true daughter of a thief, I see.'

Serena's outrage increased that Mr King would judge her so. He'd never even asked her name, let alone learnt anything about her.

'I am Serena Bellingham. And my father is no thief.' One mistake. He'd made one mistake. Must the label of thief remain forever?

'Then why are you here?'

Serena frowned. 'I don't understand. You brought me here.'

'I brought the daughter of a thief. If your father is not a thief, then you are not the person who took his place.'

Her mind whirled in confusion. 'Should I leave then?'

Mr King scowled at her. 'What is the matter with you? Have you no wits about you? Your father stole my food and attempted to steal a painting. That makes him a thief.'

'He made a mistake.' Serena ground out her words in exasperation. 'One he regrets terribly.'

'Good. So you admit to your father's crime. That is a beginning.'

'I admit no such thing. He is not a criminal.'

'No?' Mr King pulled his hands from his pockets and clasped them behind his back. He then walked the length of the room. 'I think he is. And his activities have rubbed off on you. You have not been in my house a day, Miss Bellingham, and you have already snooped where you have no business to snoop. What did you intend with that key? Find my safe and run away with my gold? Hmm?'

'What? No.' What excuse should she give for searching under the sofa? She couldn't admit the truth. 'I don't even know what that key might unlock. I merely found it and wished to return it to its rightful owner.'

Mr King approached her then. Too close. So close she caught the scent of lavender and cinnamon and what was that—tobacco? So close she could have measured the length of his unshaven beard—not even a quarter of an inch. Serena caught her breath at his penetrating gaze. 'I wish I believed you, Miss Bellingham. Time will tell.' He stepped back from her. 'One thing your father spoke true.'

'What did he say?' Serena's voice wobbled with uncertainty.

'He told me you were fair. I cannot argue it.' His lips curved a fraction at the corners.

Was that a smile? She didn't know how to respond.

'Judith will show you to your room and explain everything.' He turned to leave.

'But what am I to do?' Serena said to a closed door.

This time, Serena did not dare move an iota as she waited for Judith to enter, whoever she might be. The shame of discovery in a prostrate position, with her head underneath a sofa, was enough for one day. But the audacity of that man to accuse her of criminal intent was beyond endurance, and the longer she waited, the angrier she became.

Angry, and a little fascinated if she admitted it. His words at once confounded her and irritated her, and that dark, brooding face attracted her. He was both alarming and alluring.

Five minutes passed before the door re-opened, and the

woman she'd met earlier stepped inside. Serena clenched her fists in her lap as she realised this must be Judith.

'Come this way please, Miss Bellingham.'

Serena stood to her feet and collected her bag. At last the waiting was over.

Exiting the drawing room, they walked along a massive hallway, steps echoing through the spacious corridor. Within minutes, Serena realised why she'd spent so much time counting the candlesticks and paintings in the drawing room. The house extended forever in each direction, huge wings stretching out from the centre of the mansion. The ornate detail in the arched roof above her inspired wonder, as did the artworks that hung at intervals along the passage.

'I shall settle you at the end of this wing, where we house the staff—when we have any. There are one or two guest rooms this way, but family and friends usually have rooms in the opposite wing. You will find this comfortable though, I think.' Judith turned to her with a knowing twist to her lips.

Was this Judith staff or family, then? It was hard to know.

Moments later, she opened the door to what seemed to Serena an entire house. At least, it was as large as her home in the city. A suite? Was she to occupy her own suite? Overwhelmed, she gazed around the luxurious rooms, not knowing what to do. 'Do all staff have similar accommodations?'

'If we had any staff, yes.' Judith went to the huge four-poster bed and fluffed the pillows. 'Small rooms do not exist in Aleron. We don't house staff here these days, and we manage well without them.'

'Aleron?'

'The name of the house, child. Aleron House.'

'And you are not staff, then, Judith?'

'Not precisely. I do function somewhat as the housekeeper though, yes, and you may call me Mrs Jones.'

'Oh.' Strange. A well-born woman acting as a servant. Serena could only speculate what reasons might be behind that arrangement. She moved toward the bed and was greeted with the heady fragrance of fresh rosemary, a pouch of which had been left on the quilt. She adored the smell of rosemary and pressed the pouch to her nose. Her mouth filled with the longing for roasted lamb, seasoned with the delicious herb, something she had not tasted in several years.

Still clutching her bag, Serena remembered Mr King's behaviour in the drawing room and cleared her throat. 'Mr King—he accused me of attempted thievery.'

Mrs Jones straightened and eyed her, one brow lifting higher than the other. 'He did?'

'Yes, he thought I intended to find his safe and steal his gold.'

Mrs Jones watched her but said nothing.

Would Serena seem presumptuous speaking of the master of the house in such a way? She worried her lip between her teeth. She needed to know.

'I am wondering, Mrs Jones, if that is his normal manner?'

'Manner?'

Serena swallowed. 'Yes. Um. Gruff and scowling.'

The woman stared at her for a moment longer. Then her lips twisted in amusement again as she straightened an already perfect bedcover. 'Yes, indeed. The most cantankerous person I know. You'd best keep your distance. But in this case, I am afraid my brother was playing a charade.'

'I beg pardon?'

With a curt sigh, Mrs Jones faced Serena again. 'There is

neither safe nor gold. I suspect Mr King was baiting you.'

'*Baiting* me? Why?'

Mrs Jones approached her and took the leather bag from Serena's grasp, stopping to look her in the eye. 'If I could answer that question, we would both be wiser now, wouldn't we?'

She winked then, shocking Serena even further. She had first considered Mrs Jones to be stiff and serious, but now she had to rethink that impression. Maybe she'd discovered a friend and confidant to help her survive this time of trial. Surely Providence was at work. But then ... 'Wait. Did you say Mr King was your brother?'

'Yes. Lucky me.' Mrs Jones grinned at her droll words this time. 'My husband and I brought him out to Australia with us after ...' The smile vanished and Mrs Jones busied herself placing Serena's bag on the bed and opening it. 'After we learned what a wonderful country Australia is.'

Serena did not wish to pry but the hesitation proved Mrs Jones' answer unconvincing.

'It works for us to live here. I, as I've explained, work as the housekeeper, and my husband, Robert, acts as the butler and Eddie's personal valet.' She glanced up briefly, her face pinched as though she suffered, and then removed Serena's unmentionables and placed them in drawers. 'The groundsman and groomsman are our sons and the cook is a dear family friend. As you see, we are a close-knit group here. Apart from us, we bring in a team of maids once a week to go through the whole house and clean whatever we have missed along the way. We've closed many rooms and covered the furnishings with dust sheets, leaving little to do. The house works efficiently that way.'

Strange, but if that worked for them, who was Serena to argue? 'And what am I expected to do?'

Mrs Jones pressed the drawer shut. 'What skills do you have? I am not sure my brother thought it through when he agreed to hire you. He can be somewhat spontaneous.'

'Agreed?' Serena shook her head. 'No, he forced my hand.'

Mrs Jones stared at her, blinking. 'You must have misunderstood. Why would he do such a thing?'

'He ...' Serena almost blurted out everything, but bit on her lip instead. If Mrs Jones didn't know of Papa's attempt at thievery, Serena didn't need to advertise it. 'I know not why, but here I am.'

'And your skills?'

'I can cook and clean.' Though that seemed redundant now she understood how Aleron operated. She shrugged. 'I have experience in nursing my sickly mother, God rest her soul, and in caring for my sisters.'

Mrs Jones pressed her lips into a grim line. 'I suppose you can help with the laundry. It's too much for the maids to complete in one day. But that won't fill all your time, so it will be your duty to go from room to room and make sure everything is tidy and in place. In the meantime, I will speak with my brother.'

Oh dear. Laundry was her least favourite of household chores, but if that's what she had to do to atone for her father's mistake, then so be it. The rest should be easy enough. Serena let out a long breath. 'Very well. When shall I start?'

'Tomorrow morning will be soon enough. Take the day to acquaint yourself with your new surroundings and meet the rest of us. Just stay away from Mr King's suite at the end of the north wing. He tolerates no interruptions when he is working.'

Serena nodded.

'Governor Gipps commissioned him to design a grand theatre for the city. The governor wants it to be a lasting and outstanding landmark for Sydney.'

Impressive. Serena raised her eyebrows. Mr King's work sounded important. No wonder he had been so moody and short with her earlier if he'd been dragged away from his enterprise. 'I'll be sure not to disturb him then.'

Not that she had any wish to meet that cantankerous man so soon again, anyway. To wander the grounds and explore the house would overwhelm her enough without another confusing encounter with Mr King.

4

After spending some time exploring the suite she'd been settled in, Serena headed for the front door. It was dark when she'd arrived last night and she wondered what Aleron House looked like from the outside. Was it as grand as the interior suggested? Serena paused outside her rooms, looking in both directions. It was hard to get one's bearings in a home of this size.

Finally, she found familiar furnishings in the hallways and located the entrance, then followed the pathway a hundred or so yards to the front gate. The lonely crunch of stone beneath her feet stood out in contrast against the silent grounds. The fresh country air might have been invigorating if she wasn't so vexed by the owner of this place. She turned to gaze at her new prison.

Aleron House rose in a formidable stance before her, as fearsome as its master. Although, it more resembled a castle than a house. It presented a gothic impression with turrets, parapets, arched windows and gables. If it hadn't been her gaol she might have considered it an enchanting piece of architecture, something from her childhood dreams. And if the sky had been less threatening with its dark clouds, the sandstone walls might even be inviting. No doubt Mr King had designed and built it himself.

Serena leaned up against the closed gates. This would be her dwelling for the foreseeable future and she worried that her time here would be taxing. Although, if she were honest with herself, she feared more for her family than herself. Her sisters seemed barely capable of dressing themselves, let alone looking after the house and cooking. And with Papa heading to sea again, she pictured them lost and alone in their small cottage. If only she could go back and check on them.

She tried to drive thoughts of home from her mind, berating herself. How many times had she wished for a break from the constant routine of her life? How often had she pined for the days when she had almost married and been mistress of a grand house? If Mama hadn't died ...

Every time she thought of escaping her life, guilt nagged at her. How could she dream of such things when her family needed her? Since Mama died, and they lost their wealth, they had leaned on Serena for support. Papa needed her to be the mother of the house, and her sisters needed someone in whom to confide. But now they would have to get along without her. Julianne must be the one to manage the household. Serena drew a deep breath. Julianne would cope. She had to cope.

With a sigh, Serena continued her tour of Aleron House. The grounds were magnificent, designed with pretty flower beds, dotted here and there with larger trees. It would be a rainbow of colour come spring. In the middle of these gardens stood an imposing fig tree, which drew the eye from every angle—a magnificent centrepiece. Where the formal gardens ended, pastureland spread into the distance, bordered by a forest of eucalypts.

The vista from her tiny house in the city was nothing in comparison. Of course, a short walk from home, Serena could gaze out over the ocean and watch the ships glide into Port Jackson. But in every other direction stood buildings of stone and wood, separated only by roads. The beauty of Aleron's vista made her soul ache. Hadn't she always dreamed of living on such an estate again? And here she was, but it did not belong to her or her family. Did God mean to tease her?

Even the air was different. Gone was the tinge of the sewers on the breeze, or the fishy aroma from the port. Here, only fresh, flower-laden air met her senses. And the earthy scent of horses.

The stables stood off to her right. Mr King no doubt had several fine animals in his possession. She hastened her steps in that direction, eager to see them, and almost collided with Mr King standing beneath the fig tree.

'I'm sorry, I—'

'Do you always run about like a hoyden?' A deep frown marked his brow.

'Hoyden?' She obviously repulsed him. Indignation quickly replaced any civility Serena might have used.

'First I find you prostate on my drawing room floor and now you are careening about my garden in a careless fashion. What other description is there but hoyden?'

Serena glared at him. This was the outside of enough.

'Shall we discuss your own behaviour? You left me alone in that drawing room all night. No offer of refreshments, no bed, no warmth. What manner of host are you?'

Mr King averted his eyes, but not before Serena caught a flash of emotion in them. Was that regret? But then he stared at her again, his eyes narrowed.

'I am *not* your host. I am the one to whom you owe a debt. It would serve you well to remember that.' With those harsh words, he swivelled on his heel and strode toward the house.

Serena watched him walk away, hands clenched at her sides. 'No, you are not my host,' she mumbled, 'but it appears I am your hostage.'

She leaned up against the broad trunk of the fig, trying to calm her anger. Was he always going to be this callous and rude? How would she endure?

With a heavy sigh, she pushed away from the tree. She must put it out of her mind. The scent of horse manure drifted on the air, reminding her she'd been on her way to visit the stables. Trying to forget Mr King, she headed that way again. As she entered the dim hold, Serena paused, allowing her eyes to adjust.

'Good day, miss. May I help you?' A young man stepped out of the shadows and greeted her with a hesitant smile. Serena recalled seeing him briefly on their arrival last night.

'Oh, hello. I came to visit the horses,' Serena stammered.

'And you are?'

'Miss Bellingham's my name. I'm here to work, like you. But, not with the horses, of course.' She giggled, suddenly nervous. 'I didn't catch your name though.'

'Xavier Jones. I'm in charge of the stables.'

Mrs Jones's son, of course. The groomsman must be similar in age to herself if Serena was any judge. Mr Jones sported the same good looks as his uncle, but wore a shy smile. In fact, the similarity between them was unnerving, although the nephew did not have the melancholic air of his uncle. She offered him a brief curtsy. 'Pleased to meet you, Mr Jones.'

'If you don't mind my asking, what duties were you hired to perform? I didn't think we were hiring staff.'

Serena let out a mirthless chuckle. Did no one want her here, except Mr King, whose own acceptance seemed thin? 'I'll be working in the laundry and doing odd cleaning around the house, starting tomorrow. For now, Mrs Jones suggested I explore my new surroundings.'

Mr Jones shuffled his feet, looking awkward and then gestured toward the door. 'I am due to bring the horses in from the paddocks. You can join me if it pleases you.'

Serena glanced at her boots—the only pair she owned these days. 'Is it very muddy?'

The shy grin spread on Mr Jones's face again. 'It shouldn't be too bad. The rain has dried since yesterday.'

'Very well then. I shall enjoy a tour of the selection.'

Moments later, with two halters looped over his shoulder, Mr Jones led her from the stables. They passed through a gate in the fence which bordered the manicured gardens, and then the ground became more uneven as they entered the paddocks. Serena had to watch her every step, lest she land in a rabbit burrow and twist her ankle.

'The horses are in the lower paddock. Can you manage?'

'I think so.' Serena giggled. 'I have climbed over the rocks in the bay many times, you know.'

'Right.' Mr Jones studied her for a moment.

'My father is a merchant, so I am often at the port,' she offered by way of explanation.

'Ah.' Mr Jones's eyebrows rose.

They walked in silence for a moment and Serena worried her lip. Questions burned in her chest. She sent a furtive glance his way. He seemed friendly enough. Why not try? 'I wonder, Mr Jones, if you would care to tell me more of your uncle?'

Mr Jones lurched as his foot met with a deep furrow. Had she been too presumptuous and startled him? His brows had drawn together.

'What is it you wish to know?'

Everything. As Serena saw more of Mr King's estate, she became intrigued about the mind that created such magnificence.

Could a constantly brooding mind create such beauty? She opened her mouth to ask about his mind for architectural design, but Mr Jones spoke again.

'Or, should I ask, what have you heard?'

Serena glanced sideways at him. Was that a suspicious gaze he cast upon her? Strange, such a veil of secrecy hung about the place. She tried to offer a disarming smile. 'I've only read snippets of information about him in the newspapers. Not much. I had expected him to be older, I suppose.'

Mr Jones pressed his lips into a thin line. 'Uncle Eddie was a child prodigy. Brilliant. He entered Cambridge at a young age. Studied everything he could find to learn, but he always came back to creating and building. He designed his first building—a church—at sixteen and within a few years became the rage of London in architecture.'

'Because of his young age, do you think?'

He gave a slow nod. 'In part, but his work is quite remarkable.' Mr Jones gestured behind them to the house. 'You cannot deny it.'

Serena paused and turned toward the mansion, admiring its silhouette against the sky. No, she couldn't deny it. 'If London demanded his talents so much, though, why leave and come to Australia?'

Mr Jones expression clouded. 'I was only nine when we left, so much of it is hazy in my memory. But with respect to my uncle and my mother, that is their story to tell. I do know my uncle can be impulsive when he chooses.'

'Do you imply he came to Sydney Cove on a whim?' Serena couldn't believe a person would travel so far without careful planning or forethought.

The young horseman turned an open face to her. 'It is not

for me to say, Miss Bellingham. Perhaps you might ask him yourself if you have the opportunity.'

She intended to ask another question when a dapple-grey mare shook her silver mane in front of them, diverting Serena's attention. She admired the mare's beautiful coat with a soft moan. 'Oh, she's lovely.'

Mr Jones grinned. 'She's one of my favourites. Her name's Misty. The other dappled grey over yonder is Storm and together they pull Uncle's carriage.'

Mr Jones gestured toward Storm, thundering toward them with a loud whinny. 'Does Storm live up to his—or her—name?'

Mr Jones released a soft laugh. 'Yes. She looks like a storm cloud and behaves like one, too. But Misty keeps her in check when they're in the harness.'

'Misty's the docile one then, is she?' Serena laughed, ducking for cover behind Mr Jones as Storm skidded to a stop in front of him.

The groomsman gave a soft laugh as he pulled a carrot from his pocket and fed it to the eager horse. 'As you can tell, Storm certainly isn't.' He stroked the big mare's nose with affection. 'She can smell a carrot a mile away.' He turned and gave Serena a lopsided grin. 'Or else, she knows I bring one for her every day.'

Serena giggled at the horse's antics, then stepped closer to stroke its nose. The short hair of Storm's face was soft beneath her fingers. The mare nickered and sniffed at her hand, its warm breath leaving moisture on her fingers. Mr Jones fastened the halters to the two mares and Serena fell into step beside him once again as they headed back toward the house.

As she neared the stables, Serena noticed another young man pushing a wheelbarrow through the gardens. 'Is that your brother?' She pointed in his direction.

'It is.' Mr Jones nodded, then placed two fingers between his lips and let out an ear-piercing whistle. 'Simon!' Turning back to Serena, he added, 'I must introduce you.'

Mr Simon set down his wheelbarrow and strode toward them. Unlike Mr King and Mr Xavier Jones, he had sandy brown hair. However, he did wear his uncle's perpetual frown. If Serena thought Mr Xavier regarded her with suspicion at first, it was worse with Mr Simon. He did not remove his serious brown eyes from her as he approached.

'This is Miss Serena Bellingham, Simon. She's here to work for Uncle. Miss Bellingham, my brother Simon Jones.'

Mr Simon stared at her a moment longer before his gaze swerved to his brother. 'No one informed me we were hiring a new maid.'

Mr Xavier cleared his throat, embarrassed by his brother's rudeness. 'Apparently Uncle Ed hired her.'

'Yes, he did.' Serena forced a smile. She needed to settle the awkwardness between them and bobbed a friendly curtsy. 'Pleased to meet you, Mr Jones.'

Mr Simon eyed her with a gaze Serena could only call hostile. He stood stiff and cold, giving her only a curt nod. 'If you're to stay here, you need to know one thing. We don't care for busy bodies.'

Serena tried to hide her sharp intake of breath. Another family member who enjoyed making accusations without the right information. Swallowing her affront, she pressed her lips into a faint smile. 'I'm not here to interfere, I can assure you. I already know to leave Mr King in peace while he is working.'

Mr Simon's eyes bored right into her soul through narrow slits, as though he searched for any deception in her words. He spoke through lips curled into a sneer. 'Well, make sure you do. And no matter what you think you hear or see, it is not what it seems.'

Serena lay awake that night, an endless stream of questions running through her mind. Not even the potent smell of the rosemary could help her relax, and she'd pressed it to her nose several times.

When she first arrived, fear had gripped her—a fear brought on by the story her father had told her. Since then, she had experienced a wide array of emotions, it left her confused more than anything. Irritation, indignation, awe, wistfulness, bemusement—all had taken their turn as she surveyed her surroundings. It was like a cruel joke—the most beautiful house she'd ever seen, occupied by the most unfriendly people she'd ever met.

For all appearances they were well-born, but living as servants to Mr King. Why should they choose to do that? Why indeed, had they come to Australia in the first place? Had they run away? It made no sense to Serena.

No matter what you think you hear or see, it is not what it seems.

Mr Simon's words played over her mind. A shiver of fear rippled up her spine, despite the warm blankets, and Serena sank further into the pillows, pulling the cover up to her chin. Only a sliver of moonlight cut through the darkness where the drapes did not meet, giving the bedroom an eerie glow. She had experienced such an array of emotions today, and now she was back where she'd begun.

Fear.

She shouldn't let her mind run. Soon she would hear things that didn't exist. Her whole body stiffened at that moment. Yes, there it was now. The slow tread of footsteps along the long stone corridor, closer and closer.

Clomp. Clomp. Clomp.

With every muscle taut, Serena held her breath. Who was out there? She knew she was the only staff member who wasn't family or friend of Mr King, so, she was alone in this wing of the gothic mansion.

Clomp. Clomp. Clomp.

No matter what you think you hear or see, it is not what it appears. Mr Simon Jones's words repeated in her mind yet again.

Clomp. Clomp. Clomp.

The steps were right outside her door now and Serena sat bolt upright, hugging the quilt to her chest as though it could save her life. She stared through the shadows at the dark outline of the door. There, in the gap beneath the door, a light shone. The footsteps ceased. Whoever it was stood outside her room. Serena's heart rattled as though even it wanted to escape. Why would they stop here?

Clomp. Clomp. Clomp.

The yellow stream of light faded with the footsteps and Serena released her pent-up breath. She had expected the person to enter her room, but they had not. She slumped back onto the pillows, thankful.

Clomp. Clomp. Clomp.

The unknown person remained in the hallway, continuing their aimless journey. In that instant, Serena knew if she didn't look for herself, she would lie awake imagining each person in the house and what their motives might be. She threw back the covers and slipped her feet into her slippers, the cold night air wrapping its chilly fingers around her bare ankles and throat. Without pausing in her step, she grabbed her dressing gown and swung it around her shoulders, flinging open the door while still threading one arm into the sleeve.

Serena leaned into the dark hallway. Sure enough, a figure silhouetted by the candlelight walked back toward the central part of the house. The long shadows were frightening enough without imagining them to be anything else. Serena swallowed hard, pushing her fears aside. 'Excuse me!'

5

The figure halted in its steps, then slowly turned. The small flame sent distorted shadows over the person's face.

'Yes.'

The last of Serena's fear fled with the anchoring sound of a human voice. Pulling the front of her gown closed, she approached the person. 'I'm sorry. I heard you walking out here and, well, I was having trouble sleeping, so I thought I'd come and see who it was.' It was close enough to the truth to suffice.

He half turned away as she neared as though embarrassed to be discovered up so late. At once Serena recognised the handsome face of Mr King and her heart, which had finally settled, leapt to attention again. What kind of set-down would it be this time? She steeled herself for more of his rudeness.

'Not used to your new room, I suspect.'

'Well, no,' Serena admitted, surprised. He almost sounded civil. But it might not last if she sounded unappreciative. She needed to turn his opinion of her, even if he didn't deserve her consideration. 'Not that it is uncomfortable. On the contrary, I am grateful, for your unexpected generosity.'

Mr King waved a hand in dismissal and again half turned from her.

'And I wasn't trying to stay up till everyone else was asleep so I could rob you.' Serena ended her try at humour with a forced giggle. 'Neither was I lying there planning my escape, although I miss my family already.' If he had been indeed baiting her earlier on, perhaps he might rise to the half-hearted joke.

Instead, he turned back to her and appeared to study her. 'Personally, I find the quiet of night the best time for ideas to flow.'

'Oh. So, you're not walking to help you sleep?' What an odd thing for a person to do. Work, in the middle of the night.

'No.'

'You're designing?'

'Walking helps me think.'

Serena dipped her head in understanding. 'Right. I will let you resume your thoughts then. I'm so sorry to have interrupted you.' The genius at work. A little embarrassed, she backed away, with a slight nod of the head in deference to her host. Master. Good grief, she was still in her nightdress. 'Good night, Mr King.'

His eyebrows rose, as though he meant to say something, but then coughed lightly and turned his head aside. 'Good night, Miss Bellingham.'

She watched him for a moment, the candlelight dimming as he walked away, and then with a brief shrug, Serena ducked back into her room and closed the door.

Curious.

Mr King strolling the house in the dead of night was odd behaviour, and yet his countenance and conversation were almost normal for a change. Perhaps it was a sign that he was not the complete ogre she'd believed him to be.

'We shall see, Mr King,' she whispered into the darkness as she climbed back into bed and finally, more relaxed than she'd been all day, she fell asleep.

The morning light brought with it a sense of mixed curiosity and nervousness. She'd survived her first day at Aleron, but this would be her first day of work. As yet, she remained uncertain of her host's expectations where that was concerned, though at least he showed signs of not being the overbearing master she'd begun to believe. If last night's encounter was anything to go by, he could be amenable if he wanted to.

On her way down to the dining room, she wondered what his mood might be like today if she happened upon him. Hopefully his anger towards her and her father would not remain the entire time she stayed here. Hopefully he would learn to relent.

Since most of the staff were members of Mr King's family, they all ate in the dining room. All that is, except for Mr King, oddly enough. Mrs Jones refused to allow Serena to eat in the staff kitchen by herself, so she joined them. The formal dining room was yet another magnificent example of design, with highly polished furniture and not an item out of place. The table could seat a large dinner party as two dozen chairs surrounded it—she had counted them twice to be sure.

Serena stretched her mouth in a yawn as she selected a piece of toast for her plate, the smell of warm bread stirring her appetite.

'Did you not sleep well, Miss Bellingham?' Mrs Jones caught her ill-manners.

Serena covered her mouth. 'Oh, no. I mean, yes. But it was a while before I went to sleep.' An image of Mr King wandering the hallways flooded her mind and she tried to hide her smile.

'The strangeness of your new surroundings no doubt caused that.'

'I suppose so.' Serena bit her lip to keep the grin from her face, but she was certain the merriment in her eyes gave her away.

'What has you smiling this morning?' Mrs Jones crumpled her face in curiosity.

'I, um, encountered a phantom in the middle of the night.' *A living phantom.* Serena giggled.

Mrs Jones eyed her with a mixture of suspicion and amusement. 'A phantom?'

Unsure whether they knew of Mr King's late-night rambles, Serena sobered. 'Excuse me, Mrs Jones. You will soon learn I have a very active imagination. After lying awake for a long time, worrying over my father and sisters, I heard noises which frightened me. But I am not used to the house as you say.' She turned her focus to her toast, feigning concentration on spreading butter.

'As I thought. It must be hard to be away from your family.' Mrs Jones seemed to accept her story. 'Is it the first time you have been separated from them?'

Serena nodded, spooning jam from the pot. 'I don't quite know how they'll get on without me.' She lifted a corner of toast to her mouth, not wanting Mrs Jones to see her lips quiver.

'If I were in your shoes, no doubt I would feel precisely the same.' A faraway look washed over her face, as though she imagined exactly that. And thankfully, the woman didn't press the conversation further.

One by one, Mrs Jones's family entered the dining room to join them. First Mr Simon, who had not lost his sour expression from the previous day. Then Mr Jones Senior, who she had only met briefly at supper the night before. Even though he acted as Mr King's valet or butler, he spent much of his time running errands in town. He had the same sandy-coloured hair as Simon, but his looks were more rugged than the King side of the family, and he appeared to carry a permanent injury to his left arm. He used it very little, as though he had not the use of his fingers properly. However, his eyes twinkled with friendly humour and he winked at her as he seated himself at the table. Of the family at Aleron, he was the warmest, and didn't seem as secretive as the others.

'How did you spend your first night in the castle?'

'After discovering and conquering the ghosts haunting the south wing, I slept like a queen.'

'Ah yes. I presume no one warned you that Aleron is haunted.' Mr Jones's eyes crinkled at the corners.

'Father, must you scare the girl?' Mr Xavier entered at that moment, shaking his head.

'It's just friendly banter, isn't it, Miss Bellingham?' Mr Jones Senior winked in her direction again before tucking into his tomato and sausage with poached eggs.

'Yes, no harm done,' Serena agreed, sampling a bite of her toast and enjoying the sweetness of the jam.

She left the dining room half an hour later, with the opinion that living at Aleron house might not be a complete trial after all. Granted, they proceeded through life differently here and amidst such luxury, but apart from the odd pricklish comment, the family were pleasant enough. They could never replace her dear Papa, Julianne and Rachel, but perhaps she could relax around them. Serena sighed as she made her way to the laundry for her first day of work, sure a mountain of linen awaited her.

However, she was pleasantly surprised to find the mountain more resembled a small knoll. A few napkins, towels, dish cloths, and a few items of clothing, still made for several hours of washing, wringing, drying, starching and ironing. Not one to procrastinate, Serena fetched hot water for the copper and scrubbed with soap on the washboard. Before long, perspiration ran down her neck. Her back and shoulders ached and her hands cramped. The skin on her fingers resembled dried prunes.

Who would be doing the laundry at home? Her sisters were still learning, and Rachel had not enough strength in her hands to scrub the stains out. Until Mama had died, none of them had needed to do any domestic chores. They'd been wealthy enough to afford servants to keep house for them. But, Papa had crumbled beneath the weight of his grief and let his business flounder. Soon enough they were drowning in debt, had to sell everything and move into their small house near the port. Since then, Serena had tried to teach her young sisters how to cook and clean. But, she had failed. They fretted over the smallest thing, fearing injury or her disappointment. They were still little more than children. And now that Serena wasn't there, their naivety would cause them to suffer the harsh realities of life. She had been wrong to protect them from it. She winced as she imagined the skin peeling from their raw fingers after a day in soapy water. How terribly painful. Serena could not help but feel sorry for them. It was her fault. She should have been a better teacher.

As she finished putting the batch of freshly rinsed washing through the mangle, the big front door knocker echoed through the house. Someone to visit Mr King perhaps. Could it be regarding the theatre design commission? Did the Governor wish to know how the drawings progressed?

A few minutes passed, and the knock resounded again. When it came a third time unanswered, Serena picked up a towel. She dried her hands, dabbed her face and neck and smoothed the moist runaway strands of hair back against her crown. Straightening her skirt and blouse, she hurried to the front door. Where was everybody? Perhaps this was a common occurrence. Didn't Papa say no one answered when he sought shelter from the storm the other day?

Serena paused and smoothed her skirts one final time before opening the huge door. Hopefully she didn't look as dishevelled as she felt. 'Good morning. May I help you?'

A man dressed in a suit stood there. Nothing fancy—a common day-to-day suit she'd seen on the streets in Sydney. A business man of sorts? His mouth stretched into a smile when he saw her, although there was a blunt set to his jaw. 'Good morning. I'm here to see Mr King, if he is available.'

'Is he expecting you?' Serena had not yet been in this predicament. What was the procedure for accepting guests?

'Not exactly. But I would appreciate a moment of his time.'

'And who might I say is calling?'

One corner of his mouth lifted in a smile—or was it a smirk? 'My name is Moncrief. Caleb Moncrief.'

Caleb Moncrief. Where had she heard that name before? Serena searched her mind but couldn't place him. He didn't look familiar.

'I'll show you into the drawing room. Come this way.' Serena remembered the room Mr King had left her in yesterday. Was it only yesterday? It seemed like a week. She waved Mr Moncrief inside, closing the door behind him, then led him along the hallway.

'How is Edward, if I may ask?'

'He is well.' Serena shrugged. 'I have seen little of him. I'm new here.'

'I see.' Mr Moncrief looked at her with what she could only

describe as keen interest. 'And from what you have seen ...?'

Serena creased her brows. 'Um, he seems in good health. I'm sure you can ask him these questions yourself.'

They arrived at the drawing room then and she offered him a seat.

'Thank you, ma'am. If you don't mind my asking, what is your overall impression of Edward?'

'I beg pardon?' What an odd thing to ask.

'Bear with me. I am just the curious sort. Some people would call him eccentric. What do you think?'

For some reason, his questions made her hackles rise, and she wanted to defend Mr King. 'I think those questions are impertinent. If people don't understand the nature of a genius when they meet him, that is their misfortune.'

Mr Moncrief held up his hands in defence. 'Say no more. I have no intention of slandering the chap.' He smiled at her. Was he laughing at her? 'He chose well when he employed you.'

'Thank you, sir.' Serena didn't have the confidence she forced into her voice. 'Now, if you don't mind waiting, I shall see if he is receiving visitors.'

The first person Serena could find was Mrs Jones. She had been reluctant to go straight to Mr King's suite and disturb him, and hadn't been able to locate Mr Jones. The valet had probably gone to town on errands, and the young men worked out on the grounds. But to guess in which room Mrs Jones presently cleaned was challenging. She still had not found the time to explore the house, and knew not where the rooms the family used were. Calling as she searched, Serena finally located her on the second floor, in the library.

And what a library! Books that lined every wall to the roof. She stood gaping, her errand forgotten. Serena recalled her one book of poetry by John Keats, her worn and dog-eared copies of Jane Austen's works and the family Bible. Her mother had taught her to read using that precious book before she had even entered the school room. Those volumes, and a few of Papa's favourites, were the scant remains of their former collection. But, even before their wealth evaporated, their bookshelves numbered nowhere near Mr King's library. Her fingers itched to lift a volume from the shelf and trace over the rough paper that held such treasures of knowledge and imagination. Oh, and that smell of old leather and aged paper. It was heaven.

Serena expected to find books shelved here on any topic she chose. It was as if the whole world had just opened to her. Next time she spoke with him, she must ask him if she might borrow one or two.

'What is it you need me for, Miss Bellingham?' Mrs Jones brought Serena out of her stupor. The housekeeper was a few steps up a ladder, dusting the books.

'Oh, yes. There is a Mr Caleb Moncrief here to see Mr King. I've asked him to wait in the drawing room.'

Colour drained from Mrs Jones's face. 'What have you done?' She scrambled from the ladder, her eyes wide.

Serena frowned. 'Nothing, as far as I know. I have not interrupted Mr King if that's what you mean. I came to find you first.'

Mrs Jones clasped her elbow, hurrying out of the library and back to the staircase. 'But you left Moncrief alone?'

'Why, yes.' How did they expect her to seek help and stay with Mr Moncrief at the same time?

'For goodness sake, he's probably snooping around by now.'

Mrs Jones' frustrated words came out half mumbled as she hastened her steps even further. Serena almost needed to jog to keep pace. What was so wrong? Why the panic? Serena had no opportunity for questions in their dash to find Mr Moncrief.

At the top of the stairs, Mrs Jones paused and moved to the window. Lifting the latch, she pushed the window open, then pulled a whistle from her pocket and blew it hard. She closed the window again and continued her rush to the drawing room.

When they arrived at the door, Mrs Jones took a deep breath, and transformed into a calmer image of herself. She threw open the door and bustled inside, Serena close behind, to find an empty room. 'I knew it.' Mrs Jones spun on her heel, almost colliding with Serena in her haste to return to the hallway. 'Get out of my way, girl.'

In the corridor, they met with Simon, who'd hurried in from the gardens. 'What's wrong, Mother?'

'Moncrief's here. Somewhere.' Her lips formed a thin line.

'Right. I'll check the north wing.' With those curt words, the young gardener hurried away.

'And I'll search these central rooms. Miss Bellingham, go back and look in the south wing. If you find him, tell him firmly—but cordially—to leave.'

Serena opened her mouth to blurt out the questions running through her mind.

'Now, Miss Bellingham.'

The sound of a commotion drifted up from the front of the house, male voices rising. Serena hurried back downstairs in time to see the door close behind Mr Moncrief, and to receive a deep scowl from Mr Simon.

'Did you let him in?'

'I ...'

'It's not her fault, Simon. She is not familiar with the man. And you know how Moncrief is.' Mrs Jones sounded a trifle exasperated.

'What do you mean?' Serena glanced from one to the other. 'Excuse me, but I do not understand my error. I heard the knocker, no one came, so I answered the door. Mr Moncrief spoke of Mr King in familiar terms, and I had no reason to believe he was anything but genuine.'

'Because you are too naïve.' Mr Simon glared.

'That's enough, Simon. You may go back to work now. No harm done.'

'So you think.' His eyes flashed at Serena. 'What did you tell him?'

'Tell him?' Serena tried to recall her brief conversation with the visitor. 'I'm sure I didn't tell him anything. We exchanged a few pleasantries, that's all.' Of what was Mr Simon accusing her?

'Simon, let me deal with this.' Mrs Jones clasped her son's arm, nudging him toward the door.

With something akin to a growl, the groundskeeper yielded and headed back to his gardening.

Mrs Jones turned to Serena. 'Don't mind him too much. He is over-protective of his uncle.'

Why did Mr King need protection? Or was she referring to his privacy? 'I don't understand. What is so wrong with Mr Moncrief?'

Mrs Jones let out a heavy sigh. 'He is a journalist for the *Sydney Herald*. It is his goal to make a scandal of my brother's life. He comes here at least once every month. I'm sure he thought it serendipitous when you answered the door today. Have you ever read the *Herald*, Miss Bellingham?'

'Yes, now and then.'

'Moncrief writes most articles that involve gossip about Sydney's wealthy, powerful and notable folk. He's a scandalmonger. He thrives on it and has become notorious for it.'

So that's where Serena recognised his name. The newspapers. That's where she'd read those little titbits on Mr King. Yes, and the latest on-dits about Mr Johnathon Fordham, the son of a baron, or a whisper of gossip about Governor Gipps. *Caleb Moncrief.* And she'd let him into this house and let him fool her with his smooth words. 'Oh. I'm very sorry. I should not have let him in.'

'Like I said, you weren't to know.' Mrs Jones gripped her elbow, and they walked back toward the library. 'Anyway, he didn't find Eddie, so all is well.'

Serena tried to smile, but uncertainty made it difficult. Had they averted a crisis? Now that the chaos was over, Serena recalled Mr Moncrief asking—or insinuating—very specific details. What had her replies been? Might she have unwarily damaged Mr King's public figure? She squeezed her eyes tight and tried to replay her exact conversation with Mr Moncrief.

How angry would Mr King be if she'd tarnished his reputation further with thoughtless words? That he considered her the daughter of a thief was bad enough. Would he now also think her a gossip? So much for trying to impress Mr King so he might release her to her family soon.

6

Several times throughout the afternoon, Serena had the distinct impression someone watched her. The eerie sensation came over her as she worked outside and hung washing on the lines which crisscrossed a small courtyard. Hedges enclosed the yard on three sides, save a small gap near the wall that led onto the grounds. She supposed this design hid the unsightliness of laundering.

Why would anyone wish to spy on her pulling in linen? It baffled Serena. Surely, it must be her imagination running out of control again. Ever since the encounter with Mr Moncrief that morning, she had invented the worst scenarios for what the journalist might write, and the possible effect on Mr King. Her imaginings descended to his decommissioning for his work on the theatre. Then his reputation ruined so that no one would ever hire him again. And it would be all her fault.

Just as her sisters' demise would be her fault. Not only did she imagine tragedy for Mr King, but also for her family. Perhaps they were slowly starving with no one to cook for them. If she could run home and see they were well, it would be a salve to her, but then Mr King might hold to his promise and have Papa arrested. She couldn't take the risk.

And now she suspected a prowler watched her. As Serena unpegged and folded a towel, the uneasy sensation in the pit of her stomach grew. She glanced over her shoulder. Did someone crouch outside the hedge perhaps, watching her? She dropped the fresh towel on top of the basket and headed for the gap in the hedge. Only one thing would put her mind at rest.

Serena ducked around the corner of the hedge, which stretched in a vacant line before her. No matter, perhaps the spy hid around the corner. She hurried forward and peeked around each bend to find nothing. Not a soul. Not a sound. Not even a hint that someone had been there recently.

'There you go, Serena. It is only wicked inventiveness.' In scolding herself aloud, her fears faded even more. She returned to folding and tried humming one of her favourite hymns, *Rock of Ages*, which she'd sung often with Papa. Though humming that tune distracted her it soon made her miss her family.

'I heard you spoke to Moncrief this morning.'

Serena almost leapt out of her boots. Where had he come from so suddenly? 'Mr King! I didn't hear you come out.'

The corner of his mouth jerked upward. Was that meant to be a smile? Did he enjoy catching her unprepared? His intense gaze flickered with interest. Saints above, he was striking to behold. In the light of day, his chiselled jawline and broody mouth drew her eye like magnets. As if she didn't feel warm enough from her work already without him looking at her like that. Come to think of it, she must look a fright after laundering. Her hands fluttered to wayward strands of hair, tucking them behind her ears, then smoothed her blouse and skirt.

'I startled you. Again. At least your head is not wedged beneath my sofa this time.' Mr King's lips twitched once more.

'You have a way of sneaking up on one, Mr King.'

'Moncrief?'

He drew her back to the point of his visit. No time for

pleasantries. Even a 'how was your day' would have been nice. What was she thinking? Serena was here as his employee and for discipline, nothing else. Whatever she might have expected from him, she must disregard it now. He was toying with her, or—how did his sister put it—baiting her. Serena cleared her throat. 'Yes, he came to the door, unexpected.'

'And he gave you the slip.'

'I suppose he did.' There was no other explanation. Mr Moncrief had misled her, intending to sneak off to find Mr King. 'But your sister and nephew—Mr Simon—found him and sent him away.'

'Well and good. But in the meantime, you spoke with him. Yes?'

Why did everyone need to interrogate her? 'Yes. Briefly. He intimated a friendship with you, and not knowing who he was, I believed him.'

Mr King clasped his hands behind his back and walked a few paces away before swinging around to face her again. 'We were friends once.'

'You were? When?'

'Years ago. Before the ...'

'Before?'

Mr King let out a half laugh. 'Before the falling out we had.'

'Oh, that is a shame. Does Mr Moncrief intend revenge?' Serena bit her lip. She busied herself unpegging another towel, recognising the faint odour of lye soap still in the linen.

'I suppose you could say that. I have not spoken to him in years. But according to Judith, he is out to ruin me.'

'Well, I hope I can put your mind at rest, Mr King. I am not a tell-tale. He asked me for my opinion of you and I scolded him for his impudence. So, unless he twists my words around ...'

Serena faltered as she remembered her earlier fears and looked up from her folding. 'Would he do that?'

'Once, I would have denied he had the capacity for heartlessness. But now, I am uncertain.'

Mr King's face held not a trace of emotion. Was he angry? Sad? Afraid? He stepped closer to her again—too close for Serena to remain comfortable. Her heart skipped a beat, or maybe two, and the linen in her hand slipped from her grasp as if it were made of soap rather than coarse material.

'Did you really scold Moncrief?'

'Y--y-yes. I think impertinent was the word I used.' This close, Serena saw that Mr King had shaved today. There was only a dark shadow where his whiskers might be. And the scent of cloves tingled her senses.

He studied her face thoughtfully, for so long, she began to feel awkward. 'It seems I might be able to trust you, Miss Bellingham.'

'Of…of course you c-can.' Serena's words tumbled out in a stutter as the intimacy of the moment disturbed her composure.

'Let's hope then, that Moncrief publishes nothing sinister, shall we?' Breaking his intense gaze, Mr King moved away, relieving the tension between them.

'I shall pray he doesn't.' Serena let out her pent-up breath.

'Pray?'

'Do you not believe in Providence, Mr King?'

He seemed to stiffen. 'I believe in creating my own destiny.'

'That sounds very lonely.'

'The gods are too busy fighting amongst themselves over who is greatest for me to interest them. Greek gods, Egyptian gods, the Jewish god, Islam's Allah, Hindu gods, and that's not an exhaustive list. I don't need a god. I can look after myself.'

Serena could not ignore the hard glint in Mr King's eye as he finished. How could she argue with someone as widely educated as he was, while she had only ever learnt the basic three 'R's? She was no theologian. To Serena, faith was a simple matter of trust—not a process of deliberation. But she suspected if she tried to explain that to him, he would argue her down within moments. She shrugged. 'If you say so, Mr King.'

'Do you not agree that people should be self-sufficient, Miss Bellingham?'

'Well, no. It's nice to be needed, is it not?'

As soon as the words left her mouth, she doubted the truth of them. Indeed, hadn't she wished her sisters and Papa didn't need her quite so much; wished for space to choose her own life. But that's all they were—wishes. The truth was they *did* need her, and she was no longer there to help.

'I suppose so, now you mention it. It is pleasant when someone needs to draw from my wealth of knowledge.'

'But you never need to lean on someone else?'

'No, Miss Bellingham, I don't. In my experience, most people want to control me, and that I prefer to avoid.'

Serena glanced at him but could not read his expression. He delivered statements without sentiment, as though stating facts. She didn't know what to make of his words, and as they parted company, she wondered about this enigma of a man. With resources and intelligence like his, who would have the power to manipulate him? And why did he suspect they did?

Several days passed and Serena began to fall into a routine. In the mornings she would wash the smaller items of linen and clothing, leaving the larger items such as bed linen for the Monday maids. While the laundry dried on the lines, she would move about the house, straightening, dusting, polishing, wherever she saw the need.

For the most part, it was uneventful. She rarely saw Mr King, and if she did, he continued to be brusque, or civil at best. The rest of the family displayed varying levels of suspicion toward her, except Mr Xavier and Mr Jones Senior. She had shared several laughs with the latter, his dry wit matching her sense of humour.

But one thing made Serena more curious every night. Late into the dark hours, when all else was quiet, she heard the clomp, clomp of Mr King's footsteps pass outside her room. Every night. Sometimes it woke her, and sometimes, like tonight, she was still awake and fretting over Papa and the girls. Did the man never sleep?

Since the wind was gusting about the parapets tonight, she had little chance of falling asleep for a while. Perhaps she might see what Mr King was trying to design while he walked.

She slipped her feet into her slippers and pulled her robe over her night dress, tying it securely. Before opening the door, she smoothed her braid to make sure she wouldn't appear too dishevelled, and then stepped into the hallway.

He must have heard the door open, for he swivelled to face her before she could speak.

'Good evening, Mr King,' she aimed for a pleasant smile, 'or is it good morning?'

A rare, wry grin twisted his lips. 'Neither, Miss Bellingham. I believe I just heard the grandfather clock strike midnight.'

'Well, then. Good midnight?' Serena giggled at her own inanity.

'You are not sleeping?'

She gestured towards the roof. 'The wind. It's very noisy.' She dropped her gaze. 'And I miss my family.' Serena glanced up again. 'You are working at this hour?'

Mr King looked away from her but nodded and then shrugged. 'Have you been through the house?' He swept a hand around him.

'Pardon?' Mr King's question surprised Serena.

'Have you seen my home—in its entirety?'

'Well, I ... I've seen parts of it while I work, but I am still unfamiliar with all the rooms and areas.'

Mr King eyed her for a moment as though deciding. 'Perhaps, since you are having trouble sleeping, you might care to join me. I can take you for a tour, if you wish.'

A tour of the house in the dead of night? In her bed clothes? It sounded both improper and adventurous to Serena—a notion she usually conjured up in her imagination. Still, Mr King ought to be working, and Mrs Jones warned her not to bother him. 'Thank you for the offer, Mr King, but I do not wish to distract you from your important work.'

'But I may rest on occasion, may I not? And since I answer to no one, who will complain? Come.' He held out his arm for her to take. 'We'll start with the second level.'

'But I am not dressed, Mr King.'

He glanced over her robe and shrugged. 'I shan't tell, if you don't.'

Serena stared at him, stunned. Had he not berated her for hoydenish behaviour not three days ago? And now he was inviting her to roam the mansion in her nightdress? It didn't make sense, but neither could she deny him—she was beholden to him after all. An icy wave washed over her heart as she once again considered she might be here for his personal entertainment.

God help me. But a refusal might anger him again, and yet he appeared honest and trustworthy.

Serena's heart threatened to sink as she curled her fingers around his elbow. Was this really happening, or was it naught but a strange dream? And what had become of the accusing, curt man she had met on other occasions? This version of Mr King was almost *friendly*. In one sense, Serena knew it must be wrong to wander around a house by moonlight with a gentleman, and unchaperoned. But then, if she owned truth, the prospect of touring the house with Mr King excited her. The speed of her pulse echoed that sentiment.

'Your two nephews are very different from each other,' she ventured to begin a conversation.

'Pleasant boys, if a little simple.'

Mr King's condescension stung, strangely enough. If he belittled his own kin with such ease, it was no wonder he spoke in such rude fashion to her when they first met. Irked, Serena let her frustration show. 'I suppose everyone is simple in your eyes.'

'Well, yes, but that doesn't mean I don't appreciate them. It is a basic fact that my intelligence far exceeds theirs.' Mr King shrugged in a nonchalant fashion.

Such pride! Serena studied his profile in the dull light. Surely, there must be a twinkle in his eye or a twitch to his lips to show he jested. Yet she discerned nothing. Baffled by his attitude, she drew her brows together. 'So then, if we are dim-witted to you, does that make us dull company?' She wanted to understand this man, even if he was exasperating.

'Not at all. I can still be amused. However, if I desire intelligent conversation, then I must find a good scientist, or a philosopher—if you get my gist.'

Serena tried to hide her smile as she nodded. 'And are

there many of those in Sydney, Mr King?' Since much of the population grew through convict transportation, she thought not.

'Sadly, no.' He rolled his eyes. 'No staggering minds have arrived yet, but I will soon convince my old chums from Cambridge to immigrate. In the meantime, I must appease myself with the works of Aristotle, Newton and the likes.'

'And what do you do for enjoyment? Apart from laugh at the poor obtuse folk who surround you.' She shouldn't be goading her new employer, but he seemed to think far too highly of himself.

He stopped and turned to her. 'You are determined to poke fun at me, aren't you? It is understandable, I'm sure, that one such as yourself cannot conceive of what responsibility comes with great intelligence.'

Or perhaps you take yourself too seriously. Serena sighed. 'I'm sure I cannot.'

For all his arrogance, Serena could find nothing in him to terrify or anger her. In fact, as they walked the hallways for the next hour and he pointed out the intricacies of his design, she became more intrigued than frightened. Mr King tried to explain the mathematics involved in constructing the varied arches in the house, both in the stone windows, and the wooden interior. She nodded along, asking several questions, even if she didn't understand the answers. Everything was excessively precise, with little margin for error—at least in his eyes.

Before long he led her to the ballroom, a vast expanse of polished floor and vaulted ceilings hung with several chandeliers. At one end, a raised platform was installed to house the orchestra, and a large pianoforte waited in the darkness for skilled hands to draw magic from the keys. Above it jutted a balcony from where guests could watch the dancing below them. At the other end, a large hearth was inset in the wall to give warmth to the room in winter.

The light of one candle could not do the majestic room justice. Serena made a mental note to revisit in the daylight hours. Apart from the pianoforte, no furniture existed in the ballroom. Perhaps Mr King had never held a ball here. That was a shame for Serena might have given her left foot for an opportunity to watch men and women dance.

As if he'd read her mind, Mr King ceased his architectural monologue, placed his candle on top of the pianoforte and turned to face her. 'Do you play?' He lifted the cover from the keys and motioned toward the stool.

'Oh, Mr King,' Serena gasped, 'It's been several years since my fingers graced the keys, and poorly at that.'

'Never mind. I have enough technique for us both.' He sat at the piano and stretched his fingers.

Serena stood bemused. Did he mean to play? It didn't seem to match his crochety nature.

And yet he played. Serena immediately recognised Beethoven's Sonata number fourteen, otherwise known as *Sonata of the Moonlight*. She smiled at the aptness of his choice. A wistful tune, which he played with flawless precision—expected—and deep expression, which she did not anticipate. Perhaps he was not as heartless as he seemed.

Even more disconcerting was the fact that he stared at her face, not paying attention to where his fingers were going. How did this man switch from a lengthy explanation of building design to playing a sonata in the space of a heartbeat? Mr Xavier Jones's words returned to her then. *My uncle can be impulsive when he chooses.* Well, he was right on that count.

As her shock at the sudden turn of events wore off, Serena closed her eyes. She tried to imagine the ballroom filled with light and dancing people, the strains of music resounding in her ears. How magical it would be. Serena was caught up in the vision in her mind and noticed, too late, that he had finished and that she was still swaying.

He stood before her, too close. Once again, she caught the faint scent of tobacco and cinnamon mixed with lavender. She liked the way he smelled. Without asking or warning her, he slipped one arm around her waist, took her hand in a firm hold and began to twirl her around. On a gasp, she pulled away from him. This couldn't be right, could it? Were her darkest suspicions true? She couldn't let him know how unnerving his behaviour was, and forced a laugh.

'Well, that was diverting. You are very gifted at the piano. Thank you, sir.'

He offered her a formal, overly dramatised bow.

Now what did that mean? No wicked gleam shone in his eyes, just a calm expression of pleasure. Was his taking her in his arms innocent after all? Quite improper, but impulsive and without malice.

Afraid to challenge him, else he revert to hostile behaviour, Serena dipped an awkward curtsy. At that moment, however, she remembered her slippers and dressing gown and the inanity of the moment mixed with her unsettled feelings caused her to erupt in nervous giggles.

'I like to hear you laugh, Miss Bellingham.' His smooth voice came from the shadows, for he had stepped in front of the candle and she could not make out his face. Was he smiling?

'Well, this is rather silly, don't you think? Here, I am in my nightgown, behaving as though I'm at a ball. I should go back to bed if I'm to work tomorrow. But I have enjoyed our tour.'

'You are quite right. One mustn't overtire the staff. I shall walk you back to your room.' He gathered his candle and presented his elbow for her again.

Still giddy, Serena clasped his arm and allowed him to escort her.

Back in the main hallway, they approached a long display table against the wall. Small paintings crowded the surface. Serena drew in a sharp breath. 'The roses.'

Mr King stopped before the table as she peered at the miniatures in the flickering light. They were captivating, just as Papa had described. The reality of why she was in this house descended on her like a heavy shroud. For a moment, the wonder of the building and its occupants had engrossed her, or rather, the one occupant standing next to her. Yet, he had forced her to leave her family. How did Papa fare tonight? Did they eat at all? She knew Papa would miss her as much as she missed him. 'You know, he never meant to do you harm, Mr King.'

He stifled a frustrated sigh. 'Wrong is wrong. He chose to steal. No one steals from me, Miss Bellingham. No one.'

Serena turned to face him, searching his dark eyes for any compassion. 'Is it worth sending a man to prison, though? Or a girl away from a family that need her, to a life of servitude?' She tore her eyes away, unable to face the lack of mercy that she expected there. She didn't even wait for an answer, but pointed to the paintings. 'Which one was it?'

Mr King did not hesitate. He picked up one of the tiny roses and held it where the light of the candle fell on its facade. Serena took it from his hands. A pink rose with droplets of rain still on the petals, open and waiting for the sunshine, painted by an exceptional hand. Struck by its loveliness, and the pain of what her father's actions had caused, a tear slipped from Serena's eye. 'Papa knew precisely what would please me.' She kept her back to Mr King and brushed the moisture from her face. He mustn't see how affected she was by his heartlessness.

'It is one of the better ones.'

Serena nodded and placed it back on the table, swallowing back her emotions. 'If it makes any difference, I apologise on his behalf.'

'An apology doesn't change the facts. He stole, or tried to steal, what was not his. I may accept your apology, but the consequences remain.'

'Consequences that I alone must suffer.' Serena didn't know if she'd said the words loud enough for him to hear. And she didn't wait for a response, but hurried to her room.

7

It is three in the morning. I cannot sleep no matter how I try.

I thought my day would be the same as always—the weight, the torpidness, the endless despising, the call of the fig.

But Serena invaded every moment—Saints above, she is beautiful. The picture of sweetness.

I am aware if I spend too much time with her, Serena will discover the truth. That must not happen.

Oh, but she stirs me from this fog of aimlessness.

Might she cure me of this curse?

That damned monk. If I could find him, I would demand that he remove this scourge he laid on me. And if he refused, I would call curses on his head in retribution.

8

Serena had spent three weeks at Aleron House and had settled in well enough to know how the household operated. It took some time to get used to being on her feet so much, and her feet and back ached until her muscles became used to the constant work. At home she'd shared the load with her two sisters and that was only a tiny cottage.

On Mondays, a cart load of women was brought in from the Female Factory in Paramatta to launder, wash windows, clean rugs, polish floors and scrub every inch of the kitchen. These were convict women who were waiting to be sent out on assignment, not those who were imprisoned for serious crimes. They worked hard all day under the supervision of two guards and were driven back to the Factory in the evening.

After seeing how hard they were forced to work, Serena realised her plight was not so bad, and better than Papa's would have been had he been sent to the penal colony.

Sunday was her day off when she attended a small church service nearby. Then, in the afternoon, she wandered out to a small beach not two hundred yards north. The weather had cooled with the approach of winter, but Serena persisted in her habit of removing her boots and stockings to let her toes revel in the soft sand as she strolled. Serena had inherited her father's love of the sea. She left her shoes on a rock and sauntered along the shoreline, breathing in the salt-laden air.

Looking back toward the house, she understood Mr King's thinking in the design. His personal suite of rooms was on the second floor at the far end of the north wing. From there, his view of the beach and the sea beyond was unobstructed. The view from the south wing was lovely too—green hills scattered with trees—but Mr King must prefer the ocean.

Serena had seen little of Mr King, aside from passing him in the hallways on occasion, since that first week. In those moments, naught had transpired but an awkward nodded greeting, although she often felt as though he would have tarried longer had she encouraged him. But she assumed he was very busy with his design work, since Mrs Jones always insisted it was so. A few times at night she awoke to noises and suspected he walked the house again, stirring his creativity. Although she dared not emerge from her bedroom, afraid of both meeting with his disapproval and of another invitation to tour the house at night.

Thankfully, Mr Moncrief had published nothing about Mr King. Perhaps her prayers were answered. With no one to share her experiences, save Mr Xavier—and he said little—Serena wrote letters to her family. In the pages, she outlined the details she had kept under a buttoned lip at Aleron. Thoughts of Mr King, the house, the family-cum-staff, even that strange night-time tour of the mansion. Hopefully her sisters would laugh, and Papa mightn't miss her too much. She always finished with a few reminders or instructions, such as the special way one needed to pump the tap for the water to flow. She hoped they were faring well in her absence and she loved them dearly, sorry that she was not there to look after them. As yet, their letters had not indicated any terrible struggles—only that they missed her very much.

Serena turned and stared out to sea, allowing the rhythmical crash of the waves to massage her thoughts. Was this where Papa ran aground, changing the course of their lives forever? She let out a wistful sigh. If only she had never mentioned a rose. If only he had never discovered those paintings. She forced the regrets aside and walked on, the light breeze fluttering her skirts against her legs and tugging her hair loose from its binds.

Although it still hurt that she was forced to leave home, and though she worried about her family constantly, life at Aleron House was interesting. She could be almost content. Mr King had decided he might trust her. If that was so, perhaps she might persuade him one day to let her go. To that end, she worked hard and did everything asked of her, never raising a fuss or complaint. Serena made sure that Mr King only heard good reports concerning her.

Turning to walk back to where her shoes waited, Serena saw a figure coming toward her on the sand. From this distance, she couldn't make out if it was Mr King or Mr Xavier—they both looked so similar. Then again, Mr King never wore the garb of a horseman.

'Mr Xavier. What brings you here?' She greeted him with a warm smile.

'My uncle told me you were here. He thought I should come and keep you company.'

'He did?' Serena could not mask her surprise. 'I am curious to know who told him I was here.' Especially considering she had told no one. One of them must have seen her head in this direction.

Mr Xavier shrugged. 'I know not. He was rather engrossed

in his painting. I'm sure he just wanted to be rid of me.' He gave a self-conscious chuckle.

Serena, however, focussed on one word. 'Painting?'

'Yes. He paints. Didn't you know?'

'No.' Astounded was an understatement. How did she miss this important detail? All those roses were *his* work?

'I suppose you've inspected none of the artwork around the house then.' Mr Simon smirked at her in a knowing way.

Suddenly, Serena wanted to hurry back to Aleron and study every painting. But it would be rude to leave Mr Xavier so abruptly. Instead she tried to picture the art. After a few moments, she gave up with a suppressed groan. She had not paid enough attention to the wall decor. 'I confess, I haven't. It is excessively ignorant of me, isn't it?'

A shy laugh escaped from his mouth. 'Don't be too hard on yourself. I'm surprised Uncle Ed hasn't pointed it out to you.'

'It is a little out of character for him.' Serena giggled. 'I wonder why. We haven't spoken often though. Perhaps he never found the opportunity.'

Mr Simon pressed his mouth into a brief smile. 'What do you say to a gallery tour when we return to the house?'

'I should like that very much.' She gave him a genuine smile of gratitude.

They strode in silence for a time.

'He says you come here on occasion.'

Serena shot him a sideways glance. Was Mr King keeping track of her every move? Was he that suspicious of her?

Not wanting to express her uncertainties to Mr Xavier, she lifted her shoulders and dropped them again. 'As often as I can. But the cleaning keeps me rather busy.'

'I enjoy the sea air myself.' Mr Xavier glanced at her. 'If you need an escort, I am happy to be of service. I'm usually with the horses if you ever need to find me.'

Serena looked over at him again and a bashful expression spread on his face. He was uncomfortable making this offer, but why? Was it just his shyness, or was he acting under orders? But then, by the slight tinge to his neck, perhaps there was more to it. Was he attracted to her? Serena's eyes widened at the thought. Mr Xavier was handsome and provided pleasant company. Maybe she should spend time with him. If something developed ...

She shouldn't think so far ahead. The last time she let her imagination run in that direction, she had been severely disappointed. She tucked a stray strand of hair behind her ear again. 'I do like the solitude here, but I confess I prefer to have company. Thank you.'

They arrived at the rock which guarded her boots and Mr Xavier politely turned his back while she slipped her stockings on. Would he think her barefootedness vulgar? She hoped not. It would be a shame to have to change her ways.

'There. All done.' She straightened and brushed the sand from her hands.

Mr Xavier offered her his elbow. 'I think your method of strolling on the beach is better. I might try it myself next time.'

'Next time it might be too cold.' Serena wrapped her fingers around his arm.

'True. Then next time, perhaps we should ride the horses here.'

'I'm sure that would be enjoyable, except I've never ridden a horse. Is it hard?'

There was his gentle laugh again. 'Not really, but it does take time and practise. I guess we'll stick to walking in our boots for now.'

'Boots it is.' Serena joined him laughing. It was lovely to have found at least one friend at Aleron. If only Mr King trusted her as he said he might, her days would be satisfactory. At least, for now.

As they strolled back to the house, the ever-present questions rolled across Serena's mind.

'Do you mind if I ask you something, Mr Xavier?'

'Not at all.'

'You and your brother—you do not seem.... I mean to say …You are obviously well educated. Why is it that you are here working as servants?'

Mr Xavier kept his eyes on the ground.

'Yes, that education came from none other than Uncle Ed. Mother insisted we would learn best from him.'

'But neither of you are out and about in society like other young men. If Mr King attended Cambridge, then—and correct me if I am wrong—you all come from a wealthy family at least, if not titled. It seems odd that you would live so modestly. Pardon if I am being impertinent.'

There was that bashful smile again.

'No. You are very astute Miss Bellingham. My grandfather on my mother's side was a knight.'

'A knight?'

'Yes, but he died when I was quite young and soon after that we all came to Australia.'

'And now you all live rather quiet lives. It seems a shame.'

Mr Xavier shrugged.

'It's all right. This is the way Mother likes it. She…she worries about us overmuch.'

Overmuch seemed like an understatement. Why would a

mother keep her sons in an inferior way to that which they were born? The circumstances at Aleron House became stranger and stranger.

9

As soon as they entered the house, Mr Xavier headed straight for the hall table that displayed the miniature paintings of roses. Serena could not wait another minute to learn the truth. Picking up the small frame containing the pink rose, she carried it to the window where she could study the detail. Sure enough, there in the corner in tiny black lettering was the signature, *E King*.

'You see?' Mr Xavier smirked.

'Yes, indeed.' No wonder the man took offence when Papa tried to steal it. Hadn't he said it was one of the better ones? Maybe even his favourite work. Serena now understood why it was so valuable to him. She worried her lip with her teeth as she replaced the miniature in pride of place on the table and bent to examine the others. Yes, each one of them bore his signature.

So, Mr King had an infatuation with painting roses.

'What else has he painted?'

Serena explored the long hallways with Mr Xavier, stopping to take in every piece of art. A few hangings were the work of other artists, but several had Mr King's signature. Soon enough, she recognised his style before she saw his name, and Mr Xavier laughed at her enthusiasm. Scenery, people, animals and several buildings—all painted with an exceptional hand. There were even a few large pieces depicting rose bushes, or roses in a vase. This artist certainly had an eye for the majestic.

Mr Xavier had said his uncle was painting at present, even now as they wandered the house admiring his gift.

His gift.

Surely this was a most gifted man. Not just intelligent, but also artistic and creative. Serena saw why he weighed his talents so heavily and so seriously. It didn't excuse his conceited behaviour, but she understood why he felt burdened by his giftedness. How would one focus such a wide variety of talent? It might be hard to find specific purpose when one had so many paths of possibility from which to choose.

'He has more art in his suite. Shall we go and visit?' Mr Xavier gestured towards the north wing.

The temptation was strong. Would he be displeased if they disturbed him? Surely, he broke from his work on the Sabbath. Might he protest if they broke his concentration?

'I thought you said he wanted to be rid of you. Won't he be vexed by our interruption?'

Mr Xavier waved a dismissive hand in the air. 'He is harmless.'

Curiosity won out, and though her steps into the north wing hesitated at times, soon Serena stood with Mr Xavier in front of the doors to Mr King's suite. She chewed on her lip, while he knocked. What excuse might she give for invading Mr King's privacy? Very little besides the truth. She drew in a deep breath. *Calm down, Serena, Mr Xavier brought you here!*

His knock echoed into the hallway behind them and sent her heart rate up a notch. Too late to run away now unless he didn't answer. She'd hardly seen him since that night-time tour, and that strange moment in the ballroom. The seconds ticked by as they waited. *One, two, three …*

At twenty-three, when Serena was certain Mr King had

either not heard, or ignored the knock, footsteps approached the door and it swung open. There he stood, unshaven, dark silk shirt open at the neck with no cravat in sight, his house coat slung wide at his shoulders—not expecting visitors—and smelling of turpentine. Serena's eyes locked on the masculine hair visible at his open throat, and her heart skipped a beat. Inappropriate, that was their idea to call on him uninvited. She forced her gaze away and turned to leave, heat rising in her cheeks.

But Mr Xavier had no such qualms.

'Hello Uncle. I've brought Miss Bellingham to see your artwork.'

'Though we can come another time, when it is more suitable,' Serena added. Mr King was clearly not prepared to receive guests. 'Sorry for the intrusion, sir.'

Again, Serena turned to flee.

'Wait. Don't go. Please. Just give me a moment.'

He motioned them into his large sitting room and then disappeared into an adjoining room. Serena perched on the edge of a chair, ready to fly, and twisted her hands together. What made her so nervous she could not say, except that he stirred unwanted feelings in her. Before she could settle herself, Mr King returned, this time in appropriate attire, albeit still unshaven.

'I apologise for my untidy appearance. I have been busy.' He sat opposite her, also on the edge of a sofa. 'How was your walk on the beach?'

'Very pleasant, thank you. Mr Xavier came and joined me.'

Mr King glanced at Mr Xavier and then back at her. 'My nephew is a good sort.'

'Yes, he is.' Serena entwined her fingers in the fabric of her skirt until the twists began to cut her circulation. 'He told me you enjoy painting.'

'I do, yes. I paint a great deal. There are so many ideas up here, Miss Bellingham.' He tapped his head. 'Why, I have started three pieces today. First, a rose at the end of its life, then I pictured an image of Misty and Storm racing through the surf, so I sketched that out. And then I thought it would be grand to do portraits of my nephews. No sooner do I get an outline drawn for one idea, then another fills my head, and I'm sure each one will be a masterpiece.'

Serena stared at him, wide-eyed. The broody expression he usually wore had vanished. The man before her oozed enthusiasm and energy—and conceit—gesturing with his hands as he spoke, hands that still carried stains from the oils he'd been using. His eyes sparked with zeal for his ideas and the art of painting. Instead of clipped, precise phrases, he was chattering. Whatever she had expected from visiting Mr King, this was not it.

'Well, Mr Xavier has shown me the art around the house. I didn't realise most of the work was yours.'

Again, Mr King glanced at his nephew. 'Thank you, Xavier. You honour me.'

Mr Xavier blushed. 'You know how much I value your paintings.'

Mr King's eyes held expectation as he turned back to Serena. 'And what did you think?'

'They are wonderful.'

'Aha.' He clapped his hands. 'You see. I knew it.'

'Knew what?'

'I knew you'd appreciate my art.'

Serena quirked an eyebrow at him. He'd waited for her to notice, so he could exult in her praises?

'You are very confident.' Had he forgotten how much he'd hurt her family? Perhaps he needed a reminder. She pointed to one of his paintings. 'I don't like that one so much—it is a little dark for my taste.'

Mr Xavier choked back a laugh and then covered his mouth, but Mr King seemed to not even notice her slight.

'Come, I must show you some more.'

He grabbed her hand and jerked her to her feet in his enthusiasm, and she let out a startled 'oh'.

'Uncle!' With a single word from Mr Xavier, Mr King dropped her hand.

'Forgive me.' The words sounded sincere enough, but immediately Mr King's enthusiasm returned and he led them, almost dancing, into another room.

Mr Xavier blocked her entry for a moment, turning to whisper to her.

'Don't mind my uncle. Sometimes he has trouble controlling his … er … impulses.'

With that, he followed Mr King. What did he mean by that? Mr King acted before thinking? Was that why he'd just grabbed her hand? And was that why he'd taken her in his arms that night? Mr Xavier had implied he acted on whims before.

Serena shook her head. She would have to think about it later. Looking around her, paintings rested on easels and hung on every inch of wall space. Except for one wall, which was an entire mural of its own. Did his pride need feeding so much he had to parade his art in front of her, or was it more than that? Perhaps he relished sharing his enjoyment with another soul. After all, she supposed his family might have become quite inured to it after many years.

Whatever the reason, Serena stood dumbfounded as she

encountered one exquisite piece of work after another. The colours, the lines—every detail spoke of beauty. The wall painting portrayed a mermaid perched on dangerous rocks, beckoning to a nearby ship from which a young man stared at her with wistful longing. His imagery spoke to her of a yearning for perfection and its unattainable nature.

'What do you think?'

What could she say? That she was speechless with amazement? Serena didn't want him to know his creativity astounded her. He was still her gaoler. She pursed her lips, trying to think of a set-down.

Mr King didn't wait for her response, but strode over to two of the easels. 'Some are unfinished. Did you see this?'

No, she hadn't. Between the stands was a small pedestal, atop which sat a pretty ceramic vase with a delicate ceramic rose hanging over the lip. 'Oh, it's perfect,' Serena breathed before she remembered she was trying to hide her enjoyment. 'Where did you find that?'

Mr King's mouth stretched into the first full smile Serena had seen, and her heart thumped despite her determination to remain indifferent. 'I made it.'

'You made it? Is there nothing you can't do?'

'Very little.' Mr Xavier answered for him.

It had to be an exaggeration, but right now, Serena was overwhelmed. It was a bad idea to have come here. As much as she wanted to find more faults with him, the brilliance he accomplished outweighed any social ineptitude. She searched the room again. Sure enough, there were several more pedestals with delightful ceramic sculptures, and even wood carvings on them. 'You made those too, I expect?' She rolled her eyes and ran her fingers over the perfectly smooth wood.

'I did.'

Serena sucked in a deep breath and released it with a loud sigh. 'Well, Mr King. I never imagined you'd surprise me again, but I confess I am quite astonished.'

That evening at the family dinner table, the cook, as always, brought out covered platters and everyone began serving themselves food. When the door opened and Mr King entered the room, the whole family seemed surprised.

'Ed, what brings you down here to us mere mortals?' Mr Jones winked at him.

'Robert, don't be a tease.' Mrs Jones scolded her husband playfully, then turned to her brother. 'It is nice to see you here, dear.'

'Yes, I thought I might join you for supper this evening,' Mr King said as he pulled out the chair at the head of the table and sat. 'What has Becker delivered up tonight? Something delicious I hope. It smells divine at any rate.' He glanced up and saw that everyone stared at him. 'What? Cannot a man enjoy a meal in his own dining room?'

'Of course, dear.' Mrs Jones sent reproachful glares at her sons and husband, who then returned to dishing up food as if nothing strange had taken place.

Serena watched the entire exchange with piqued interest, whilst forking succulent duck and greens into her mouth. That was definitely one benefit of being stuck at Aleron—exceptional food.

The family seemed unaccustomed to Mr King's presence in the room. Indeed, Serena had not seen him in the dining room once in the three weeks she'd been here. Clearly it was not a common occurrence. Was it as Mr Jones insinuated—Mr King thought himself so far above the others that he secluded himself? Or did he never have time to leave his work and eat with his family?

'Have we all had a pleasant day?' If Mr King noticed his family's awkwardness, he did not show it.

A round of 'yes, thank yous' followed, but only Mr Jones continued. 'Reverend Phillips gave a stirring sermon this morning. He spoke about the prophet Ezekiel. Did you know he prophesied the destruction of several ruling powers well before they took place? Fascinating stuff.'

'He was probably an intellect of his time. You would only need to study a nation and how it managed its affairs to figure out its downfall was inevitable. Prophecy is overrated. Pass me the duck, please.'

Mr Simon sent the requested platter along the table.

Mr Jones would not be dissuaded. 'And yet their destruction was not always from internal mismanagement. Many were decimated when overtaken by foreign nations. How could you predict that? Besides, he would have to be well travelled to study every nation he prophesied against. But he was just an exile living in Babylon.'

'Nevertheless, Robert, there would be a logical explanation. To say he heard the voice of God is absurd.' Mr King selected a leg, before spooning greens onto his plate.

'You are very adamant for someone who has studied almost every work of ancient writing except for the Bible.'

Serena didn't miss the twinkle in Mr Jones's eyes. He enjoyed baiting his brother-in-law.

'And you are rather adamant for one who chose not to take orders, but joined the military instead.'

The twinkle in Mr Jones eyes died, replaced with a flash of regret. Had Mr King just insulted his brother-in-law?

Mr King, ignoring the effect of his words, turned to his nephew, his fork poised near his mouth.

'What have you been up to this afternoon, Simon?'

'I worked on my project.' Although the young gardener brightened with his uncle in the room, he remained somewhat sullen, and kept a suspicious eye on Serena.

Mr Jones nodded toward Serena. 'He works with wood as a hobby. He's building a roosting box for the local birds at present, and he's got other projects in motion, too.'

'Oh.' Serena nodded. So, the creativity didn't stop with Mr King.

'He made me a brilliant rocker last year.' Mr Xavier beamed with pride.

'And I received a lovely carved trinket box for my last birthday,' said Mrs Jones.

Did Mr King teach his nephew how to carve the wood, or to design his projects? Mr Simon turned crimson after the flood of compliments. 'It was nothing. Not like Uncle Ed's work, anyhow.' He tried to divert the attention away from himself.

'It is not nothing. And you should not compare yourself to Eddie,' Mrs Jones chided.

'No, you shouldn't.' Mr King agreed.

Because he was unmatched? Mr King didn't show humility, or even false humility.

By the time supper finished, Serena had a stronger understanding of the dynamics between Mr King and the family members who lived at Aleron House. There was much affection between them, although there was a slight undercurrent of tension. Mr King didn't belittle his family, but neither did he act as though he were their equal. It was rather condescending, in fact. But Serena did not doubt that he cared for them.

Mr King had gone off to play cards and smoke with the menfolk, which was sociable of him, leaving Serena to keep company with Mrs Jones. Mrs Jones, however, had letters to write, so Serena had to fend for herself. She remembered the vast library Mr King kept. She should ask him for permission before borrowing any volumes. How would he react to yet another imposition? He'd been receptive this afternoon, but he had been alone then and now he was with his nephews. She shrugged to herself. There was no harm in trying.

Serena hurried after the gentlemen, hoping to catch Mr King before they settled in the drawing room. She rounded a corner in time to see them filing through the doorway.

'Excuse me, Mr King.'

They all looked back at her, questions written on their faces. She approached hesitantly. 'I wanted to speak to Mr King.'

He nodded to her and stepped aside, leaving the others to continue. 'Yes, Miss Bellingham?'

'I was wondering if I might borrow a book from your library.'

'By all means.' He seemed pleased at the request. 'Although, if you're looking for one of those three volume travesties by Jane Austen or the like, you will be disappointed. I keep only quality reading in my library.'

'Oh,' Serena swallowed her embarrassment. She had hoped for something romantic. 'Do you have any recommendations?'

He nodded enthusiastically. 'There are several wonderful histories in there. But, if you prefer something more fictional, I have the complete works of Shakespeare. And, of course, there's poetry. You may try Lord Byron if you prefer.'

'Thank you, sir.' Serena offered him a light curtsy.

For a moment, she thought he might follow her, but after a slight hesitation, he turned back to the gentlemen and re-joined them as they lit pipes and laughed. Serena paused and looked through the gap as she pulled the door closed. Mr King lifted a small silver box from his pocket and flicked it open. He took a pinch of powder from it and put it to his nose, sniffing hard and loud. Ah, he didn't smoke like the others, he took snuff instead. Thoughtful, she shut the door and headed for the library.

Strange, the difference between Mr King and Mr Xavier. While the latter was comfortable company and easy to talk to, she was more drawn to the unsettling presence of Mr King. Mr Xavier made a good companion, but her thoughts turned to Mr King more often. Serena let out a groan. She shouldn't be thinking in this direction. Mr King only saw her as a prisoner and Mr Xavier, well, who knew if he saw her as anything else, either? She needed to get a book and busy herself with reading it. That would keep her runaway mind in check. She hoped.

10

Simon calls me a fool. Why did I bring her here? Can I not see she is my ruin? And if she doesn't ruin me by her machinations, Xavier will with his chatter. Xavier must be warned.

But no! He cannot see. She is the cure for this curse.

The fig mocks me also. It will have me yet, it says. But it no longer draws me, instead Serena does.

I am filled with ideas, plans for the future—buildings to design, paintings to draw, sculptures, words—the list is endless and continues to grow with every waking minute. I can't sleep for the excitement. Need forces me to write them down before they vanish into the ether. I write and sketch until my fingers cramp, but still they come. The next thing I know, the sun is sending its rays through my window.

And rising with the sun is Serena. Soon she will be in the yard, hanging washing. I can watch her from the second-floor parlour.

When Serena worries, or is concentrating, she has an endearing way of clamping her lip between her teeth. It makes me wish to puzzle her, just to see it.

Stay away. Stay away. Stay away.

She must not learn of the curse. I must speak with Xavier.

11

Serena strolled along the colonnade that spanned the length of the south wing. Another colonnade mirrored the covered walkway on the north wing, giving the mansion its symmetry. Her heels clicked on the pavers and she allowed her hand to brush the smooth stone pillars that reached up to form pointed arches above her head. Mr King was in the elegant detail of every part of this building. Everywhere she looked, fastidious design met her gaze.

She released a sigh as she leaned up against a column. The house held her in an enchantment, she could no longer deny it. It always had. But, perhaps it was not just the house that had gripped her. Mr King. How she yearned to know him more—the intricate ways of his mind. Serena was still unsure whether his exhibition of art the other day was a display of self-importance, or a simple sharing of interests. Did he mean to convince her of his exceeding craftsmanship by overwhelming her with it? Or did his passion for art overflow to any who might lend him a willing ear?

And then there was the matter of those sudden and strange impulses, which the family hinted at, but which she had experienced as well. Did Mr King really have trouble with self-control or was it simply ill-mannered behaviour? She had never encountered anyone like him before.

Serena was not certain of anything at Aleron. The seeming changeable nature of Mr King—at first irritable and rude and then open and cordial, even at times charming. The protectiveness of his family. It sat at odds with her experience of a normal household. But then, normal in a house this size might be quite different.

Oh, but she missed her family near the docks. She never imagined she would pine for the smell of brine and fish—or the noise of city living, with its constant stream of carts grating in the laneways, the 'hoy' of warning shouted here and there. And the people. On top of missing her father and sisters, she yearned for her morning visits to the baker, or the butcher, if they had extra coins that week. There was much colour in her old routine that sadly lacked here at Aleron house. And at home, her family needed her. She served only one purpose at Aleron.

For several weeks now it had been breakfast, then washing—wringing, hanging, starching, folding, ironing—and dusting and polishing all day with only a few breaks to eat and drink. At the end of the day, she fell exhausted into bed. After supper, Serena was free to do as she wished, but too often she was so depleted, she could only read a page or two of Lord Byron before falling asleep.

The only change to this routine came with the occasional visit from Mr King, or a walk on the beach with Mr Xavier. The two men caused such opposing emotions in her. Whenever Mr King intercepted her, her heart fluttered and the familiar attraction drew her, but then he always left her baffled. When she strolled on the sand with Mr Xavier, she was at peace, but apart from his well-looking face, he aroused little more in her than friendly affection.

With another sigh, Serena straightened from the pillar and pulled her shawl tighter around her shoulders. The late afternoon breeze became chillier by the day. Footsteps scuffed on the stone flagging to her right, causing her to turn to greet whomever came her way.

'Mr King. What brings you out here?'

He approached in a manner that Serena could only describe as jogging, or was it skipping? Perhaps a cross between the two.

'I might ask you the same, Miss Bellingham.' Mr King drew her attention to the fading light with a sweep of his hand. 'It is getting cold out.'

'Oh, I don't mind the cold so much, and I wanted fresh air before supper.' She fell into step beside him as they walked back toward the entrance. 'I'm used to a draughty house and thin garments, you know.'

He appeared to study her shawl for a moment with an intense gaze. Did he think her lack of the finer things made her lesser somehow? Even her austere circumstances were only a recent happening. Once, she'd been wealthy, with many prospects for the future.

Serena swallowed those dashed dreams of the past and reached out to run a hand over one of the smooth columns. 'I must confess I was out here admiring your architecture.' She released a wistful sigh for effect.

Mr King stopped walking and turned to stare at her as if reading her sincerity. 'You have an interest in structure?'

Serena let out a self-conscious laugh and continued toward the door. 'Well, I've always loved beautiful homes. Truth be told, I dreamt of living in such a place. Aleron is so majestic, I can't help it.'

'It pleases me to hear you say that.' Within a few strides he was at her side again, grinning broadly.

Another boost to his ego, Serena supposed, but suppressed the sigh of frustration that rose in her. And yet, he surprised her as he leaned closer to speak.

'Meet me in the library after supper. I wish to show you something.'

Serena's heart rate leapt at his nearness, and at his suggestion of a secret meeting. Before she could ask him what he wanted to show her, he had hurried off toward his rooms. What treasure did the library hold that he was eager to show her?

Supper was tedious, despite the delicacies that enriched her plate. Serena found it hard to concentrate on the conversations taking place around her. She nodded absently here and there when one of the family addressed her directly. When Mr Xavier asked her if aught was the matter, she pleaded weariness from the day's work—which was not entirely untrue. It warmed her heart that he cared enough to ask. If only Mr King showed her such compassion, then she might be more certain of his approval.

Finally, after making her excuses to Mrs Jones, Serena made her way to the library. More than a little excited, she checked over her shoulder several times to make sure she wasn't being followed. Was she committing an indiscretion? Guilt had a way of creeping in—unwelcome. Mr King hadn't suggested anything untoward, after all. Glancing behind her once more, she turned the knob and pushed open the library door.

There he sat, lounging on a sofa, an open book on his lap. He did not appear to be waiting for an arranged appointment at all, let alone a secret one.

A little breathless, she greeted him. 'Good evening, Mr King.'

His eyes shot up and he snapped the book closed. 'Ah, Miss Bellingham.' He rose to his feet and approached her.

'What is it you wanted to show me?' Serena scanned the dimly lit room for anything out of the ordinary.

Mr King's gaze ran over her entire being. 'Do you have warmer clothes to wear?'

'No, but I'm all right. It's not excessively cold in here.'

'Hmm. We shall have to remedy that. Wait here. I'll return momentarily.' With those words, he hurried from the room.

Had he heard her?

When he returned a few minutes later, he carried a heavy cloak and a scarf over his arm. 'These should keep you warm enough.' He presented them to her.

'I don't understand, Mr King. I am comfortable in here.'

'But we are not staying in here,' he announced with animation. 'I have asked Xavier to hitch the greys to my curricle. I want to take you for a drive.'

Serena opened her mouth in a silent 'oh'. He was taking her out. In his carriage. At night.

A tiny thrill shot through her body. She did not expect he had anything in mind other than sharing an interesting book, but she was not inclined to refuse any time with him.

Mr King held the coat up for her and then draped the scarf around her neck.

'Thank you, sir.'

'Shall we, then?' He proffered his arm.

With a smile, she hooked her hand through his elbow and let him lead her to the stables.

A serious-faced Mr Xavier greeted them. 'Uncle, I wish you wouldn't take the curricle out at night. There is no moon this evening and the clouds obscure the stars.'

'Nonsense, Xavier. I have a bright lantern and I am not racing. And besides, we are not going far. Just to the lighthouse. We shall be back before you know it.'

Mr Xavier looked as though he had much more to say, but held his tongue and nodded instead, fiddling with the reins in his hand.

Mr King turned to Serena and assisted her into the light carriage, then climbed up beside her. The young horseman handed him the reins without a smile and bid them a safe drive. Mr King tipped his hat to his nephew and flicked the reins.

'Did you mention a lighthouse?' The exchange between the two men piqued Serena's interest.

Mr King shot her a sideways glance. 'I thought since you appreciated Aleron, I would show you other interesting architecture in the region.'

'Oh.'

'Yes. Francis Greenway built the lighthouse nearby. He died five years ago, but his work lives on.' He briefly looked at her again. 'That's the great thing about buildings. They outlive their creators.'

Serena smirked at him. 'Unless they burn down.'

Mr Kings eyebrows drew together. 'What a thing to say. Miss Bellingham, I declare that was most irreverent of you.'

As if the structures themselves were deities. Serena turned her face away, so he did not notice her roll her eyes.

'Anyway, as I was saying, Mr Greenway designed several buildings around Sydney. He originally came to Australia as a prisoner. Fraud I think it was. But while still incarcerated, he showed his ability in design and soon received a commission to build the Macquarie Lighthouse. He wasn't happy just to create buildings in the standard way, he aspired for something greater.

No box-like structures for him, no. He built in grand Palladian style as you shall soon see.'

'Will I see, sir? In the dark?'

Mr King turned to her with a quirked eyebrow as though in disbelief. 'It's a lighthouse, m'dear. Of course you'll see it.'

Serena suppressed a giggle and pulled the cloak tighter around her shoulders. Even if Mr King thought too highly of himself, he certainly possessed a wealth of knowledge. She could learn a deal of information from him. Indeed, it would be akin to receiving an education—something she had experienced little of before Mama passed. And what a teacher he would be.

Once again, Mr King shifted his face toward her, this time with a gentle smile. Serena bit on her lip and dipped her head. Thankfully it was too dark for him to see her blush. He mustn't know the attraction she felt. Surely, he would think her more the fool for it.

'Here we are,' he declared, rounding a bend, and Serena saw the aura of light shining from the lighthouse out to the ocean beyond them.

12

The lighthouse was a whitewashed construction, tall and stately. Similar arches to those at Aleron graced the base of the lighthouse. 'These arches are more rounded than yours,' Serena noted as her escort handed her from the curricle.

'Yes, I follow a more gothic approach than Mr Greenway did, more reminiscent of churches and cathedrals.' His fingers lingered over hers for a moment, making Serena's heart quicken. She tugged her hand away and walked toward the edifice.

Mr King, having secured the horses, jogged up beside her with the lantern and offered her his arm. Serena hesitated. She could become too comfortable with this closeness.

'We can't have you stumbling in the dark.' He gave her a cajoling wink.

Serena capitulated and took his arm, but kept her gaze fixed on the lighthouse. 'Why use a design trait usually devoted to glorifying God?'

Mr King eyed her askance. 'Why should God be stingy with the grand architecture? Are we not worthy to live with as elegant design as He?'

Serena tried not to frown at his arrogance. 'None of us is worthy, Mr King. Not in the least.'

'Humph.' He gave her a dubious look. 'And do you suppose such humility impresses the Almighty?' His words held a hint of scorn.

Serena carefully chose her reply. 'The Scriptures say a man's pride shall bring him low, but honour shall uphold the humble in spirit.'

'They say that?' Mr King looked more doubtful than ever.

'Yes, they do. In Proverbs, I think.'

He shrugged. 'I put little stock in the Bible. So, what is your impression of this lighthouse?'

Like that, he dismissed the subject, without a blink of his brown eyes. Did he realise that King David called God a light to his path—a guiding light similar as a lighthouse to a sailor? Serena determined not to press Mr King on the matter though, and turned her full attention to the tall building before her. They now stood at the base of it, and she leaned her head back to admire the majesty of the smooth stone tower—a herald to ships on the sea to find safety. An important structure that must stand the test of time.

As if reading her mind, Mr King spoke. 'I daresay this lighthouse will stand for several hundred years yet. It is soundly built, even if I had naught to do with its construction.'

Serena's lips twitched with amusement at his superiority again. 'Does it pain you to admit another architect has done well?'

He arched an eyebrow at her. 'Why should it pain me? Credit where credit is due, you know. Aleron house will survive at least as long as this lighthouse, if not longer.'

'You are that confident?'

Mr King seemed surprised at the question. 'Of course I am. Were I not confident, I should have torn it down by now and rebuilt it.'

How was it possible to enjoy someone's company when they

often spouted sentiments of self-importance? And yet, Serena did. She shook her head in amusement. 'Well, this lighthouse is remarkable. For a building so necessary to seafarers, it is surprisingly graceful.'

Mr King rounded on her, peering into her face in the dim light. 'Would you like to see more?'

'Well, I—'

'It shan't take long. And I promise they are at least as interesting as this.'

'But it must be almost midnight. Doesn't the darkness concern you?'

Mr King grimaced. 'I am adept at handling the reins you know, and the night is yet young. Come, it will be diverting, I promise you.'

He appeared so genuine and his face held such wide-eyed expectancy that Serena could hardly say no. However, she doubted she had much wakefulness left in her. 'Very well. Lead the way, Mr King.'

It turned out that Mr King grossly underestimated his idea of 'it won't take long'. Five miles and almost an hour later, he steered the curricle into the sparsely lit streets of Sydney. Oh, so close to her family, her heart was drawn toward the docks, as though an invisible string tugged it in that direction. Dare she ask him to visit?

'Mr King…' she swallowed the question before she blurted it out, too afraid.

Perhaps this hadn't been the wisest idea, after all. No one chaperoned them, and their 'short outing' was now several hours long. Serena smothered a yawn as he handed her from the vehicle outside another intimidating piece of architecture.

'This one, I think you will appreciate.'

Serena looked up and focused in the semi-darkness. 'Why it is St James.' She'd walked past this church countless times over the years. 'I am very familiar with it.'

'But did you know Greenway designed this building?'

She shrugged. 'No, I never thought about it.' Serena gazed up at the towering spire, although it was difficult to see on such a dark night, and then studied the rest of the building. 'I do recognise similarities to the lighthouse. The curved arches, for instance.'

'You are quite insightful, Miss Bellingham. Walk with me.' He thrust his elbow out.

'Mr King. It is the middle of the night. Should we not—'

'Nonsense. Those rules on the proper times for an excursion are the fabrications of stuffy individuals with no imagination. You only live once.' He turned to her as he finished this rebuke and such animation lit his eyes, she could not argue with him. Mr King wrung an exorbitant amount of life from every moment. Overawed by it, Serena could only nod her compliance.

They had barely turned the corner when Mr King pointed out the Barracks building. 'That is also a Greenway design.'

Serena had little to say. The arches were represented again, but the total construction was square and less interesting than the lighthouse and the church.

'Did you know he also designed the Female Factory at Paramatta, where the maids come from every Monday?'

'No, I didn't know that. I'm sure Mr Greenway must have been very busy with all of these buildings.'

The two walked on in the darkness and Serena pulled the coat tighter around her shoulders. As the night deepened, the air grew colder still. Few other souls roamed the streets at this hour. Serena gasped at two men staggering in a drunken stupor, presumably back to their homes for the night. The occasional horse and carriage trundled by, but the streets were quiet, save for the howling of dogs in the distance. They were nearing the shoreline—Serena sensed it in the salt on the air, and pangs of longing for home arose within her again.

'You are quiet of a sudden, Miss Bellingham.'

'I was just reminded of home. The smell of the ocean brings it back.' Serena swallowed the lump in her throat as she glanced up at him.

As they approached one of the street lamps, she noted a frown creased the small space between Mr King's brows. Was he perturbed by her admission?

'You miss living in a hovel surrounded by the stench of fish?'

'I've never called it a hovel … and my family must miss me as much as I miss them.'

'You found happiness with needy siblings and a pilfering father?'

As quick as the pangs of homesickness had risen, a burst of anger now overrode them. 'Mr King! You go too far. I love my father, even though he made one mistake, and I love my sisters, even though they have been my responsibility these past few years. My home was, well, *my home*. Until you took it away from me. Do you never care for anything save yourself?'

The words were out before she could stop them, but then she clamped a hand over her mouth. 'I'm sorry. I …'

A distant look came over Mr King's features. A memory perhaps, or maybe he didn't care for her tirade.

'I should not have spoken so boldly.'

Mr King said nothing, but continued to walk toward the harbour.

'It appears you consider me ungrateful.' Serena wanted him

to know how his words had affected her.

He shrugged—a noncommittal lift of his shoulders—which told her nothing.

'It is hard to be grateful when an injustice has been done to me and my papa.'

'I could have had him imprisoned.'

Serena wanted to groan. So, she should appreciate that one reprieve? 'Instead *I* am imprisoned. In luxury, yes, but a prison nonetheless.'

'There must be consequences. That is true justice.'

'And what of grace?'

'Was it not grace to allow your father to continue to provide for your family, instead of rotting in gaol while you starved?'

Serena let out a long, frustrated sigh. She was not intelligent enough to keep arguing with him. And to be honest, he had a point—although, it would be preferable if Mr King could extend enough grace to pardon the whole incident. After all, Father did not actually succeed in stealing the painting.

'And here we are at another of Greenway's buildings.' He stopped and gestured with his arms at the walls before them, closing the topic of justice versus grace.

Still churning with frustration, Serena looked up at the structure before her and tried to put aside her annoyance. 'Why, it is a castle.'

Mr King made a mirthless noise that might have been a laugh—and a scornful one at that. 'Yes, a very elaborate design. However, it is a stable.'

Serena gaped at him, dumbfounded. 'A stable? Why create a stable that resembles a castle?'

He made a face. 'I imagine the government house they planned would have dwarfed it by comparison. But they never completed the rest. I believe Mr Greenway thought too much of himself and in time, he lost his position.'

She had to use great restraint to not compare one architect with the other standing before her. Could Mr King not see the similarity? Would he be in danger of losing his commission if he continued to act so superior?

'If I were him, I would have stuck to my ideals, too. Perhaps I might have suffered the same fate.'

Had he read her mind?

'But then, I possess an advantage over Francis Greenway.'

Serena cocked her head at him. 'And what is that?'

His face split into a wide grin and he winked at her. 'I have charm.' In an unexpected movement, he grasped her by the hand and pulled her along the street. 'Come, I feel like a dip in the ocean.'

How was she supposed to convince Mr King to go home? He did not appear weary in the slightest, but skipped down the lane ahead, while she stumbled behind, exhaustion dragging at her every step. One moment he had been the harsh master, the next a proud architect, and now an excited little boy. But then, she switched and changed almost as much—from fatigued, to exasperated, to intrigued and even entranced. His boundless enthusiasm was infectious.

Serena had no idea of the time, except from the way her eyelids drooped the moment she stopped moving. Like now, when she sat upon a rock whilst Mr King peeled off his shoes and socks, and frolicked in the shallows, mindless of the cold.

'Come, Miss Bellingham. Come and join me.' He ran along the shoreline, kicking up water and sending spray high into the air. He would be soaked through in moments if she didn't discourage him.

'No, no, Mr King. I am content to sit here for now. But we must leave soon, I think.' She smothered another yawn.

Mr King was enjoying himself so much that guilt nagged at her for wanting him to stop. Serena panicked when it appeared he might strip to his underclothes and dive right into the water, but he must have had second thoughts as moments later he turned and ran back up the beach.

Breathless, he paused before her. 'We should return to the horses, yes?'

Serena gave him a definite nod. If she'd known the welfare of his animals might draw him home, she would have used that excuse earlier. When she gazed at him in the moonlight, his eyes were bright with zeal. Water dripped from the ends of his dark hair and gleamed on his coat. He must be saturated, but seemed unperturbed. Mr King pulled on his shoes and walked her back to their waiting curricle.

If she assumed they had finished their tour—that they would return to Aleron—she was wrong again. No sooner were they seated and he'd taken up the reins than Mr King turned to her with wide eyes. 'I'll take you there.'

Fighting the sleep that dragged at her senses, Serena blinked at him. 'Where?'

'This home you love so much.'

'Really, Mr King. It is the middle of the night. There is little point.' If only he'd shown this interest earlier. She might have seen her dear sisters. Now she was beyond tired and they would no doubt be asleep.

'We shan't knock on the door.'

He didn't seem capable of reason. She let out a sigh under

her breath. 'Well then, if you must. Do you remember the direction? Head East on King Street.'

Five minutes later, he drew up in front of Serena's house. 'This is it. This is where I live—lived.' Being this close and yet not being able to see her beloved family made her stomach swirl with longing. How were they? No light emanated from the windows, not even from the rooms where her sisters would be snuggled in their beds. If only she could jump down and bang on the door, begging Father to rescue her. But what good would that serve? Mr King would drag her back or threaten to throw Papa into gaol. She kept her gaze averted from him. She refused to allow him to see her suffering again tonight. Instead she gazed with longing at the narrow path to the front door.

'It is even tinier than I recall.'

'But filled with love.'

Mr King was silent for a moment. 'So, when there is love, other things don't matter? For instance, comfort, warmth, decent food.'

Serena let out a harrumph. 'When you are surrounded by love, you can endure many discomforts. Trust me, I know. I once enjoyed the luxuries you mentioned. Papa's business declined after my mother passed away. Eventually we lost our fine home, nice furniture and warmer clothes. But, we still had each other, so we were—*are*—happy.'

Silence again. This time for so long that Serena wondered what occupied his thoughts. She turned to face him.

'You have a point there, Miss Bellingham.'

Wonder of wonders. She offered him a small smile, tired as she was.

'I remember a time when I perhaps knew that happiness you speak of. When my parents lived.' Sadness crept into his features for a moment, but just as quickly it was replaced with a hard glint. 'But sometimes love can be suffocating.'

Her head spun, on the point of drifting off to sleep, no matter that she was sitting up in a curricle. Too sluggish to respond in any sensible fashion, she sat there staring at him. She was aware enough, however, to note that his vibrant gaze travelled over her face and paused at her lips. His eyelids dropped a little and his expression became serious.

'Do you know how alluring you are in the moonlight, Serena?'

Was she dreaming? Had she slipped into sleep and now her mind played out intimate fantasies? Was he really leaning that close to her? She shook herself awake with a jerk. 'What?'

Mr King straightened and cleared his throat. 'Nothing.' He flicked the reins and gestured with his head toward the horizon. 'Look. The sun is rising.'

Serena followed his gaze. Sure enough, the sky out over the sea was greying as the sun heralded its coming. 'Oh dear. We've been touring all night. Won't your family worry?'

He pursed his lips. 'They shouldn't. They know I can look after myself.'

'How am I to work today when I've had no sleep?'

Mr King flung her a wide smile. 'Have the day off. I'm the master, you know.'

'But what will Mrs Jones think?'

'Do you regret coming out with me, Miss Bellingham?'

From where did that question come? And what was the answer? It was tiring when one wanted to sleep, and Mr King had annoyed her at times, but mostly it had been an adventure. 'No. No regrets.'

'Well then, do not worry what my sister or anyone else

might think.'

Serena did not reply. It might be a simple thing to say, but it still gnawed at her conscience. What would his family think of her now she'd been together with him all night, unchaperoned?

As they headed back through the city, Mr King sat up straighter, his nose in the air. 'Do you smell that?'

'Smell what?' Serena could barely take in anything at this point.

'Freshly baked bread, that's what.' The next moment, he drew up before a baker's shop and jumped down. 'I'll be back anon.'

True to his word, a few minutes later the small carriage swayed as he climbed up beside her. Mr King handed her a small package wrapped in linen. 'I'm sure you must be hungry.'

Serena peeled back the cloth to reveal a delicate pastry. Heat from the fresh-out-of-the-oven package warmed her hands and the aromas of cinnamon and apple tickled her nose. She peeked at Mr King holding his own pastry, but also watching her.

'Go on.'

She bit off a corner of the pastry and groaned with delight at the buttery sweetness. She had eaten nothing quite like it. 'This is wonderful.'

Mr King grinned and began his own breakfast.

Serena could only shake her head after each morsel. The pastry was so crisp and light, she couldn't get enough of it. When she finished, she could not resist licking the sticky remainders from her fingers, as ill-mannered as it made her appear. 'Thank you, Mr King. I've never had a breakfast to equal it.'

His smile spread wider than she'd seen yet, and his eyes sparked with animation again. Without a word, he leapt from the carriage again and ducked into the store. He returned soon after with two large bundles.

'What do you have there?'

Mr King gave her an indulgent smile. 'I bought all they had.'

Serena's pressed a hand over her open mouth. 'You didn't.'

'Yes. If you enjoyed them so much, you should have more.'

'You bought them for me?'

'Well, I may eat one or two myself.'

Serena was left speechless. Extravagant. That was the only word for it. Surely those pastries would spoil before she could eat them, and she wasn't enough of a glutton to eat them all in a day. 'You needn't do that, Mr King.'

He shrugged. 'I wanted to.'

Again, he left no room for argument. Mr King flicked the reins and, at long last, they headed for Aleron. Soon, the sway of the carriage rocked Serena into a senseless trance and sleep dragged her away from wakefulness. She was only vaguely aware of an arm around her shoulders that pulled her into a warm chest, where she snuggled in and relaxed with a sigh.

13

Serena woke up in her bed at Aleron and sat up, groggy, her head pounding, and still wearing her day dress. What was the time? She stumbled out of bed and drew the drapes back. The sky remained bright, although there was plenty of cloud cover. Massaging her temples, she moved to the mantel, above which hung a clock. Almost one o'clock. She'd slept half the day away. Well, with thick curtains and little noise, it was easy to do.

She trudged back over to the bed and flopped onto the mattress. What had possessed Mr King to stay out the entire night? Not that their tour was dull in the least. Serena groaned. What possessed her to join him in the first place? Did she fall asleep on his shoulder? How embarrassing. He would judge her as presumptuous now, added to being the daughter of a thief. She could not face him today, or any day soon. With any luck, she could stay in this room forever. And yet, the dryness of her throat and her aching head told her she needed a drink, and her stomach rumbled. Apart from the pastry early this morning, she hadn't eaten since supper last night.

Serena resigned herself to visiting the dining room, hoping Mr King kept to his suite. His presence would only disquiet her further. She pushed herself to her feet and changed her dress, pausing at the basin in the corner to freshen her face.

The dining room was deserted. The family had probably

eaten and gone on with their chores for the afternoon. No matter. Serena headed for the kitchen. Becker undoubtedly kept leftovers for her. As she entered, the cook turned and at once frowned.

'Four pounds of pastries. What does the master think I will do with four pounds of them?' His German accent stood out in his ire. He turned back to continue unceremoniously banging pots and utensils as he worked.

Serena blanched. It was her fault for admitting how much she liked them. 'It was very spontaneous. I did not expect him to buy every one of them.'

Becker waved a hand in dismissal. 'Never mind. It's not your fault.'

'I'll have one now if that will make it easier. I came looking for dinner.' Serena gave him a hopeful look.

The cook grunted. 'I kept food for you. I expected you'd be down here sometime. Lucky, it's still warm.' He moved to the stove and returned with a covered plate. 'Roasted fowl, green beans, potatoes and pumpkin. I trust it is to your liking.'

'Your cooking has not failed me yet.' Serena tried to sweeten his mood. She lifted the cover and drank in the savoury aromas.

'Humph. Well, you go and eat. I shall bring one of those blasted pastries shortly.'

She took her plate to the dining room and sat in the quietness to enjoy her meal. As promised, Becker soon entered with another plate, a glass and a carafe of water. He placed them on the table without ceremony. But he didn't leave.

'Thank you, Becker. I appreciate you looking after me.'

He grunted again. 'Doesn't Edward know, I could have baked those pastries, and better? He only had to ask.'

So, it was jealousy that had roused his ire. Serena raised her brows at Becker. 'Better, you say?'

'Ya. Much better.'

'You have yourself a challenge then, Becker, because I have never tasted the likes of them.'

The cook stared at her briefly then offered a short bow. 'Challenge accepted, Miss Bellingham.'

Serena still smothered giggles minutes later when Mrs Jones entered.

The housekeeper—or was she playing sister to the master today—stood inside the doorway, fidgeting as if she didn't know what to say. Serena nodded to her, equally uncomfortable. What did one say to excuse oneself in this situation? And where to start?

'Are you rested?' An abrupt beginning from Mrs Jones. No greeting first. The woman paced the floor.

'I suppose. I have a touch of headache, but otherwise, I am well.'

With a rush of movement Mrs Jones pulled out the chair beside her and sat. 'Are you all right? My brother didn't … wasn't … inappropriate, was he?'

'No.' Serena shook her head. 'Unless you count running barefoot along the beach inappropriate.'

Mrs Jones dropped her head into her hands. 'He didn't!'

'Yes, quite.' Serena tried to cover a smile by putting a forkful of chicken in her mouth. Mrs Jones was serious. 'But that's nothing *I* haven't done before, so it didn't bother me. I am aware that Mr King can be impulsive.'

'Did anyone see him?'

Serena furrowed her brows as she thought back. 'No, I don't think so.'

Mrs Jones' stiff frame relaxed a little at that.

'Didn't you tell him to bring you home?'

Serena lifted her shoulders. 'Once or twice. But he was so excited to be showing me the architecture in Sydney, I didn't have the heart to complain.'

Mrs Jones put out a hand and covered hers. 'I'm so sorry, Serena. It was poor judgement on his behalf to drag you around all night.'

Sorry? Why should Mrs Jones apologise for her brother? It wasn't her fault. Mr King made his own decisions, even if it seems he put little thought into them. Besides, wasn't it her own fault for agreeing to go, knowing they were without an escort? 'There is nothing to forgive, Mrs Jones. I enjoyed his company most of the time.'

The housekeeper stiffened in the chair and her eyes sparked with dismay. 'Most of the time? What did he do?'

Serena removed her hand from beneath Mrs Jones's and patted it. 'Nothing so alarming. Mr King will not relent over... over a disagreement we had, that is all.'

Mrs Jones breathed out long and hard as though a huge relief fell from her shoulders. 'So, you enjoyed your tour with him except for his arrogance from time to time, is that right?'

'Yes, exactly.'

Her smile brightened. 'Well, I'm glad. But it shouldn't happen again—not without a chaperone.' She let out a laugh that sounded forced and rose from the table, her chair scraping against the wooden floor. 'Eddie has given you the day off, so I will leave you to your freedom.'

'Thank you, Mrs Jones.'

Serena watched her leave, still pondering their conversation. Mrs Jones was more anxious over her brother's behaviour than Serena's own. That was a change about, since she'd met with much suspicion over her motives since arriving at Aleron. But she was too tired to make sense of it.

Fresh air is what she needed. Once she finished her late dinner, she collected a wrap and headed outdoors into the gardens. She strolled across the manicured lawns and roamed amongst the garden beds. Strange. Just as she often felt someone watching her while she laundered, she sensed it again now in the garden. She shivered while looking around her. There was nowhere to hide, and she stood quite out in the open. But nothing disturbed the serenity aside from the chirping of birds. Did her imagination play tricks on her yet again?

Serena forced her thoughts back to the trouble at hand. What would she say to Mr King next time she saw him? She had not mentioned it to Mrs Jones, but she had been the inappropriate one—resting on Mr King's shoulder, indeed. And didn't they share a moment in front of Papa's house? Or was that just a dream? Whatever the case, she must learn to control her runaway feelings for Mr King. There was something about him that constantly drew her, even though he wouldn't forget the almost-stolen-painting issue. He was smart—well, more than smart—gifted, vibrant and full of passion, and yes, charm as he'd told her. And all on top of his brooding good looks.

But naught could develop from infatuation with his kind, surely. She was nobody—not any more. A servant. Mr King was rich and famous. She was uneducated compared to him. He was a genius. Why should her heart yearn for what could never be?

Before Papa's business failed, she might have been equal to one of his ilk. Her mind drifted back to that awful evening outside Papa's study, when she had eavesdropped on James asking for her hand. Good and kind James, who was more than able to provide for her. But Papa had denied him, claiming *he* needed Serena more. What a crushing blow it had been. Since then she had scarcely hoped for anything. At every turn, her family's needs outweighed her own desires. Why should her fortunes change now? It was her family's needs that placed her here at Aleron in the first place.

Serena turned toward the stables to search for Mr Xavier. She could, at the least, continue a friendship with him. However, as she looked up, not he but Mr Simon strode toward her. And he wore an unpleasant scowl on his face.

'What game are you playing at, Miss Bellingham?' No greeting, no pleasantries. Mr Simon launched straight into accusations.

Thrown off guard, Serena opened and closed her mouth, then shook her head in confusion. 'I cannot think what you mean by that, Mr Simon.'

'That you encouraged Uncle Ed to stay out an entire night, what else would I mean?'

Serena almost released a snort of disdain. He couldn't be further from the truth. And even if he wasn't, what business was it of his? She gave him a direct look. '*I* encouraged *him*. Is that what you think?'

'Well, you've wheedled your way into employment here, even though no staff were needed. You were the one who allowed Moncrief to roam the house. And now you've kept him out wandering the streets of Sydney till the sun rose. What more is there to assume but that you either plan to bring about his ruin, or you are what they call a fortune hunter? Can you deny it?'

Shocked and gaping, Serena scrambled for a response. Of course, she could deny it. *Should* deny it. Mr Simon had jumped to extreme conclusions. And yet, she couldn't admit the truth, lest she hurt Papa. A fortune hunter of all things! Serena forced aside her annoyance to meet Mr Simon with a little logic. 'Moncrief was a misunderstanding, when will you realise that? And as for Mr King, you make him sound as if he has no mind of his own.'

At that, Mr Simon backed off a little—his shoulders straightened and his scowl transformed more into a mask of confusion. 'Of course he does.'

'Then give him some credit, will you? Don't assume a servant such as myself can wrap him around her little finger, not that I even wish to do so.'

He thrust his hands in his pockets. 'Of course you can't. Uncle Ed's too smart for that.'

Interesting. In the space of a few sentences, Serena had made Mr Simon defend his uncle from a different angle. That might be something to remember. She pressed her lips together to hide a smile. 'Precisely.'

Mr Simon half-turned away, gave her a sidelong glance that said he was not convinced of her innocence, and then trudged back to wherever he'd been.

Serena watched after him with narrowed eyes while releasing a long breath through her nose. Fortune hunter, indeed. Or, what was the other thing he'd suggested—that she intended to ruin Mr King. She folded her arms across her chest. It was beyond enduring. She had half a mind to go straight to Mr Simon's uncle and repeat their conversation. How would Mr King react to that? On second thoughts, that mightn't be a good idea. Mr King was likely to agree with Mr Simon. After all, he *had* accused her of thievery like her father more than once, even though his belief was misconstrued.

Turning toward the stables as she had done only a few

minutes earlier, she recommenced her mission to find Mr Xavier. This time though, she had more in mind than pleasant company. Serena found him mucking out the stalls and Mr Xavier noticed her seconds before raking a pile of rank-smelling hay and dung onto her feet.

'I beg pardon, Miss Bellingham.' Colour marked his cheeks as he stopped the rake just in time. 'I did not hear you coming.'

'Never mind, Mr Xavier. No harm done.' Serena offered him a benign smile and leaned against one of the rough wooden posts, careful not to splinter her hands.

The handsome groom leaned on the rake. 'How do you fare after, er, last night?'

There, it was foremost in his mind as well. It should not have surprised Serena. 'I'm a little tired, though I shouldn't complain. I have slept half the day away.'

'Yes, you were fast asleep when Uncle Ed carried you inside this morning.'

Serena tried to smother a gasp. Mr King had carried her to bed? That was even more embarrassing than falling asleep on his shoulder. She studied Mr Xavier's face, trying to read his judgement on the incident. He, in turn, studied her. She steeled her features. She must not allow Mr Xavier to learn how tumultuous Mr King made her feel. She cleared her throat. 'Well, I have no recollection of that, so I must have been.' On another whim, she arched her brows and smirked. 'Serves him right for keeping me up till dawn.'

Mr Xavier let out a gentle chuckle. 'Don't be too hard on Uncle Ed. He gets enthusiastic around architecture.' He moulded his features into a thoughtful expression. 'My guess is, the lighthouse was not enough, so he dragged you off to see every building in Sydney of architectural significance. According to him, that is.'

It was Serena's turn to giggle. 'You have been on the same tour then, I assume.'

'A few weeks after Mr Greenway died. I was old enough to find staying up all night thrilling, but not old enough to actually remain awake.' Mr Xavier raked at the straw again, the stubble rustling as he dragged at it. 'You are more fortunate than I though, Miss Bellingham. Uncle Ed made me wake up and take myself to bed when we got home.'

Serena grinned at him and then fell serious as she remembered Mr Simon's accusations. 'Your brother assumes I'm trying to corrupt him.' She glanced surreptitiously at Mr Xavier to gauge his response.

He frowned before he raised his face to hers, pausing with the rake. 'Simon is protective of Uncle Ed. We all are.'

Serena searched his face, trying to understand. 'But why does he need so much protection?' The answer came to her as he opened his mouth to reply. 'Don't tell me. It's the burden of his genius?'

Mr Xavier sighed as though a great weight rested on his shoulders. 'There are people who take advantage of intelligence and creativity. Mother is always ranting about it—how people won't understand his genius.' He turned to her and a small smile turned the corners of his mouth. 'If it's any consolation, I don't believe the same as Simon.' Colour infused his cheeks again as he looked away and continued his work, the rake scraping against the floor.

'It is a relief to know I have one friend around here.' She demurred then, realising the bold nature of her statement. 'That is, if I may call you a friend?'

He faced her once again with earnest conviction in his eyes.

'Yes, you can. If you ever need anything—help, or even someone to talk to—please remember I am here.'

'Thank you for that. It is nice to know. May I ask you something?'

'Of course.'

'Do you remember much of your grandparents? I only ask because Mr King mentioned them last night, and it sounded like they were good people.'

'He did?' His eyebrows went up. 'He doesn't often talk of them. But, yes they were good sorts. Grandmama always had sweets hidden away for us, while pretending she was very strict. Grandpapa was much like Uncle Ed—generous, playful, energetic. He would talk to us for hours, and take us on outrageous adventures. That was when he was home. He would be away on business at times. But it was a happy home, to be sure.'

'What happened to them?'

Mr Xavier's eyes shuttered. 'Grandpapa died in a tragic accident. Grandmama died soon after. They said she had a broken heart.'

'It must have been a terrible time for you all.' Serena's heart swelled with compassion.

'Yes, I think that is partly why Mother is so protective now.' He looked aside. 'But I should not be speaking like that. It is not my place to speak of her so. I'm sorry.'

'It is well, Mr Xavier,' Serena reached out to touch his forearm. 'I'll not broadcast what you have said.'

'Thank you, Miss Bellingham,' he seemed relieved. 'I should be getting back to cleaning these stables though.'

For a moment, she suspected he had more to say, but instead he shrugged and continued working.

Before she turned to leave, Serena wanted to accomplish one more thing. 'If the weather remains fair, I will go walking on the shore on Sunday. Might you be free to accompany me?' Mr Xavier showed signs he might find her pleasing, but he showed many more signs that he was too shy to act.

His head lifted again at her request. 'Certainly. If you wish. As I said—'

'You're here to help if I need it. Yes. Thank you again.' Well, if he was determined to make nothing more of it than that, so be it, but she would enjoy his companionship nonetheless.

14

For the briefest of moments I held her. She fit in my arms like the final stroke of an artist's brush, or the last tile in a mosaic—snug and perfect. Oh, the softness of her hair against my chin. I wanted to bury my face in its lemon-scented loveliness.

Simon has not spoken two words to me since this morning. And Judith—her face mottled when I lifted Miss Bellingham from the curricle and carried her to her room.

Can I not do anything without her hovering, fretting, fussing over whether I will tarnish her good name forever? It is only me who bears the curse.

No-one can know, Eddie. No-one can know.

I acknowledge my family care for me and it feels good to have their devotion. But they care so much I cannot breathe. Like being in a trap of sorts. But Serena, her family love her enough to let her go.

15

After Sunday's breakfast and a delicious pastry Becker had made—he had surpassed the challenge—Serena sought Mr Xavier for his promised escort to the beach. As she strolled toward the stables, her mind travelled—as it often did—to Mr King. She had not seen him since their all-night escapade and wondered if his determination to avoid her matched her own. To be honest, she was disappointed she had not met him in the halls, or that he hadn't joined the family at mealtimes. Nor had he accosted her out of doors anywhere. Why should that make her feel deflated? To see scorn in his face after falling asleep on his shoulder would be humiliating. And yet, part of her wanted to see him despite the embarrassment.

Serena groaned. This obsession with Mr King needed to stop. His position, intellect, status in society, why, everything about him far exceeded her. And then there was the problem of his judgement of her and Papa.

Mr Xavier was more her equal, and that is who she must focus on now. Serena quickened her steps to the horse yards, eyes searching for the groom. There he was, in one of the smaller enclosures, hand feeding a young roan foal. He had told the family that the horse's health had declined since being weaned from its mother and Mr Xavier worried for the foal.

'Is the young fellow faring better?' Serena said by way of greeting.

Mr Xavier glanced up, then bent his head back to watch what he was doing. 'He's been improving since I've made sure he's eating well.' He stroked the foal's white nose, inciting a soft whinny from the young horse. 'Aren't you, boy?'

Serena watched the pair for a moment. 'Mr Xavier, are you free to join me for a walk on the beach today?'

A flush of colour spread on Mr Xavier's face, but he did not look at her. 'I'm sorry, Miss Bellingham. I can't get away today.'

Serena opened her mouth to postpone their outing until the morrow when he continued.

'Don't let my busyness stop you though. I know how much you enjoy your Sunday constitutional.' This time he glanced up with a brief smile. Something in his expression told Serena there was more to his detachment than business. Did she imagine she saw a flash of regret on his face?

'Well, if you're certain.'

Mr Xavier gave a curt nod and then turned his back. What happened to 'I'm here for you'? She thought they were becoming friends at last. That was just two days ago and now here he was practically ignoring her.

With hesitant steps, Serena backed away. Mr Xavier did not glance at her again, not even briefly.

Frowning, she lifted her shoulders and headed for the shore. If she must walk alone, so be it. A deep sigh rose from her chest. Serena never expected loneliness to trouble her in such a large house, but there it was. She missed the constant chatter of her sisters and their warm hugs and quiet conversation with Papa. At Aleron there was only business-like discussions and hours of silence—except for those times with Mr King. But she couldn't rely on those moments. The genius was busy with architectural design—as the family had told her repeatedly—and he could not afford to spend hours with her.

A cold, blustery wind whipped her skirts around her legs, making her steps slower. Serena leaned into the wind, pulling her thin wrap tighter around her. It was not the best weather for a walk, but as Mr Xavier mentioned, her Sunday walk was important.

White caps covered the usually calm bay. Keeping her boots on, Serena trudged along the water's edge. Salt spray dampened her hair and clothes, but Serena didn't mind. She had experienced this type of weather many a time. Papa always said sailing in strong winds was an adventure—there was nothing like sea air to blow away one's troubles.

Serena felt a pang of longing as she remembered his words. How she longed to see him. She had received a letter from him, but he only responded to her stories of life at Aleron. He wrote no tidings of life at home. No news should mean good news, but what if it meant things were so bad he couldn't mention them for fear of upsetting her? Anxiety rose within, along with guilt for leaving them, as it did most times she thought of her family.

Serena spread her arms wide, face to the wind, and tilted her head back toward the sky. She breathed the briny air deeply, allowing the strong breeze to blow against her.

*Lord, grant me peace. Cleanse my troubled thought*s. Yes, God could help her even more than a refreshing wind. She must trust in Him to guide her.

Serena leaned into the breeze and continued along the sea shore. As she absorbed the beautiful scenery around her, she soon realised a figure sat on the small bluff at the far end of the beach. It was hard to make out any features in the haze of the sea spray. When the figure raised an arm and waved to her, however, she knew him at once. Mr King. Strange to discover him in the exact place she visited. Could it be possible he orchestrated these meetings? It had happened too many times to be coincidental. Could it be that he sought her out—that *he* was interested in *her* company? It was more than she ever expected, but she could not deny the thrill that ran through her body. Perhaps he did not hold against her the indiscretion of falling asleep on his shoulder.

Waving back to him, she made her way to the bluff, partly in trepidation, and partly excited to learn more about Mr King today. In all truth, even if he spoke utter nonsense, she wouldn't mind. Just being near him with his emotive eyes would satisfy her fascination. By the time she'd scrambled up the modest bank, she stood before him slightly breathless. 'Good afternoon to you, Mr King.' She tugged at a loosened strand of hair which had blown across her face and tried to tuck it back into the bun at her neck.

His face turned up to hers with a broad grin, though he squinted against the glare of cloud-filled skies behind her. 'And to you, Miss Bellingham.'

Mr King held what seemed to be a white card across his knees. 'What have you there?' She nodded toward it.

'I have been sketching.'

'Oh.' Serena then saw the pencil tucked behind his ear. 'May I see?'

Mr King shifted over on the rock, motioning for her to join him. The rock was not large enough for there to be much space between them and Serena found that her hip and thigh pressed up against his. The physical nearness sent more thrills through her body. He was so very attractive. She bit on her lip. She must not allow herself to dwell on his attributes. Serena forced herself to focus on Mr King's drawing.

The sketch encompassed the scene below—the beach with several pretty eucalypts bordering the cove, including the white-capped waves tumbling into shore. It almost looked as though they were in motion. But the real surprise was the image of herself as she had been but fifteen minutes earlier, with arms outspread in the wind. The only difference was that he had drawn her hair loose, blowing free in the breeze. Serena gasped and her hand fluttered over her mouth.

'You drew me?' Her eyes swerved to his expressive brown ones.

'I drew a free-spirited water nymph. You are inspiring, Serena.' His eyes locked on her gaze, a wealth of meaning written in their depths.

Is that how he saw her? But what of all those accusations? What had changed? 'But, I thought ...' She faltered, unable to finish the question. Her mind quickly became a fuzzy mess. She started when his hand lightly covered hers.

All rational thought fled as he drew her hand to his lips. Tiny explosions of pleasure invaded her head and her heart, and it seemed every other part of her body, right to her toes. The heady scent of lavender and tobacco filled her senses. At length he drew back, and his eyes told her he longed to kiss more than her hand. She closed her eyes and imagined what those kisses would be like, arousing sensations in Serena that she felt sure must be wrong.

Finally, she opened her eyes and pulled back, but the intensity in his gaze remained. 'I cannot stop thinking about you.'

Serena scrambled to find a coherent response. 'Nor I you.'

His eyes roamed her face and he did not release her hand which still burned where his lips had been. 'Come to my rooms tonight.' The invitation burst from him.

'Mr King.' Serena sucked in her breath. 'What can you mean? You must know that is improper.' He had not even mentioned marriage, let alone love or anything close to that.

'No. I ...' He shook his head as though a fog filled his mind.

Did he mean to feign innocence, did he? Perhaps he was a womaniser as previous newspapers had hinted. The fluttering in her heart transformed to an offended, pounding throb. She wrenched her hand away from his and stood. 'I don't know what kind of woman you think I am.' No wait. She knew exactly what he believed about her. Her shoulders fell. 'Is this a trap? You want to prove that I'm a criminal or even a wanton?' She stalked away from him.

'Serena!'

Serena flung back toward him with a hand stretched out before her. 'Stay away from me.' She left him and didn't turn back.

Serena headed straight to her room. Right now, she was in no mood to speak with any household member. How dare Mr King! She had half a mind to pack her belongings and walk home. The only thing that stopped her was the possibility, no the probability, that Mr King would have her father taken to the penal settlement. And added to that, he would likely have her denounced as a harlot. Water nymph indeed!

Angrier than she'd been in years, Serena slammed the door. She threw herself onto the bed, thumping the pillows to vent her humiliation and groaned in frustration. Rosemary burst from the sachet, filling the air with its fragrance.

She remembered how Mr Xavier refused to accompany her to the beach. Had he known Mr King sat on the bluff, sketching? Was he involved in this?

And Mr Simon. When he found out what had transpired there on the rocks, he would feel justified in his assessment of her character, wouldn't he? And what about Mrs and Mr Jones? It didn't bear imagining. They were all ready to judge and condemn her it seemed. Perhaps every day had been a test to bring out her true character—a character they'd already determined as wicked.

But they were wrong. So very wrong. And Serena held no illusions that she could change their point of view. They had damned her without a fair hearing.

Harmless indeed. With another groan, she stood up from the bed and paced the room, her ire still stirred. Shouldn't a girl's first moments of intimacy be something she could treasure? But Mr King had ruined it with his unchaste suggestion. An idea struck her—not a solution precisely—but it might help relieve her anxiety.

Serena sat at the bureau and withdrew a sheet of paper, then several more sheets. This promised to be a long letter. She opened the ink pot, dipped her quill, and wrote out all that had happened. She started with the night-long tour with Mr King and ended with the episode at the beach—minus the kiss of her hand—and the strange attitudes of the family. Only Papa might understand her side of the issue. He knew her nature, that she bore no guilt for any immorality.

As her pen scrawled across the page, her indignation calmed to only the dull ache of disappointment. When did she begin to expect more from this position than an extended punishment?

It was her own fault for letting her imagination run away with her. The possibility that Mr King, or even Mr Xavier, would show any interest in her was a delusion. She existed at Aleron as a slave and should have only expected treatment as such. Serena shook her head as she signed off and let out a long breath.

She blotted the page then rose to stretch her back and legs. As Serena crossed the room to fetch a glass of water, she noted an envelope on the floor just this side of it.

How long had that been there? Days? Hours? Minutes? She had no idea. From whom could it be? What if it came from Mr King? It might hold a message of accusation or apology, and she didn't want to read either. More accusation would hurt and she wasn't ready to forgive him. Serena heaved a sigh. There would be no apology. What a foolish thing to expect.

If it came from one of the Joneses, nothing better would be inside the envelope. But then, what if it was mail from her family? Serena hurried over to it, but there was no postmark on the envelope. Just her name in flowing script—Serena.

Heavens above, it was from Mr King. She knew it at once. For a few moments Serena couldn't even bring herself to pick it up. Biting on her lip, she made herself collect the letter and open it. Within the first two lines, her knees became weak, and she sank onto the bed.

Poetry. Rhyme depicting Athena, the goddess of wisdom, and elaborate comparisons of herself to this goddess filled the page. The words sounded almost worshipful, they were so exaggerated in their praise. Serena shifted uncomfortably on the bed. As beautiful and artistic as the poem was, it seemed excessive. Mr King didn't think of her this way, did he? Or was it his intention to make sport of her? When did he write it? Before or after today on the beach?

Serena swallowed, confused. Had she not just berated herself for over-imagining things? But here was Mr King's own hand, testifying that she hadn't imagined his interest. The paper scrunched in her hand as she groaned yet again. He wrote a poem for her—which normally would be romantic. Well, it was romantic, but, oh, so overwhelming, her stomach churned.

She didn't know what to make of it. With a deep breath, she went back to the desk and straightened the page out beside her. On another page added to her letter to Papa, she copied out a phrase or two of the poem and asked what he thought it all meant. Papa should be able to give her an objective answer.

In the meantime, she must figure out what to do next. Once again, she feared facing the man behind the words lest he scorn or embarrass her.

16

As it turned out, the decision was eventually made for her. Serena did avoid Mr King, and any depth of conversation with the rest of the family, for two days. During those days, while working, her mind often drifted to the memory of Mr King's lips on her hand and the warm glow it created. Every time she forced herself to shake it off and try to forget, she'd find her thoughts heading in that direction again moments later. And, when free, her hand involuntarily delved into her pocket for the written sonnet, which she read repeatedly. She almost knew it by heart now, and yet it still swept her into a dizzy spin.

On Tuesday afternoon, Mr King accosted her in the hallway and drew her into the library. Accosted was an apt description because he appeared wild, and she had not heard his steps behind her. His unoiled hair stood out at all angles, a crumpled coat hung loose on his shoulders, and he clearly had not shaved in several days. On top of that, dark rings circled his eyes, even though those eyes still sparked with vitality.

'I cannot go on like this.' His glance darted from her to the floor and then at everything else but her.

Serena remembered her parting words to Mr King on Sunday and bit her lip. He probably thought she hated him—she had made no effort to apologise. He still gripped her elbow and Serena pulled away from his grasp. 'You refer to Sunday, I suppose.'

'Yes. I've been avoiding you. But not because of what you said. Because of what I did.' He rubbed a hand over his face. 'I'm so terribly embarrassed about the way I'—he winced—'took liberties with you.' He turned and walked across to the hearth. 'I don't know what came over me. Sometimes, I ...' Instead of finishing his sentence he thumped a fist into his thigh, then covered the few steps between them to stand near her again. 'I'm sorry.'

'But Mr King, you asked me to come to your room. How else was I to interpret that but that you question my virtue? It is bad enough that you considered me a thief when I first arrived. But, this, this is—'

'Unforgivable.' He hung his head. 'I know.' He slowly raised his eyes again and ran a shaky hand through his unkempt hair. 'I do not think so base of you, you must know that. It is just that I...' His words trailed off as he swallowed.

Serena, still shocked at his haggard appearance, scanned his face. 'Are you well, Mr King?'

A laugh that almost sounded hysterical erupted from Mr King. 'No. I think not.'

A sense of unease stirred in Serena's gut. 'Do you have a fever?' Although hesitant, she reached up to press the back of her hand to his forehead.

Mr King captured her hand and held it to his cheek. 'Of sorts. I cannot stop thinking about you.'

Serena's concern for him transformed to a flutter in her stomach, as though a flock of birds had taken up residence there. She did not imagine this. His own mouth now betrayed him. 'You, you can't?'

'Every second, of every minute, of every hour.' Mr King edged closer. Close enough Serena had to tilt her head to see his face, and stale tobacco and lavender met her nose. 'Of every day, of every week.'

Once again, Serena found herself caught up in his fervent expression. There was a desperate, pleading in his look as he leaned closer as if to kiss her. Instead, he drew her hand to his lips again, his kiss searing her fingers. Serena equally knew both bliss and a deep conviction that this was improper. She pulled her hand free and drew the courage to push him away. Hadn't he just apologised for the self-same behaviour at the beach?

He released her, but his eyes gazed at her with burning intensity. 'Marry me?'

Serena's mouth dropped open. It wasn't an invitation to his bed this time, but it was still shocking in the extreme. 'We hardly know one another.' Shouldn't he have broached the subject of love first? Heavens, he hadn't even courted her. Unless he considered the midnight house tour, and all-night city drive courting. Certainly, she found him mesmerising, and attractive, but was it love? She admired him, yes, and thought him rather impressive, but was that enough? Perhaps she even cared for him, and yet there were times she almost hated him because of what he had done to Papa. How could they build a bond of love with that hanging over their heads? Serena took a few stumbling steps backward. 'No. No we can't.'

'No?' The wild expression returned to his face. 'You don't feel the same way?'

Serena breathed in deeply. 'I ... I ... No.'

'No?' He repeated.

Regretful that he seemed unable to comprehend her denial, Serena bit her lip and shook her head. Mr King stared at her momentarily then left the room, banging the door behind him.

Serena hung her head. Part of her wished she could say

yes. He exhibited countless wonderful qualities and she couldn't deny the pull between them. But what did he see in her? He was her captor, her master, after all.

With a deep sigh, Serena trudged back to the laundry to complete her work. She was still frowning over the afternoon when she sat at the dining table for supper. Mrs Jones glanced at her with concern several times during the meal. As soon as the menfolk went off to smoke and drink, she beckoned Serena to join her in the parlour.

'You seem troubled, my dear,' she said as soon as they were comfortably seated opposite each other, with warm cups of tea.

Serena attempted a carefree smile and waved a hand in dismissal. 'Oh, it's nothing. Just homesickness, I suppose.' She held the cup close to her nose to inhale the leafy aroma.

Mrs Jones studied her face as though trying to read the truth there. 'Are you sure?'

Serena nodded, forcing another smile.

'Because if my brother has made you uncomfortable, you may confide in me. I shall not accuse you of untoward behaviour, I promise. I'm well acquainted with Eddie's…faults.'

Did Mrs Jones realise exactly what had been happening over the past week? Including the altercation with Mr Simon? Serena swallowed a gulp of tea, barely tasting the sweet brew. Should she mention Mr King's fervent and impulsive behaviour? Not enough time had passed for Papa to receive and respond to her letter yet, and Serena remained confused to a certain extent. But what should she tell Mrs Jones? How much of the truth should she reveal?

'He…he wrote me a sonnet.' That was a beginning. Serena watched Mrs Jones's face for her reaction, but not a muscle twitched. Instead, she nodded.

'I thought as much.' It seemed more of a murmur to herself than a confirmation to Serena. But then Mrs Jones made direct eye contact again. 'I shall be blunt, Miss Bellingham. Has he made advances toward you?'

The woman's forthrightness surprised Serena. She hadn't expected such candour. She drew in a deep breath and, releasing it slowly, nodded. Serena's hopes fell though. If Mrs Jones had the boldness to ask such a direct question, incidents like this must have happened previously. So then, Serena was not the first Mr King had proposed to, or propositioned, or kissed. What a deflating revelation.

Mrs Jones must have sensed her dismay for she shifted to the sofa next to her and clasped one of her hands. 'Don't you worry, Miss Bellingham. Eddie can be too familiar sometimes, but he is harmless. He would never actually do anything—never follow through with action. It's mostly thoughtless words. His tongue is loose, if you know what I mean.'

Serena didn't know whether to feel better or worse with that. Mr King didn't want her at all? His mouth was just running away with him? It was a relief she'd had the presence of mind to refuse him. She glanced at her hands where she still imagined the feel of his lips burning on her fingers. But what about that? Serena would have defined those kisses as 'following through'.

'Eddie has a weakness for a pretty face.' Mrs Jones sighed. 'I suspect that's why you're still here. But like I said, don't worry. I'll sort him out. But, I do beg of you not to mention this to anyone else. He really is quite harmless.'

Better to keep the secret of his kiss to herself. If Mrs Jones intended to scold her brother, Serena did not wish her to mention that detail. It was a mortifying thought, and heat rose in her cheeks.

'What is it, Miss Bellingham?'

Serena pressed her hands to her face to cool the flush. 'How do you suggest I respond if he approaches me again?'

'Well, my advice is to stay away from him, as I think I instructed you from the beginning.'

Hadn't she been doing that? And yet, Mr King had 'come across' her too many times for coincidence sake. 'And if he seeks me out?'

Mrs Jones shook her head. 'Oh, he won't seek you out anymore. You can trust me on that.'

17

Wednesday 25th May, 1842

...what a fool I am.

Blasted curse.

How to fix this. Serena will not wish to speak to me again. Not after bombarding her with affection twice within a week. And yet, I hardly know myself.

Serena. Serena. Serena.

Xavier knows it all now. I made him swear not to speak to Serena again. I daresay, he didn't like it, but it can't be helped. He's a good lad.

And Judith must insist I not speak with Serena again, lest the curse be known and I am ruined.

How she suffocates me.

I must escape this house, these bounds. Feel the wind in my face. Feel free...

18

'Miss Bellingham! Quickly, you must come.' Mr Xavier's somewhat breathless voice beckoned her from where she stood at the washing lines, pegging up linen.

'What is it?' She matched his expression of concern as she approached, wiping her damp hands on her apron.

'Uncle Ed.' Mr Xavier rolled his eyes. 'He insists on going out to the lighthouse, even though it threatens to rain.'

Rain? She peered at the cloud-ridden sky, something she should have done before hanging washing out to dry. The dark, heaviness of the clouds testified to Mr Xavier's words. With a sigh of frustration, Serena fell into step beside him as he hurried around the house toward the stables. The linen would not dry today.

'I'm happy to go with him, but you are important to him and I sense you need to be there.'

She stopped mid-step, baffled by his cryptic explanation. 'How can you know that? And besides, I am not attired for an outing.' Serena gestured to her servant's garb, which was no longer fresh. Saints above, she probably reeked of lye and bore smudges of dust as well.

'Never mind your appearance. Just come.' He reached out and clasped her hand, tugging her along with him. 'And I know because he told me.'

Told him? Too bemused to argue, Serena stumbled behind the young stable-hand. How was a visit to the lighthouse urgent, anyway? And why was it so significant for her to join them? Hadn't Mrs Jones told her to stay away from Mr King, and that she promised to keep the charmer away from Serena? Well, so much for that.

Rounding the corner, Serena saw Mr King seated in his curricle, with the reins in hand. He was just as dishevelled as she had last seen him. 'Ah, good for you, Xavier. You thought to bring the lovely Miss Bellingham, I see. Come along then.' His eyes were bright with impatience.

As Mr Xavier handed her up into the carriage, Serena saw Mr King pull his snuff box from a pocket. He flicked it open and took a pinch, sniffing hard at each nostril. She must have frowned for his face spread into a wide grin. 'Nothing like a pinch of snuff to refresh the senses.'

Serena turned back to Mr Xavier, a question on her lips. Before she could speak, it seemed he read her mind.

'I shall catch up on my horse.'

She had only framed her mouth into an 'O' before Mr King flicked the reins and the horses lunged forward. And not at a calm walk either. He urged them straight into a run. Serena knew there was no point in trying to slow him. Mr King loved the speed and, on all accounts, it was likely to pour with rain at any moment, so there was reason to hurry. Rather than comment, she gripped the side of the curricle hard enough to make her knuckles white. She tried not to fall against Mr King when they bumped through a rut or rounded a bend.

When they arrived at the stately lighthouse, however, Mr King raced right by it, heading straight for the grey sky. Serena sucked in her breath and held on with both hands, visions of the curricle soaring over the edge flashing through her mind. Did the man intend to stop? At the last moment, Mr King pulled Misty and Storm to a sudden halt, laughing with his head thrown back.

'Your face was worth the dramatic stop, Serena.'

It was funny? He thought it a great joke to scare her? The corners of her mouth curved upward, even as she scolded him. 'Mr King, that was not very genteel of you.' If she had a fan in her hand, she might have rapped him over the knuckles.

He handed her from the curricle, civilised to perfection now. 'Perhaps not. But don't you think it would be marvellous to fly over the edge?'

Serena gurgled a chuckle. 'If I had wings, maybe.'

Mr King tucked her hand through his elbow and led her closer to the edge. The wind whipped at their clothing as the storm clouds rolled in from the sea, dark and menacing. Seagulls gleamed white against the darkness, playing in the gale, their cry a stark reminder that nature would have its way. Serena shivered and pulled her thin wrap tighter around her body.

Mr King's arm slipped around her shoulders and rubbed up and down her arm. 'Too cold for you, my dear?'

Serena shrugged away from him, not willing to encourage his attentions. Surely he'd understood her refusal. But both Mr Xavier and Mrs Jones did say Mr King was too impulsive. She shook her head free of these troubling thoughts and focused on the view.

'A storm is coming.'

'I enjoy a good storm.'

Serena shuddered again, remembering they had almost lost Papa several times to storms like this.

He continued. 'They speak to me.'

'What? Storms?'

'Yes. Well, it is as if they speak my language.'

Serena turned to watch his profile as he stared at the approaching dark clouds. His eyes were fervent with excitement, as though he would hasten the storm's approach if he could. How did he derive so much energy from thunder and lightning? Even as the question entered her mind, the clouds answered with a rumble and a flash.

Mr King closed his eyes and breathed in deeply. In the next moment, his eyes snapped open and turned to her. 'I feel like flying.'

Serena chuckled, unsure of what he meant, but she became aware when he stepped right to the edge of the precipice and stretched his hands out. Alarm shot through her as though struck by the lightning currently slicing through the sky into sea. 'Mr King!'

'Come and try it,' he shouted into the wind.

Dear God, what was he thinking? This was more than reckless, but she dared not chastise him. If he became angry and slipped ...

Serena forced a merry smile. 'No, no. I can feel it from right here.' She spread her arms out to mimic him. In truth, she could imagine taking flight with only ocean below, and the wind in her face.

For a moment, thunder seemed to approach from both directions, but when Serena looked over her shoulder, she realised the noise behind her was Mr Xavier arriving. She let out a breath of relief. He would know what to do. He leapt from his horse and hurried over, his face pale.

'Saints above, we have to get him away from the edge.'

Mr King made a sudden movement, turning to scowl at his

nephew, and Serena gasped as he seemed to lose his balance. Time hung in that moment. Would he fall? Serena's entire body tensed, her breath caught, ready to lunge and pull him to safety, even though she knew she would never get to him in time. What was likely two seconds, stretched into an eternity of dread, until, with a rush of relief, Mr King regained his footing. Serena breathed out her tension, her hands pressed against her cheeks. But how to get him away from there?

She sensed the answer was not in growling at him. 'Mr King is flying, can you not see, Mr Xavier?' She gave Mr Xavier a loaded glance. 'Put your arms out too. Isn't it wonderful?'

Serena took two hesitant steps toward Mr King and pressed a hand across her heart. 'Mr King, I must say, though this is exhilarating, I am quite frightened. Will you come and hold my hand?'

She was taking advantage of his affection for her, she knew, but she needed to get him to safety. And so did Mr Xavier.

Almost carelessly, Mr King spun away from the precipice and closed the distance between them, taking both of her hands in his. 'Always, my dear.'

His fierce gaze locked on hers until a large drop splashed on their clasped hands, soon followed by another.

'Race you back to the house.' Mr Xavier seemed to take his cues of misdirection from Serena and bolted to his horse.

Mr King needed no further encouragement. Without releasing her hand, he darted for the curricle. Serena kept up as best she could, only relieved that they had averted a disaster.

19

Serena stared out the window at the linen now sagging on the line with rain. The washing was wetter now than before she fed it through the wringer. She pressed her hand flat up against the glass pane as rivulets streamed down the other side. What had just happened?

Aside from the hair-raising, hell-for-leather flight for Aleron house, which Mr King won by a breath. Aside from the way Mr King spun her in a jig at the joy of the win. And aside from the hard rain that pelted them, or the whispered thanks from Mr Xavier as they darted for the cover of the house.

More than all of that, the experience on the cliff top had ruptured her equilibrium. Serena wiped at a droplet of water that even now trickled from her hair. Something had shifted within her. In that moment when it seemed Mr King might topple over the edge and plunge to his death, something deep inside screamed for a halt to his fall. The world should not be robbed of a man so full of life, enthusiasm and vibrancy. No, it was more than that. She herself—Serena Bellingham—did not wish to be robbed of him. He was like a living rainbow to her. Life without him would become colourless. For surely, before she knew him it had been naught but blanched.

Yes, Edward King was overbearing at times, and proud, even arrogant and improper. But for all that, he was a charming, passionate man to whom she would like to belong. As he teetered on the precipice for less than a second, her confusion and doubt became certainty. If he asked her now, in this moment, to be his wife, she would be tempted to say yes.

Serena started at a clap of thunder that cracked right overhead. Even the walls shuddered at the sound. Shaking herself free of her reverie, she made her way toward her room. Wind howled around the gables as rain hissed and thunder rolled. At times like these she sent thanks to God for a roof over her head and a warm hearth, even if they weren't in her own home. How would Papa and her sisters fare in this weather? She could imagine the little cottage rattling and shaking through the storm. They probably feared the roof would leak. *Keep them safe, Lord.*

She halted in her walk and turned her head. What was that? A high-pitched noise. Was it someone crying out for help? Serena stood still and listened. It was faint against the cacophony that drowned out her own footsteps. No, there it was again, a strangled cry. Who was so troubled? Was someone stuck outside in the squall? Serena hurried in the direction she thought the sound came from, although finding direction in this noise was ambiguous at best.

When she arrived back at the main entryway she faltered. From which way had the sound come? She strained her ears, but there were no more cries. Serena fiddled with the damp tendrils of hair which stuck to her neck, turning this way then that in confusion.

Just as she was about to decide, Mr Xavier appeared from around a corner, breathless. When he saw her, he straightened his coat and slowed his steps, flashing her an uncertain smile. 'Have you not changed yet? You'll catch a chill.'

Serena let her gaze travel over his wet coat. 'As will you.'

Mr Xavier shuffled his feet and dipped his head. 'I had an urgent task to complete as soon as I returned. Mother insisted.'

Serena nodded then remembered her mission. 'Did you hear someone crying out? I came to help.'

'You did?' Mr Xavier's eyes widened, and he looked over his shoulder and then in each direction before shrugging. 'This storm is deafening. Are you sure it wasn't the wind howling?'

'No. I'm certain it was something else.'

Mr Xavier listened again. 'Well, it's not there now. Perhaps an owl, or even a fox.'

Serena studied his face. Weren't those animals nocturnal? It was the middle of the afternoon, even though a dark gloom descended with the menacing weather. It seemed odd that the usually sensitive Mr Xavier would shrug something off with such a cavalier attitude.

'If you hear it again, come and tell me. We'll search it out together.' A half smile turned his mouth as though he realised how nonchalant he sounded and now tried to make up for it. 'But for now, we should change our sodden garments.'

He turned to leave, but Serena reached toward him, almost taking him by the sleeve before she remembered decorum. 'Wait. What happened out there? At the lighthouse.' She shook her damp hair to clear her head. 'That is, you seemed scared well-nigh to death he would jump.'

Mr Xavier drew in a long breath and let it out, his eyes darting all about the hallway. Was he calming his emotions or choosing his words? 'His father died falling from a cliff.'

'Oh dear.' Serena's hand flew to her mouth in horror. 'That is awful.'

Mr Xavier's head dipped, and he scuffed at the floor with

his shoe. 'Yes, it was.' He jerked his head up again, lips pursed together. 'Now and then, my uncle tries to tempt fate. I don't know why.' He shoved his hands deep into his pockets then smiled. 'Although you have the knack of doing what I could never do.'

'What is that?' Serena frowned at him, still trying to take in the tragedy of Mr King's father.

'Uncle Ed listens to you.'

It was a simple statement, but one that brought heat to Serena's cheeks and she demurred. 'Well, I don't know. I have spent little time with him, but I have discovered that bringing the danger or impropriety of his actions to his attention has very little effect. Somehow, appealing to a different side of his nature seems to divert his mind.'

His intense gaze rested on her face. 'I can see why.' Mr Xavier continued to stare at her for a moment before clearing his throat and averting his eyes. 'I mean, it is obvious my uncle esteems you. I suspect that is why he heeds you.'

Serena reached out and touched his forearm, wanting to reassure him. 'He esteems you as well. He sings your praises often.'

This time, colour infused Mr Xavier's neck and he pulled his arm away from her touch. 'It pleases me to know.'

Serena smiled at him until she realised an awkward silence had fallen between them. She feigned a shiver. 'I am off to my room to change. Good afternoon to you, Mr Xavier.'

'And to you, Miss Bellingham.' He bent his head in deference as she turned away.

Days passed, and true to Mrs Jones's word, Serena had neither sight nor sound of Mr King. Whatever the woman had said to her brother, he had ceased searching Serena out. Not even during her walk on the shore on Sunday. He appeared at none of the family meals. Serena had even listened at the library door after supper to see if he had joined the menfolk to no avail. She shouldn't have been watching for him. It was better this way, wasn't it? But although Mr King had been inappropriate, forward and even taken liberties with her, Serena missed him.

On Monday, she put all hope aside of glimpsing her captor. On Mondays, the extra staff came to give the house a thorough clean, and he never showed his face. Why, Serena could not say. That is how it had been since she'd arrived. Perhaps, he wanted to keep out of their way. An implausible reasoning. Perhaps he didn't care for them. Maybe they were too far beneath his genius to approach. That sounded more characteristic of him, particularly set alongside his attitude towards her father's attempted theft. Criminals in the house must be distasteful to him. And yet, at the same time, it didn't fit with the man she had begun to know.

Serena fought the temptation to go to his rooms and see how he fared. Why should she wish to attend him? She'd wanted this distance, hadn't she? Then why was she continually drawn to him? Serena groaned as she hurried from her room to the laundry. A busy day of work might purge her of such thoughts. Not that she had high hopes for any success. Mr King had invaded her every waking moment.

It was nearing the dinner bell when the front door resounded with a heavy knock. She straightened but made no move to answer it. She refused to get herself into trouble again. Anybody might be at the door ready to cause strife.

She eased out a slow breath when soon enough voices

drifted from the open door. A small commotion erupted, followed by Mrs Jones calling out in a sharp tone.

'Miss Bellingham!'

Who would call at the house for her? Serena stiffened, but wiped her hands and smoothed her skirts before making her way to the entryway. Dare she hope Papa, Julianne and Rachel visited. Oh, how wonderful that would be. But most likely Mrs Jones needed her help with something.

'I'm here, Mrs Jones. What can I do for you?'

'It's not for me, but it's what these folks can do for you.'

Although the words sounded clear enough, the meaning was lost on Serena. A slight frown creased Mrs Jones's brow. Serena dragged her gaze from the housekeeper to the visitors—a man and a woman, dressed well and wearing broad smiles.

Mrs Jones made the introduction. 'Mr Thomas Broughton and, pardon, what did you say your name was again? Madame ...?'

'Madame la Monde.' A sultry voice purred from the woman whose skirts stretched as wide as fashion allowed, and whose hair tumbled in thick curls beside her heart-shaped face.

'Pleased to meet you, ma'am. Sir.' Serena dipped a brief curtsy, still at a loss as to why they wished to call on her.

Mr Broughton nodded in response. 'Miss Bellingham. Mr King has commissioned us to create you a new wardrobe.'

'A cupboard for my clothes? I already have one.'

Madame la Monde tittered behind gloved fingers. 'No, my dear. New clothes for your cupboard.' It might have sounded like an insult, but her expression was warm and friendly. In fact, she reached out her hand to clasp Serena's fingertips, a flimsy shake if ever she felt one. But the action sent a waft of what must be a French ambergris perfume to her nostrils. Oddly though, Madame la Monde did not have a French accent as

Serena expected by that name. Curious.

'I don't understand,' Mrs Jones yet frowned. 'How did Mr King commission you when he has not left the house for weeks?'

Mr Broughton chuckled at that. 'Well, you see, he wrote to me several weeks ago. But I was amid an elaborate wedding trousseau and then there was the Honourable Mr Fordham. Of course, *he* must have the most up-to-date styles for his current mistress. I suppose Mr King wishes to keep up with that set.'

Since Mr King held none of that 'set,' as he called them, in high enough esteem to wish to compete with them, Serena could not agree. Instead, she gave him her own opinion. 'I suspect his want of fashion comes from his own creative instinct and from his charitable nature.' Glancing at Mrs Jones, she caught a brief flash of admiration in her eyes.

'What goes on here?'

Serena craned her neck around Mr Broughton to see Mr Simon almost charge through the door.

'Your uncle has asked Mr Broughton here to make Miss Bellingham new clothes.' Mrs Jones gave her son an intense look.

Was she trying to convey something? Whatever it was, the meaning was elusive to Serena.

'How is that possible?'

'They were just explaining that Eddie wrote to them weeks ago.'

'I see. But he doesn't have—'

'What my son is trying to say, Mr Broughton, is this commission must be rather expensive. Are you sure he requested a whole wardrobe of clothes?'

'Yes. As sure as I have two feet.'

'Then he made a mistake,' Mr Simon blustered, his cheeks

becoming red. 'Why would he pay for a whole swathe of clothes for a servant girl?'

'Why indeed?' Mr Broughton rocked back and forth on his heels. 'And yet, he sent along with his letter, rather a large draught on his bank account. I can assure you he was in earnest.'

'Then you should return it. Obviously, the girl has bewitched him.' Mr Simon's temper grew.

Serena had watched this interaction as if from afar, as though it weren't even about her. But this last comment snapped her out of her stupor. Bewitched him, indeed. How dare Mr Simon insult her so! And what had Mr King been thinking? Was it after the night he noticed how thin her shawl was? Even though she had insisted she did not suffer for it. Once again, Mr King had behaved with extravagant generosity, and as a result, she found herself in strife. But she could not allow it. 'Am I permitted to speak on the matter?'

Suddenly all eyes were on her and the heat rose in her cheeks, though her chest remained tight with frustration.

'While it is wonderfully openhanded of Mr King, I am in no need of new apparel. I was unaware of his intentions to order a wardrobe for me, nor did I ask him to, or even wish it. I am more than happy to cancel his request. However, I am also loath to dishonour him by doing so. He meant it as a gift, I am certain of that, though extravagant it may be. Perhaps we can agree on one dress and a warm coat, and I shall be more than happy.'

For a moment, they gaped at her. Had she said something too outrageous? Serena swallowed, uncomfortable.

Mr Simon turned to his mother with a tight-lipped grimace, while his finger pointed at Serena. 'You see how she has wormed her way into his affections.'

'Simon, that is enough. You are being quite rude and it's

not befitting of one of my sons.' Colour now infused Mrs Jones's face as well. Serena knew the feeling well, her own sisters having embarrassed her on more than one occasion with their silliness.

'Perhaps we could ask Mr King himself. I'm sure he could set things straight.'

Now all eyes swerved to the tailor. Yes, that was the idea. Serena preferred to hear the words from Mr King's mouth, especially in front of Mr Simon, even if his words dripped sonnets of Athena. Embarrassing, but not as uncomfortable as this fiasco.

'I'm afraid that is out of the question.' Mrs Jones did not hesitate. 'He is working on a commission for the governor and cannot be disturbed. It interrupts his creativity and puts him behind schedule.'

That was the same explanation Mrs Jones had given Serena when she first arrived at Aleron. And yet from her experience, Mr King never minded being disturbed and often left his workroom of his own accord. So, why the pretence? Why refuse to fetch him? Something did not seem right, and yet, Serena refrained from saying so while strangers were in the house.

'That is a shame. I should have enjoyed meeting this Mr King of yours.' Madame la Monde's lips curled into a sensuous smile. 'Mr Broughton has told me so much about him.'

Mrs Jones gave her a half smile. 'Sorry to disappoint you, ma'am.' She turned back to Mr Broughton. 'I am inclined to agree with Miss Bellingham. A whole wardrobe is simply unnecessary for a maid. But it was my brother's wish to give her a gift, so it shall be as she says. An evening dress and a warm pelisse shall do nicely.'

20

Serena determined to seek Mr King and thank him for the new clothes at the earliest opportunity, despite Mrs Jones's warnings to the contrary, but the chance never came. The hour of the day demanded they welcome the visitors to join them for dinner. After that, Madame Le Monde fussed over Serena's measurements, and of course, had to show her a variety of fabrics. According to the estimable dressmaker, each specimen of material 'becomes you to perfection, my dearest Serena.' A statement which Serena met with veiled doubt, especially upon viewing one such fabric draped across her shoulders in the long mirror. It turned her face a hideous shade of grey—not becoming in the slightest. However, she finally agreed upon a vibrant blue silk for the evening gown and a beige velvet for the pelisse.

By the time they'd decided on these details, Serena had little time left for her work. What little sunshine had struggled from behind the clouds, now diminished quickly. She must bring in the linen from the morning, fold it and put it away, before the air became too chilled for further airing that day. She had no choice but to leave any dusting and polishing until the morrow, instead setting out to accomplish her mission to find Mr King and thank him for his generosity.

Her heart pounded louder with each step that drew her

nearer to Mr King's rooms. Why should she be so nervous? Or did another emotion beset her? Excitement? Anticipation? She couldn't admit it. Wouldn't admit it. Serena only wished to see the man to discuss his benevolence toward her—a kindness which belied his original actions in keeping her at Aleron. Oh, it was too confusing. She shook her head, attempting to clear her muddled thoughts.

Serena paused at his door, smoothed her skirts and tucked loose strands of hair back into the chignon at her nape. She straightened her bodice and, drawing in a deep breath, knocked on the wooden panelling. With any luck, it would please him to see her, rather than anger him at her interruption—as Mrs Jones always insinuated he would. Several heartbeats ticked by, however, and no response came from within the room. Serena knocked again, a little louder and, after waiting another minute, pressed her ear against the door. Not a sound came from within. Not even the shuffling of papers.

Was Mr King even inside? Was he well? Perhaps he slept soundly and didn't hear her. He'd looked rather tired of late. No wonder with the late nights he'd been keeping. A smile tugged at Serena's lips. She had enjoyed some of those evenings with him. Curious, she tried the door handle. It was unlocked, but did that hold any significance?

Serena only hesitated for a moment, then gently pushed the door open. This might be a foolish idea that would find her in deep trouble, or ...

She never finished the thought, for what she saw sent her mind spinning. Even though deep shadows met her eyes—not a single candle lit the room—it was plain to Serena that chaos ruled, and the breath caught in her throat. How long had it been since she visited Mr King here? Two weeks, perhaps. But what a change.

Collecting herself, Serena glanced around for the man, but he was nowhere in sight. His bedroom door stood ajar, and no sound came from within there either. She crept closer to see if there might be any movement, or at least the shape of Mr King asleep in his bed. A single floor board creak could mean discovery, and the improper nature of her visit would be exposed. Heat rose in Serena's neck at the thought of being caught in his rooms, but every feeling convinced her he was not here. The bed remained empty, the dark bedroom and the hearth cold.

Serena released an unsteady breath as she turned and gazed over the adjoining apartment again. The air was stale, filled with the faint odour of uncleanliness. Several empty drinking glasses and the occasional plate were discarded haphazardly around the room. The floor was strewn with crumpled up pieces of paper, and items of clothing which were tossed carelessly. Why, even his desk was a mess: quills and wafers, open books and the remains of burnt-out candles were scattered over the surface. It seemed odd, in a house where the family kept everything in spotless order, that one room could be left in a state of disarray. Did Mr King not allow maids into his apartments?

With a frown, she approached the messy desk for a closer look. Strange. There was little evidence of architectural design in progress, unless it hid beneath everything else. She lifted a corner of parchment to see what might be underneath, but an open book in the centre of the desk weighed down the reams of paper. Serena moved to shift it when she recognised Mr King's writing filled the pages, and dates headed the text. A journal?

Serena pressed her hand across her mouth to stifle a gasp as she recognised her own name on the page. She shouldn't read it. It would be ill-mannered, not to mention intrusive and presumptuous. She ran a hand over the smooth pages engraved with the pen's scratchings. Although intrigued over what Mr King might have written about her, Serena tore her eyes away from the book. It was a personal journal, and had she not already invaded his privacy simply by being there? With one final glance around the room, she returned to the door, closing it behind her.

She let out a long breath. What had happened to Mr King? And why did his apartments lie in such a mess? As she thought about it more, something seemed at odds. Mrs Jones insisted to the dressmakers that he was currently at work, and yet to Serena, it seemed he hadn't been in there for days. The room was cold—not even an ember glowed in the grate—and no fresh candles laid anywhere. So, where was he? And how long had he been away? And why did his room resemble a frantic mind, rather than a meticulous genius?

Might that be the reason he hadn't sought her out for days? He wasn't home. Perhaps he had gone to spend a week or two in town, or even further away. But again, Mrs Jones had told their visitors he was working. Maybe he did work, but somewhere else altogether. That made sense to a certain extent, and perhaps it even explained the lack of architectural work on Mr King's desk. And yet, Serena's conclusions still did not convince her.

She needed to think. Serena was lost in her reasonings, chewing on her lip all the way to her room. As she perched herself on the edge of her bed, her mind continued to churn over details. The family usually discouraged Mr King's outings. Why? And why would this occasion be any different? They constantly behaved protectively over him, even to the point of secrecy. But, why? So many questions remained and Serena knew that if she could just find Mr King, perhaps he could answer them. Unfortunately, she had no clue where to start.

Serena entered the dining room to an uproar the following morning. From outside the door, raised voices met her ears, and although hesitant to enter, she did so anyway. Mr Simon, red-faced and wearing and angry scowl, leaned over an open newspaper on the table. Mrs Jones's face had drained of colour and Mr Xavier looked ashen, while Mr Jones wore a grim expression. Their voices ceased the instant she stepped into the room and all eyes focused on her.

Before she could ask what was the matter, Mr Simon rounded on her.

'What did you do?' Turning to his mother, he continued. 'I knew she would be the ruin of him. Didn't I tell you? But none of you listened.'

At a loss, Serena gaped at him. 'What is it you think I have done?' Coldness crept down her spine, making the hairs on her arms stand on end. Did they discover she'd been in Mr King's room? Mr Simon seemed more agitated than the incident warranted though.

'Simon.' Mr Jones had the knack of pulling his son into line. With one word and a warning glance, the gardener pursed his lips together and stood stiffly aside.

Mr Jones then turned a softer gaze toward Serena. 'I'm sorry, Miss Bellingham. We've just discovered some disturbing news.' He glanced down at the newspaper and as if just deciding the matter, pushed the sheets across the table to her.

Serena locked eyes with him momentarily, trying to understand what terrible news lay in the print. All she could read in his expression was sadness. She let her gaze drop to the paper and searched the black and white maze for the terrible news. When she saw it, her stomach dropped. 'Oh, dear. Oh, no.'

Genius or Lunatic? Was the title. That alone was enough to make her heart lurch.

> *The estimable Edward King has of late been seen in public, behaving in an odd manner. The Herald has been informed that he visits the streets of Sydney in the wee hours of the night. In one moment, he might be full of charm, purchasing extravagant gifts, and in the next, might fly into a rage, making irrational threats. Are these simply the actions of an eccentric, or are they symptoms of a mind slipping from reality? Investigations continue, and we assure the public that if Mr King is considered a danger to himself or society, our information shall be passed to the magistrate. Caleb Moncrief.*

Serena felt the colour drain from her face to match that of Mrs Jones's. 'But how?'

'How did Moncrief learn of this, you mean? That is a good question.' Mr Jones studied her. Was that accusation in his eyes?

'You think I did this?'

'It is the obvious choice.' Simon blurted out, his colour rising once again. 'No one else in this house would have dared.'

'But I didn't! I swear!' Serena shook her head. 'Other people may have easily seen us in Sydney that night. Anyone might have recognised him. Mr King didn't exactly hide his identity.'

Serena looked at Mr Jones again who continued to appraise her. After holding her gaze for a long moment, he seemed satisfied and shrugged. 'That is a possibility, I cannot deny it.'

Mrs Jones rose and paced the room, wringing her hands. 'What is to be done? What is to be done? We will be ruined.'

To Serena, ruin seemed an overreaction. 'But it's only a newspaper article. Everybody knows gossip and untruth fill the papers. And we know Mr Moncrief is a troublemaker. Why would anyone take any notice?'

She looked at each of them in turn, but they avoided her gaze, appearing awkward.

'Unless ... oh.' Serena sank into a chair herself, her voice only coming as a murmur. 'Unless you think there is truth in it.'

At once it all made sense. Their protectiveness. Their secrecy. And now their devastation. They believed Mr King was unstable. Serena reflected on the moments she'd spent with Mr King. Yes, there were odd moments, and strange behaviour, but was it so bad that this article spelt ruin for him?

'He's not ... unhinged ... is he?'

The family's silence confirmed their belief.

All except Mr Simon, who glared at her again. 'Don't you ever speak of my uncle that way!'

Serena sucked back her breath. Clearly, Mr Simon still held her at fault and would not see otherwise any time soon. 'I'm sorry. I didn't mean—'

'It's all right, Miss Bellingham,' Mr Jones interrupted. 'I suppose it's time you heard the truth.'

'Really, Father?' Mr Simon balled his hands into fists at his side. 'She is behind this.'

'It's time you went to work, son.' Mr Jones took Mr Simon by the arm and led him grudgingly from the room.

Silence filled the dining room for a long moment while the four remaining people contemplated the heaviness that surrounded them.

'Perhaps you should serve yourself breakfast, Miss Bellingham.' Mr Xavier offered a grim smile, which did nothing to soften her drawn face.

'I'm not sure I can eat now.'

'You should try.' Mr Xavier collected her plate and filled it with a pair of steaming eggs and warm, buttered bread before placing it before her and taking the chair beside her. It looked enticing, but even the aroma turned her stomach.

Mrs Jones cleared her throat and began. 'We've tried to keep it a secret—not just from you, from everybody. The last thing we wish is for the magistrate to incarcerate him at Bedlam Point. He really is harmless, you know.'

'How ... how long has he been, er, sick?' Serena forked a small bite of egg into her mouth, but it was tasteless considering their conversation, the texture of cardboard on her tongue.

'Since he was twenty-two. Off and on.'

Mr Xavier cleared his throat. 'When his father died in a fall from a cliff ...' His eyes swerved to Mrs Jones, whose face contorted with grief and she shook her head.

'She need not know that, Xavier.' A sharp edge grated her voice. 'If it gets out—'

'There's no sense in hiding it from Miss Bellingham.' Mr Jones squeezed his wife's hand. 'Now she knows about Ed, she might as well understand the truth.' He nodded to Mr Xavier to continue.

'The truth is Grandpapa insisted he could fly.' He reached out and put a hand on his mother's shoulder. 'Isn't that right?'

Mrs Jones swallowed hard and nodded again.

'In the height of elation, he ran off the edge, hollering with delight. No one expected it. No one stopped him. Not that they could have, anyway.'

A single tear tipped over Mrs Jones's eyelid and slid down her cheek.

Serena placed her fork on her plate. 'His father suffered the same malady?' She swallowed back rising nausea.

'Yes. We didn't realise Eddie carried it.' Mr Jones offered

a sad smile. 'He was always such a bright lad, so smart. He is so full of creativity and enthusiasm and energy, we didn't even see it coming. We have worked very hard to keep him calm and stable, but—'

'But since I arrived, it has come undone. Is that what you intended to say?' It all became clear to Serena—why Mr Simon blamed her, why they tried to keep her away from Mr King—her presence unbalanced his mind.

'It's not your fault, please, Miss Bellingham.' Mr Xavier shook his head. 'Uncle wanted you here, despite our fears.' He looked away from her and murmured. 'And who could blame him?'

Before Serena could respond, Mrs Jones interjected. 'Unfortunately, his interest in you has agitated his mind considerably.' Her gaze held a level of gravity Serena had not yet seen.

'You don't mean to blame it all on Miss Bellingham, do you, dear?' Mr Jones seemed surprised.

Mrs Jones gaze faltered, and she stared at her hands. 'Of course not. I'm sorry.'

Serena looked from one to the other. 'But, you think I should leave?'

Mrs Jones let out a long breath. 'I think it would be for the best.'

Serena clenched her hands, her thoughts spinning. 'Are you aware that he swore to have my father imprisoned if I returned home?'

'Your father?' The couple said in unison, confusion marking their brows.

'Mr King caught my father intending to steal one of his paintings.'

'Devil, take me.'

'Xavier, that language is unacceptable.' Mrs Jones turned back to Serena. 'I did not know this. But I can assure you, Eddie will not have your father imprisoned. I think you have well and truly paid your dues.'

'If you're certain. I shall leave tomorrow.' Serena searched their faces. Strangely, she hoped they would beg her to stay, to say it was all a misunderstanding.

'I'm sorry it has to be this way. And you must swear, by all you hold sacred, not to speak a word of this to anyone. Not even your family.'

Serena understood the gravity this time and she nodded. Then her gaze fell to the newspaper once again, fighting her way through mixed feelings. 'But what will you do about this?'

'Moncrief will have Eddie locked away if he can. We must stop him.' Mrs Jones seemed sure about that fact.

'Incarcerated?'

'Yes. At the Gladesville Asylum.'

'The asylum? Surely not.' Horror crept up Serena's spine.

'That is why we must make him well as soon as possible.'

'But where is Mr King?'

'He is safe, my dear. That is all you need to know. Edward is safe.'

21

She couldn't sleep. How was one supposed to sleep having just learned the man they had fallen in love with was in fact insane? For that is what she had started to believe—that she might be in love with Mr King, Edward. But in an instant, her fate had changed and she must leave, perhaps forever. It was a cruel irony. All she had desired since arriving at Aleron was returning to her father and sisters, to help them and care for them. When had her heart changed? Now she felt drawn to stay.

Edward was *mad*? It was hard to believe. Yes, sometimes he had behaved with definite eccentricity, but to label him unsound seemed exaggerated. Odd. Strange. Weren't they terms strong enough to describe him? Why should anyone lock Edward up for being an oddity?

And what about the other times? His fervour, his passion for the artistic, his generosity and sensitivity. Surely, they weren't the actions of a lunatic? Oh, what should she make of it all? If only she could give Edward the chance to defend himself, to help her form her own judgement. Now she possessed the truth, knowing the facts, she could make an informed assessment. She wanted so much for them to be wrong. Although, considering they had known him for much longer than she, there was little chance they were.

Serena threw back the covers with a groan. Her attempts to

sleep were fruitless. She slipped her feet into her cold slippers and threw a robe around her shoulders. This time, she would search the whole house and by the saints she would find him. For a certainty, Edward was still somewhere in Aleron. If the family feared discovery, there was no way they would take him anywhere else. She grabbed a candle and headed out.

She knew he was not in his own apartments, so she began her search in the servants' wing. Supposedly, this section of the house was empty as no servants resided there. Another detail that made sense at last. Servants with loose tongues would have brought Mr King's illness to light many years ago, so they only allowed them in once per week. And Mr King never showed his face on those days. And his rooms were obviously never cleaned by them.

Careful to remain silent, Serena searched every room in the wing, softly calling for Mr King as she went. The servants' quarters were cold and empty. Not a sign of life.

Not dissuaded, Serena began a search of the family's wing. Here, she must be more careful, for fear of waking them. She must not call out for Edward, and she could only search for rooms that might otherwise be empty. It proved to be difficult, and she eventually left the wing, unsure if she had missed him there somewhere.

If the family did not keep him near their quarters, then where would they put him? Serena stood still and closed her eyes to think. If Edward's mind was truly disturbed, might he make tremendous and frightening noise? Her eyes shot open as she gasped in realisation. That scream she'd thought she heard so many days ago! Might it have been Edward? Yes, and if the family did not wish for people to hear such a blood-curdling sound, they must hide him somewhere away from listening ears. Deep in the earth would be safest. Serena drew in a sharp breath. The cellar.

With her slippers making little more than a breath of sound on the smooth floors, Serena tip-toed down the stairwell by the kitchen. As expected, she found the cellar door bolted, a great brass padlock ensuring it would not open easily. She pressed her ear to the door, her fingers splayed against the rough wood panelling as though she might sense his presence on the other side. Did she dare call out?

'Edward?' Not much above a whisper. 'Are you in there?'

When no answer came, Serena swallowed her fears and tapped with her knuckles, raising her voice a little. 'Mr King? It's me. Serena.'

She turned her ear back to the door and this time heard a rustle, the shuffling of feet across the floor. Then a rattle as the door shook on its hinges. 'Serena? Help me. Help me, please.'

His voice was feeble, scratchy, not his usual sound.

'What can I do? The door is locked. I have no key.'

A thud came against the door. Not as though he attacked it in aggression, but as if he slumped against it. 'The key.' Muffled words followed that she could not make out.

'What is it you are trying to say, Edward?'

'I cannot think. Mind is foggy. Where is the key?'

'I don't know where it is.'

'Where is the key?' He mumbled again.

Serena shook her head. At a loss, she turned and leaned her back against the door.

'It's on the hook.'

'What?' She straightened again. 'What hook?'

'Hook.' There was a long pause. 'In the kitchen.'

The kitchen. Determination surged through Serena again

and she hurried back up the stairs. With the candle held high, she searched for a hook with a key, or keys, on it. The flickering light fell on pots, pans and utensils, all reflecting an eerie gleam. At long last, when she feared the thumping of her heart would surely wake the household, she saw the key. Lifting it from the hook so as not to make any clunking or jingling noise, Serena then raced back to the cellar.

'I'm here, Edward. I have the key,' she murmured against the door.

She needed to set the candle on the floor to manoeuvre the lock in its flickering light. After much fumbling and jiggling, Serena recognised the click as the lock released, and she removed it then pulled the bolt. She retrieved her candle, then pushed open the door and stepped inside.

An ache wrapped around her heart at the sight she beheld. Aside from the common cellar occupants—bottles of wine, wheels of cheese, fruit and vegetables, and the odd rat—a paltry cot filled the corner, on which lay a dishevelled Mr King. The damp and cold of the cellar made her draw her robe tighter. The air in the underground room was dank and stale.

Serena sank to her knees beside Mr King, horror filling her chest. How could the family lock him in the darkness, alone? By the odour drifting from his shirt, they had not given him the chance to bathe either. 'You poor man.' The words jerked from her throat, almost resembling sobs, and she clasped one of his chilly hands in hers, pressing it to her cheek.

Edward groaned and rolled toward her. 'Serena.'

Even in the light of the single candle, she saw the glaze over his great dark eyes. They were clouded by blood shot veins. Drugged. Sedated. Imprisoned. The knowledge that his family did this to one they loved shocked and hurt her more than the knowledge that Mr King might be insane.

'You ... angel. My angel.' He smiled up at her.

Oh dear. He was delusional. How much of the drug had they given him? And what drug was it? Common sense told her laudanum. She'd seen the effects of it before on her mother. The memory of Mama assailed her then. And all that her death had meant for her family. So much loss. Serena had told Mrs Jones she would leave in the morning, and part of her wanted to do just that. To be with her family. To escape from this terrible house. But another part of her couldn't leave knowing Mr King was suffering. She let out a long sigh.

'I love you, Serena,' Mr King mumbled, his words slurred. 'Marry me.'

Serena pressed her lips together in a grim line. Even in his delirium, he persisted in making advances. It both pleased her and made her ache even more. She wanted to laugh and cry at the same time. 'What am I to do with you?'

'Rescue me. Save me. That's what angels do.'

When he told her his mind was foggy, he had been understating it. Serena sighed again. Delirious. She released his hand. 'Only God can truly save. But I can help you to your suite where you will be comfortable. Can you get up?'

In response, he pushed himself to a sitting position. Serena gripped his arm as he stood up, steadying him. Despite his apparent weakness, the muscles beneath her fingers felt firm, tense even, making her catch her breath. Touching him did strange things to her stomach.

Ignoring those flutters, Serena slowly led Mr King to his room where she let him sink onto his bed. He groaned. In pain or relief, she wasn't sure. As she busied herself making him comfortable, she wondered how the family would react come morning. Indeed, what would she say to them?

It may have been awkward to care for Edward last night—
even if he was insensible at the time—but facing the family
today, especially Mr Simon, was infinitely more so. Serena had
gathered warm water and a cloth, to do her best to bathe Edward
without crossing too many borders of propriety. In truth, the
whole episode was improper. The sensations sponging his chest
aroused in her were alarming. And the way her heart pounded
as she spoon-fed him thin soup she'd rummaged up from the
kitchen. By the time she left the room, agitation kept her from
sleeping.

But now this … this unavoidable and wretched confrontation.

'Who gave you the right to meddle in our affairs?' Mr
Simon glared.

His words provoked Serena to anger, despite a herculean
effort to remain calm after what she had witnessed. Still she
kept her voice low. 'And what, may I ask, gives *you* the right to
lock up your uncle like a common criminal?'

Mr Xavier stepped between them then, a hand stretched
out to Mr Simon to ward him off, as he looked back to her
in supplication. Mr and Mrs Jones watched on with pale faces.
'You do not understand. Please, Miss Bellingham.'

'Not understand?' Serena frowned. 'I understand perfectly. I
can recognise the effects of laudanum and lack of care.'

Now Mrs Jones stepped forward, eyes pleading. 'You have
not lived with Edward enough to comprehend completely. It
is as though his mind soars higher and higher in a frenzy of
thought. Thoughts that are beyond reality. He does not sleep.
He … he is not safe.' She swallowed, as though trying to ingest

a whole plum. 'We put him in the cellar with the laudanum to settle him again.'

'Without a decent meal? Without water for bathing? You punish him for his illness. It is cruel and inhumane.'

'We intended to bring him out today, I swear it,' Mr Xavier uttered, his head hung low. 'We never leave him there for too long.'

'And what is your estimation of too long? A week? Two weeks? Why can you not confine him in his suite when he is like this?'

'This is what I mean by meddling.' Mr Simon scowled. 'Do you not think we have tried everything possible? His room makes him worse, and then he—'

'She need not know the unpleasant details of his illness, son.' Mr Jones cut him off then turned to Serena. He appeared ashen, weary, as though he carried a heavy burden on his shoulders. 'They speak truth, my dear. This is a heart-breaking condition for us as well as for poor Edward. We do what we can, however desperate and unnatural it may seem, to keep him away from the asylum. I doubt we can say much to convince you that what we do is for the best. And because the best is what is in our hearts, I am convinced it is best that you pack your things and return to your family's home.'

Serena stood agape for a moment, her mouth working, but no words forming. She'd expected this from Mr Simon, and perhaps even from Mrs Jones, but never from Mr Jones. 'You're sending me away because I tried to help him?'

Mr Jones released a heavy sigh. 'I'm sending you away because your presence brings more heartache to an already traumatic situation.'

Tears pricked behind her eyes. The words hurt. They

blamed her for Edward's sickness, at least this episode of it. They blamed her for interfering. They blamed her for caring. It was not fair, but there was no strong point to argue, except for Edward himself. 'But what does Mr King want? He told me if I returned home, he would imprison my father. I am afraid to leave without his consent.'

Truth be told, she was not afraid that Edward would condemn her father. Not anymore. Somehow, she didn't believe he would do it. But she couldn't walk away without an effort to fight. She feared they would lock him in the cellar again. He didn't deserve it, even if he was brain sick. There had to be a better way.

'We can take care of Edward, Miss Bellingham. We shall see that he does not contact the police about your father. My wife already spoke to you regarding this yesterday.'

Serena let out a long breath and let her hands drop to her sides. 'Well, it seems I am no longer welcome here. I shall do as you ask and leave right away. I always regretted leaving my family, so I suppose it is for the best.' Somehow, it didn't feel like the best though. She dropped into a deep curtsy and summoned as much gratitude as she could find. 'Thank you for having me here for as long as you did. I know it must have been a trial for you as I was unaware of Mr King's condition. Not a word of this will leave my lips, I can assure you. I have no intention of causing any of you, especially Mr King, further heartache.'

As Serena took her leave of them half an hour later, she knew every word she had spoken was true. She cared about this family, even if they thought her an interfering domestic. Mrs Jones looked relieved in a grim way, Mr Jones wore a resigned expression. but Mr Simon, well, he smiled for the first time she'd noticed. Mr Xavier appeared to be a trifle sad as he handed her into the carriage to drive her home. Serena swallowed her disappointment and turned to face the road ahead.

Emotions warred within her. On the one hand, it would be grand to see Papa and her beloved sisters again. She could play games with her sisters, or walk to the docks whenever she wanted. She would be free. But, on the other hand, she would miss that magnificent house of Aleron, almost magical in its design. And especially she would miss its eccentric owner. That is how she determined to remember Mr King. Eccentric and wonderful. Never would the words insane or lunatic enter her head again. He was no more than an outlandish, very generous, darkly handsome genius who may even love her given half a chance.

Serena sighed as Mr Xavier drove away from her front gate with no more than a curt nod. No sense in dwelling on 'what ifs', or allowing her imagination to take flight. Home was her reality now. A loving family who needed her.

'Serena!' Papa came bursting out of the house and wrapped her in a bear-like embrace filled with warmth and smelling of home. 'What are you doing here? I thought you were to serve Mr King for many more months.'

She opened her mouth. What could she tell him? Very little in fact. 'I've been dismissed.'

Confusion creased Papa's forehead. 'Did you do something wrong?'

Serena shrugged. 'Not precisely.' Now to make it sound convincing. 'They weren't happy with my work.'

'They?'

'Mr King's family.'

Papa's expression clouded. 'But what of his threat? He was most emphatic about reporting me to the authorities. He didn't let you go so easily, surely.'

Serena tried to shrug and forced a bright laugh. 'His family overruled him, you see. They assure me Mr King will not go to the authorities.'

'That is something, I suppose.' His face brightened a little, and then his brow furrowed again. 'But to say you weren't good enough ...I've never known a girl who worked harder or more selflessly than you, my dear.'

'Thank you, Papa. That means so much.' Serena squeezed his hands. 'Aleron House is kept in such pristine order. In comparison, our home might be called a rubbish heap.' Her thoughts travelled to Edward's chaotic rooms. Perhaps she had grossly overstated the matter—for that one section of Aleron, anyhow.

Papa let out a deep sigh. 'You cannot realise what a relief it is to have you home, Serena.' He tucked her hand through his arm and led her toward the door. 'I think a celebration is in order. Your sisters will be so pleased to see you home again.'

'Yes, I'm sure they will.' Serena's smile covered a nagging doubt. Pleased because they truly missed her, or pleased because she would be there to coddle them again?

22

Thursday, 2nd June, 1842

Gone.

She is gone.

The light.

The life.

No more, no more.

Grey.

Dull shadow.

Nothing remains.

But the curse.

The curse.

Always the curse.

23

Serena sat around the kitchen table with her family as they shared their first supper together in months. As Papa suggested, they celebrated with mutton stew that Serena, for the most part, cooked herself, although it tasted nothing compared to Becker's masterpieces. It didn't even smell as good. So, her sisters had learned little in the cooking department.

As if reading her mind, Papa closed his eyes, savouring a mouthful. 'I have not had food this tasty in weeks.'

Curious. 'What did you eat these past weeks?'

'A lot of bread.' Papa chuckled. 'From the bakery, of course. None of your wonderful home-baked goodness.'

Julianne pouted. 'I made you food, Papa.'

'Of course you did, my dear. Just nothing like this.'

Serena waited for more details, but none came. Probably boiled eggs, cuts of preserved meat, and a few vegetables, if she were to guess. Knowing Julianne's fear of the stove, it would have fallen on Rachel to prepare any hot food.

'Well, at least you're home now. And sooner than I expected, too.' Julianne wore a wide grin.

'Sooner than we all expected.' Papa corrected. 'You girls should tell Serena your news.' He waved his fork in their direction.

'What news?' Serena sat straighter.

Julianne's grin widened. Serena wasn't sure her sister could look more excited.

'I have a beau.'

Serena had expected an announcement of sorts, but not that kind.

'And I am to attend school,' Rachel's eyes shone. 'At least, I will next year. Papa says so.'

'You have? You are?' Serena almost choked on a piece of mutton.

The girls nodded so vigorously, their curls bobbed.

'My dear Reynold has been the greatest support without you here,' Julianne sighed. 'We met in the store, while I was attempting to buy sugar and flour. I cannot tell you how silly I felt. I was so uncertain about how many pounds to buy. Just when I wished that you were still home—because you know all about that kind of thing—Reynold approached me. He must have seen what a pickle I was in and most helpfully suggested quantities. After I made the purchase, he asked if he could call on me, and, well, that's how it started.'

There were no words. This was the last news Serena had expected. 'So ... you like him very much?'

'Yes.' She demurred. 'When I am seventeen, I hope he may make an offer.'

Still nonplussed, Serena turned to Rachel. 'And you? School?'

'Papa says I am good with numbers and that I should learn.' Her younger sister bit her lip, appearing nervous. 'He says perhaps I might one day help him with the ledgers for his merchant business.'

'You're to keep ledgers?'

'Oh, Papa thinks I am quite capable, and since his business

is doing better again—'

'It is?' Serena's eyes swerved to her father who wore an indulgent smile, rather than the expected shamefaced guilt or regret over his own failings. Surely their situation couldn't have changed so much. And yet, he did not indicate opposition. He sat there, proud as a rooster strutting in front of his hens. Yet, Serena had been away for almost two months, and they hadn't written her a single detail about any of this.

'Why have I not heard anything from you?'

She wrote to them. She wrote often. And she had written *everything*. In return, they had written nothing. Nothing of consequence.

'Well, we thought it might upset you, since you wouldn't be able to return to see us, stuck in that terrible place.' The three of them exchanged glances, flashes of guilt in their expressions.

So, they had moved on with their lives, never expecting to see Serena home again. Julianne was looking toward marriage and Papa would replace Serena with Rachel to administrate his merchant business. *How vain I have been.* She assumed they were at home pining after her, not managing without her—and they'd more than managed. The truth stung. And they had not considered telling her any of this, they put her out of their minds and continued with life. Well, that's how it felt.

Trying to think about it from their perspective, she understood a little. They assumed she would not be home for a long time. 'Aleron is not so bad, but I suppose you make sense.' It was still disappointing though. After all, she had bared her soul in her letters, held nothing back.

Serena's stomach lurched. She had written *everything*. Oh, dear God, what had she done? With a sense of panic rising, she searched Papa's face. 'Did you tell anyone what I wrote to you?'

She held her breath, waiting for an answer.

'Well, no. I only read your letters to the girls. Why?'

She breathed out in relief. 'A nasty report about Mr King found its way into the paper, and we don't know how.'

'We?'

'Mr King's family and I.'

'Oh, that was me,' Julianne announced in a matter-of-fact tone, then popped a piece of meat in her mouth.

Serena stared at her, shock and confusion warring in her mind. 'What? Why?'

'Well, it was dreadful here without you at first, and Papa was pining so. When he read that letter to us I worried so much about you. I thought, if everyone knew what a beast Mr King is, he would be locked away, rather than you or Papa. And then you would come home to us.' She grinned with naïve innocence as she eyed each family member. 'See how well it worked, and sooner than I'd hoped, too.'

Serena's body trembled, nausea swirling in her stomach. 'What did you do?' She placed her hands beneath her thighs in order to stop their shaking.

'I went to the newspaper and a lovely chap was very obliging and listened to my story.'

Serena bit on her lip. This did not bode well.

'He was very friendly. I told him all about you in that great house with that odious Mr King acting so strangely toward you, and how terrifying it must be for you. Of course, little did I know that we would manage quite well without you in the end, so it seems a little unnecessary now. Not for you to be away from that terrible place, I mean, for us needing you. Oh, dear, I am not explaining myself well at all, am I?'

Serena groaned. 'Do you recall the man's name, Julianne?

The man with whom you discussed me?'

'Um, yes. I think so. He gave me his card, if I ever needed to talk again.' She hopped up from the table and almost-skipped to her room, returning moments later with the promised card.

Serena covered her eyes with her hands. She didn't want to recognise the name she knew was inscribed there in printer's ink. If only she could cover her ears as well, and never hear what she knew was coming.

'It was Mr Caleb Moncrief.'

Serena tried to focus on a book, one of those—what did Mr King call them—three volume travesties. She bit back a guilty smile, but seconds later remembered why she was reading. The dewy-eyed actions of her impetuous sister. Serena wanted distraction from her tumbling emotions. Serena had excused herself from the dinner table within moments of hearing the name of Caleb Moncrief. She felt she might explode at Julianne and say something regrettable. As an older sister, she had failed miserably. Serena had not taught them the ways of the world, and now she was paying a hefty price.

She let out a long sigh as she paused at the end of a page— one which she didn't remember reading anyway—and slammed the book shut.

'What is bothering you, pet?' Papa's voice interrupted her thoughts. Serena hadn't even noticed him enter the parlour.

How could she tell him that Julianne had caused the trouble at Aleron? That Serena didn't know whether to be angry with her sister or thankful for the intentions to bring her home? It had only been a few hours, but since Julianne mentioned Caleb Moncrief, Serena fought the urge to run back to Aleron and apologise to the family. After all, it was practically her fault that report had appeared in the paper.

If Serena hadn't written everything in her letters, Papa would not have read it to her sisters and Julianne would not have gone near the newspaper. And now she may have inadvertently brought the ruin to Edward and his family that they had desperately tried to avoid. Society was unforgiving toward brain-sick folk, vindictive even, treating them and their families as outcasts. Therein, perhaps lay the reason the Jones family had moved to Australia in the first place. But, Serena couldn't tell her father any of this and she worried her lip, searching for a response.

'Nothing important, Papa. There are moments I miss Aleron House, that's all.' It was true, although not the complete truth.

'You miss that awful place? But I thought you hated it there.' Confusion, understandably, marked his brow.

Serena traced the title of the book with her finger, feeling the imprint of the words in the leather binding. 'At first I did, but although Mr King was a trifle strange, he was rather engaging most of the time.'

'Engaging, you say?' Surprise widened Papa's eyes.

'Yes, Papa.' And extremely handsome, talented beyond words and romantic. If she allowed herself, she would gush about Edward for hours. Oh, but she couldn't tell Papa about the proposal. Serena bit back the wonderful words she wanted to say about him.

Papa fiddled with a loose thread on the sofa, silent for a time. 'I feel I ought to apologise, my dear girl.'

Serena shook her head. 'Papa, there is no need. I forgive you for trying to steal from Mr King and all that followed. There is no need to revisit that day.' If Papa had never entered Aleron

House and touched those paintings, she might never have met Edward.

'That's not what I'm talking about, lass. You should be free. You might have been married with your own family by now, if not for my selfishness.'

Ah, that night in the study with James. Yes, life may have been very different now had Papa given his consent to their marriage back then.

'The proposal came too soon after your mother's passing and I could not bear losing you at the time. But, I fear I ruined your happiness. We've turned you into a drudge when you're made for finer things.'

'Do you really think so?' Tears stung Serena's eyes. Papa's words meant so much.

'Yes, I do. You've always been so selfless and thoughtful. You deserve better and I'm sorry we caused you pain. I believe you ought to be free to choose your future now.'

Serena patted her father's hand and offered a grateful smile, blinking away tears. 'One day, perhaps. But for now, I am happy to stay here.'

'You are a good girl. I am fortunate to be the father of such wonderful young lasses.'

There was no use remaining angry with her father or sisters. Serena was the fortunate one, surrounded by family who loved and appreciated her, even if they showed it in odd ways.

Two days later, as Serena was putting bread in the oven, a knock came at the front door. The door creaked as it opened and the low murmur of voices met her ears.

Serena closed the oven door quietly, straining to hear who

the visitor might be, and wiped the traces of flour from her hands. That loaf promised to be mouth-watering.

Moments later, Papa called her name. *Who would visit me?*

After tucking stray tresses of hair into her chignon, she made her way to the front, pressing her skirts and twisting her bodice so she did not appear too dishevelled. To her surprise, Mr Xavier Jones stood in the open doorway, fidgeting with a hat in his hands.

'Mr Xavier!' Serena could not hide her astonishment. After being sent away, he was the last person she expected to visit.

Mr Xavier's mouth stretched into what she assumed was an attempt at a smile, but he only succeeded at a nervous grimace. 'Good afternoon, Miss Bellingham.' He dipped his head. 'I wondered if you might accompany me on a short walk. Just to the corner and back.'

Mr Xavier must have something of import to discuss, for the corner was mere minutes away. Certainly not enough time for a social call, and even less for courtship.

Serena shifted her gaze to Papa who nodded. 'I shall keep an eye on the bread, lass.'

Serena turned back to Mr Xavier and bobbed a curtsey. 'Let me collect a shawl and hat.'

With the thin garment draped around her shoulders and her golden locks under the charge of a bonnet, Serena strolled along the street with Mr Xavier. The familiar sounds of wheels grinding on the earthy street, and the ever-present scent of brine on the air, kept her grounded as she walked. Sneaking a sideways glance at him, she noted he appeared solemn, making him almost identical in looks to his uncle. This revelation sent a tingle up and down Serena's spine as memories of Edward flashed through her mind.

Mr Xavier seemed reluctant to talk, so Serena tried to start a conversation. 'How are things at Aleron?'

'All is well,' he said. But then his face twisted into a grimace. 'That is, all is *not* well, to be honest.'

Serena stopped walking and turned to face him. 'What has happened?'

'It's not so much as what has happened, but what has *not* happened.' After uttering this obscure reply, Mr Xavier continued walking, forcing Serena to follow.

'My uncle has not improved.'

'Mr King?'

'Of course. We thought ... believed ...' He let out a frustrated sigh. 'May I be candid with you, Miss Bellingham?'

'I don't see why you shouldn't.'

'You may not appreciate what I have to say.'

Serena pressed her lips together, remembering other things this family had said that had not pleased her. 'I am sure I shall survive. Be as candid as you wish.' Mr Xavier clasped his hands together behind his back and slowed his strides. 'We hoped your absence might help Uncle Ed's mind settle. After all, we— *they*—were convinced your presence made him overwrought in the beginning.'

'But you don't agree?' Serena realised he'd used the word 'they'.

Mr Xavier dropped his gaze for a moment. 'I have always considered you good for Uncle Ed; you have a way with him. I suppose that is why they chose me to come and visit today.'

'Oh. I see.'

Suddenly stopping, he turned and gripped her forearms with an impassioned plea in his eyes. 'Please believe me when I say everything we do we are sure is for my uncle's best, but sometimes we make mistakes. And, it seems, sending you away was one of those mistakes.'

'So, what is it you want from me? To return with you?' Serena's heart rate leapt to double its normal pace, gently wrenching her arms from his grip.

'He is begging for you. Uncle Ed flew into a rage when he discovered your absence—never mind that Mother told him it was her fault—and since then has fallen into a deep melancholy. He refuses to eat or get out of his bed and he swears he would rather die if you do not come back. So, you see, he has left us with little choice. Mother is beside herself, although she is the only one who doesn't want you to return, and Simon is ...' he left the sentence unfinished, but his eyes spoke volumes. 'You know how Simon is.'

Serena knew all too well. What would the atmosphere be like if she returned? Could she, in fact, help Edward's state of mind? Or would her presence make him even worse?

For some strange reason, her heart pounded for Edward. He was sick and he needed her and now, she was surprised to realise, his needs outweighed those of her family. And, hadn't they done well while she was gone before?

Breathless, she looked up into Mr Xavier's eyes. 'I will do it. I will come back with you. Are you willing to wait for me to gather provisions and say goodbye to my family again?'

'I will wait as long as you need.' He lowered his head in an attitude of thanks and respect.

'Let us hurry back to the house then.'

They turned immediately and walked at a faster pace than before.

'I had a thought yesterday, Mr Xavier, and I wonder if I can ask you about it.'

'Of course.'

'Did your family come to Australia because of what happened with your grandfather.'

Mr Xavier turned his face away, but answered her anyway.

'I cannot deny it. Grandpapa's title and property became forfeit to the crown. Mother could not abide the stain his illness brought, and so they decided to start afresh here. That is why she has tried so hard to keep Uncle Ed's illness quiet since it became obvious he suffered in the same way.'

What a tragedy the family had suffered. It all began to make sense to Serena and she pondered his words as they finished their walk back to the house.

The fine china and silver on the tea-tray chattered as Serena approached Edward's rooms, a clear announcement of her jitters. The family had suggested she present herself with food as the troubled man had not eaten for some time. Mrs Jones had placed Serena back in the same room as before, her mood somewhat restrained. Mr Jones had welcomed her as affably as a man could be expected to in the circumstances, and she had yet to see Mr Simon whom, she suspected, would be sulky and disapproving of her return to Aleron. Serena braced herself for the inevitable meeting where no doubt he would subject her to a list of her faults and transgressions.

For now, though, she must face Edward, and a jumble of emotions left her quite anxious. Part of her was glad to see him again, and if she dared to admit it, even ached to see him. But then the uncertainty of his current mood turned her wanting upside down, making her stomach swirl with apprehension. Pushing down her queasiness, Serena set the tray on the hall table and tapped on the door with a hesitant knock.

A muffled groan came from within the suite of rooms. 'I have told you before, Judy, don't bother me unless Serena is back.'

Serena's breath caught in her throat, nerves kicking up a notch. 'It *is* me.' The words had little volume.

'I can't hear you. Whatever excuse you are trying to make now, I don't want to hear it. Leave me alone!'

Serena cleared her throat and drew in a deep breath to steady her nerves and voice. 'It is Serena, Mr King. I have returned.'

Silence then, for several heart beats at least, followed by scrambling, tumbling, hurried noises. And suddenly the door whooshed open to reveal Edward, wearing no shirt at all. There was only a robe hanging in a haphazard fashion from his shoulders. Serena's eyes could not help but lock onto his bare chest, the curves of his breast bone and sunken stomach, her breath suspended. In the same way, her mind had jolted to a stop, sensible thoughts flown, replaced by—by nothing she cared to admit. Somehow, she forced her gaze up to meet his face. 'I'm here.'

She grimaced at this statement of the obvious, but there was no way to redeem it.

'You're here.'

Edward appeared no less speechless and countless, wordless breaths passed before he shook his tousled hair and stepped back from the doorway. 'Come in.'

In a fumbling movement, Serena gathered the tray and, averting her eyes, stepped by him. Mercifully, by the time she had set the tea-tray on a side table and turned, Edward had drawn the robe closed.

'Your family worry, Mr King. I brought some food. Will

you please eat?' *And please refrain from looking so handsome.*

'For you, anything.' He at once sat and nibbled at a thick slice of buttered bread. Not the actions of a man starving for sustenance. But his words made her stomach flip. Perhaps it would be better if he did not speak.

'Would you like tea?'

Serena nodded. 'Please.'

Was there any chance the tea would calm her nerves? Maybe, if it was one of those herbal teas. But this was not. A sigh escaped as she watched Edward pour the brown liquid into a china cup. Serena studied his face as he added milk and two lumps of sugar. Dark rings still shadowed his eyes and the smile that briefly curved his mouth had vanished. He looked tired. And not just lack-of-sleep tired. Drained-and-weary-of-soul tired. What could weigh him down so? He handed her the cup, his fingers lingering on hers during the exchange. Why was it so hard to breathe in here? She should open a window or two.

'What made you return, Serena?' Although he addressed her, his eyes focused on the small repast in front of him.

Serena drew in a deep breath and held it. Should she explain by way of Mr Xavier's visit?

'Did you finally realise you belong with me?' Now his eyes lifted, pinning her, almost accusing in their forcefulness.

Did she? It was a question even she couldn't answer. How much of Edward's attraction was real, and how much of it was fevered illness? Her own attraction was real enough it scared her. For what future might she have with someone of his nature? Serena drank half the lukewarm tea in one big gulp, the teacup rattling against the saucer as she set it on the table.

'I missed you.' That admission might cost her. But was it enough to appease him? 'I thought about you often.'

'You thought of me,' he repeated in a hushed voice, and the corner of his mouth twitched.

Was that gratitude, or relief, or mockery? Serena could not be sure, and he had lowered his gaze again. She finished the rest of the tea and set the cup and saucer on the table, glad to have it out of her hands.

'Judy was wrong to send you away. She had no authority.' He pushed the words out through gritted teeth. He was angry with his sister. Furious, in fact.

'Edward. She loves you.'

'No. She *controls* me,' he growled.

Serena was startled by his vehemence and she opened and closed her mouth several times before finding the right words.

'She won't always make the right decisions, but she does love you. As does the rest of your family.' Serena tried to add gravity to her words by reaching out to touch his hand. Big mistake. He responded by grasping her outstretched fingers and once again, those wild, intense eyes met hers.

'But do *you* love me, Serena?'

She was powerless beneath such profound fixation. 'Yes.' The word escaped before wisdom held her back.

As much as her answer surprised her, it seemed to surprise Edward twice so. His deep brown eyes widened, his eyebrows went up and his voice caught. 'You do?'

In the next moment, he knelt before her, his hand cupped around her jawline, fingers roaming into her hair. Oh, the warmth that spread through her, starting from where his hand rested on her cheek, right to her toes. Serena closed her eyes, unable and unwilling to resist this feeling. His lips caressed her hands and wrists, ever so gently at first, adding tingles to the heat that already consumed her. Until she realised that if she didn't put a stop to this, she would end up compromising herself beyond remedy.

Sensibility surfaced and she tugged her hand back, even as her heart cried for more.

Edward was still close enough to catch the scent of lavender in his hair. He whispered as he stroked the hair at her temple. 'Marry me.'

Reality crashed around her. What was she doing? She had led him to believe, what, that she loved him? Yes, it was true. But to him, that meant marriage. Of course it should. *Of course it should.* How dare she break his heart? Again.

'I ... I cannot. Edward, please do not ask.'

He jerked backwards as though she had punched him in the face. 'You cannot?'

How could she explain this? The uncertainty of marriage to a man who might be insane. She was a fool. This exchange would not end well. 'You are unwell. Perhaps you should wait to ask when you are feeling better.'

His face became dark, insulted. 'You think I don't know my own mind? My own heart?'

When she didn't answer, his scowl grew.

'I thought you were better than that, Serena. I thought you knew me better. So, you are just like the rest of them? Ready to lock me up in the asylum where you can forget about me?'

'No, Edward. Please—'

'Get out!'

'Edward. You don't—'

'Now! I said get out!'

The roar in his voice left her with no choice but to retreat. And retreat she did, all the way to her bed chamber, where she locked the door.

24

Monday, 6th June, 1842

She rejects me.

The curse turns her away despite her affection.

How can I convince her to stay? How can I assure her of my love? Can I even make her understand?

Serena.

I am repulsive to her. She sees only the curse in me, and not the truth of me. I shall never be enough.

If only she knew...

It is Judith's doing. At the very least. She has turned her against me with her lies. How I hate her pretence of care. How I wish she would leave me alone. But I am held like a prisoner. She watches my every move, judges my every word and action. Judges me as unhinged. Judges me as a heathen sinner, deserving of this curse.

This is my judgment. The condemnation of their god. This curse.

I hate them. They can all burn in the hell they preach.

The darkness surrounds me, thicker than ever. Heavy. Weighing on me as though I am buried alive. And yet breath comes, even if I will it to cease. There are times I cannot lift my head, much less my limbs. And they want me to eat? To walk in the garden? Even the thought exhausts me.

But then there is the fig. Its strength draws me, calls me. It can carry me, hold me. I am sure. Confounded curse. Be gone! Leave me.

25

Serena paused by the table of miniature paintings—the one containing the infamous rose—her head heavy. She had slept little, and poorly at that. The clock showed it was well past the breakfast hour and she would likely receive rebuke for tardiness. At this present moment, however, she cared not. It would be easier to receive another dismissal.

And to think, that tiny painting had started it all. A beautiful, delicate depiction of a rose had set into motion a chain of events that had brought so much upheaval and pain, and even confusion. Serena picked up the miniature and ran her finger over the carved wooden frame. Part of her wanted to throw it hard on the tiled floor, and yet she wanted to hold the painting to her heart.

So much for her return bringing healing, or at least stability to Edward's life. After her experience last night she could only believe things were much worse. The family was unaware of what had transpired. Serena carefully replaced the painting and pressed her hands over her face. She was despicable, and she deserved whatever they might say or do to her. Serena swallowed a groan as she turned toward the dining room. And they still didn't know about her part in the newspaper article by Caleb Moncrief, or Julianne's part anyway.

With a resigned sigh, she pushed open the door and trudged

through to her trial. Yes, they were still there, probably waiting for her. Four faces turned to her in expectation, some wearing frowns, others expressions of hope or question. Serena drew in a deep breath and took the seat withdrawn for her by Mr Xavier.

'Thank you and good morning,' she nodded to him.

'I assume things did not go so well last night.' Mr Jones watched her face. He must have seen the lack of sleep or smile in her gaze.

'No. They did not.'

'Can I offer you some eggs, some bacon perhaps?' Mr Xavier still stood beside her, lifting lids from trays to serve her.

If there was anything Serena needed, it was sustenance. Something to give her strength, and she could almost taste the salty goodness of that bacon just by its smoky aroma. She nodded. 'Thank you.'

'What happened?' No time for trivial conversation.

'He tasted the food, but I would not call it eating. He seemed happy to welcome me at first. But ...' *But what?* Then they'd shared a profound moment of intimacy and now he wanted nothing to do with her. Because she was no better than everyone who had no faith in him. 'I cannot be what he wants me to be. I cannot give him what he is asking.'

Resignation registered in Mrs Jones's eyes and she nodded, but Mr Simon's face showed only distrust.

'I told you there was no point in bringing her back.'

'Simon. Keep your thoughts to yourself,' his father chided.

'It's true. She has been bad news from the beginning. Why am I the only one who can see it?' With a scowl, he scraped his chair back, dumped the napkin on the table and strode from the room.

Mr Jones's brows knitted together. 'I apologise for Simon's

ill manners, Miss Bellingham. Xavier, go after him and have a word, will you?'

Mr Xavier nodded. 'Yes, Father.' He gave Serena what might have been a wink of encouragement, if it wasn't for the grimness of his countenance, and then followed his brother.

Serena forked perfectly-cooked egg into her mouth and waited for the Joneses to berate her. The couple shared a glance which she couldn't read, and Mr Jones covered his wife's hand with his, before excusing himself. 'I must be about my business, ladies. I'm sure you have many things to discuss.'

No sound remained besides the clinking of china. Mrs Jones turned to her with a sympathetic expression.

'It will pass.'

Serena paused, fork half way to her mouth, confused. 'I'm sorry? What will pass?'

'Eddie's infatuation.'

'Oh.' Serena let her gaze fall, along with the fork. 'How can you be so sure?'

'It always does.'

Wonderful. She was naught but the latest infatuation in a long string of them. But what if her infatuation did not pass? What then? Would this misery last forever?

'He will settle down. Give him time. You are still the best person, in my opinion, to help raise him out of his despair.'

Serena blinked at her. Less than a week ago, this woman thought the best was for her to leave. 'You've had a change of heart, I see.' She was too tired, too upset to hide her anger. 'You all thought I was a bad influence on him last week, and now you want me to be his saviour? Well, only God can save him from his despair. I have no such power, as much as I wish I did.' It was too much pressure. Too much expectation. And her refusal of

Edward's proposal would not help matters.

Mrs Jones broke eye contact and appeared to be studying her empty plate. 'I was overly hasty in my judgement, I admit. But Xavier tells me of the way Eddie responds to you. You appear to have more power over him than you realise. But you should consider carefully. Even if he returns to his right mind, there is no guarantee that he will still hold you in affection, or that he will remain stable. Or, indeed, if he will still attend you. He doesn't take notice of me, and I am his sister.'

Mrs Jones clearly believed Serena had strong influence over Edward at present. But she didn't. Unless she agreed to marry him, perhaps. But then she had no idea how long his happiness would last if she said yes. True happiness needed to come from within. From peace with God. A peace he most certainly did not have. Serena drew in another deep breath and released it slowly. Perhaps that was the answer. She must convince him he needed God. She could not walk away from him without at least trying to help. Serena cared too much for that. But Mrs Jones also made an important point. Edward's mental and emotional state could not be trusted.

'I will endeavour to speak to him again, Mrs Jones. Beyond that, I stake no claim.' The words came out sounding resigned.

'Thank you, my dear.' Mrs Jones looked relieved.

Serena tried to form a smile but was sure she failed. How she would do any good, she could not foresee or comprehend.

Once again, Edward met her at the door in disarray, as though he cared not for his appearance. His eyes were shuttered; not closed, but void of energy and vibrancy. Defeat hung like a weight from his shoulders, and they slumped even more when he looked at her. He turned and shuffled back to the chaise, where he flopped into a recumbent position, leaving her standing there.

She soon realised Edward had no wish to see her. That thought sent regret spiralling to the pit of her stomach. Had she hurt him so deeply? Serena gazed at the food tray the family had insisted she bring again and sighed. 'Should I leave this for you?' She doubted he would eat, even though Becker had filled it with his favourite foods.

Edward waved a dismissive arm, but said nothing.

Unsure whether that meant he wanted the food, she scanned the room for a space to put it. The tray from last night remained just where she'd left it. A sideboard stood mostly empty against the wall. Biting her lip, she set the new tray down and hurried for the open door, flames of heat rising on her neck and face. Shame for her behaviour. Embarrassment over his sudden reproach. Serena couldn't escape fast enough. Her hand was on the doorknob, pulling it closed behind her when he spoke.

'It is not my fault, you know.'

Serena halted in her rush, eased the door open again, not letting go of the handle, and hung her head. 'Of course it isn't. I should never have ... I should have made it clear ... I never wanted to ...' She lifted her face to see him frowning. A frown of incomprehension.

Then, as understanding lit his eyes, he shook his head. 'I am not speaking of last night. I'm talking about me.'

Now it was Serena's turn to frown in confusion. 'About you?'

'You all assume I'm unhinged. But I'm not. I mean ... maybe I am, but, it is not me. It is the curse.'

'The curse?' What was he talking about? Curious, Serena stepped further into the room and shut the door. She sat opposite him, on the edge of a chair, her back stiff, ready to fly again if needed. Her fingers found a loose thread on the chair's upholstery, and she nervously fidgeted with it.

Edward sat up and looked her directly in the eye, one of those intense gazes she should have been used to by now. Nevertheless, she wasn't, and now her stomach lurched with nervous anticipation.

'I am under a curse, Serena.'

She opened her mouth and closed it again. How was one supposed to respond to that? Was it madness speaking? Would she encourage his insanity by continuing this conversation? Perhaps. But, his words intrigued her enough to learn more. What convinced him he was cursed? 'Tell me.'

Edward's eyes lost their intensity and became hooded again. He reclined on the chaise and dropped his forearm across his brow. For several moments, it seemed he might say nothing further.

'Several years ago, I met a travelling monk in town. We sat in a coffee house and discussed philosophies at great length. Yes, I remember that day. At first, I recognised him as someone of equal intellect and logic. I enjoyed our conversation and debate. But in the end, when he could not sway me to his way of thinking, he placed a curse on me.'

What kind of brother or saint would curse a person? The notion offended Serena's senses. 'Of what faith was this monk?' Surely he must have been from a strange sect. Perhaps one that mixed religion with ancient pagan practices. Not godly in the least.

'Does it matter? The point is he cursed me.'

'Of course it matters. If the cleric abused his office, something ought to have been done.'

Edward swung his legs around and sat up, eyeing her. Suspicion? Doubt? Serena couldn't be sure. He waved a hand dismissively. 'Well, I remember not in any case. We deliberated over the teachings and ideas of Pythagoras, Augustine, Plato, Luther and Voltaire, to name a few.'

'He must have studied extensively.' Serena only recognised one or two of those names.

'Yes. Our discourse lasted several hours, and we became rather animated at times. I argued my beliefs, much as I outlined them to you.'

'Will you refresh my memory, Edward?'

He frowned at her, as though repeating himself would be an annoyance. But he skimmed over his conviction—too many gods were fighting for supremacy—and he was happy to take care of himself.

'And this is what you told the monk?'

'Precisely.'

'And then he cursed you?'

'When it came time to say farewell, he told me of King Nebuchadnezzar.'

'King who?'

'Nebuchadnezzar. From your Christian Bible, the writings of Daniel.' Edward frowned again.

Heat spread up Serena's neck. She had not read the Bible enough. She shook her head. 'I'm sorry. I do not remember his story.'

'He was a great king of the Babylonians. Nebuchadnezzar defeated many nations, creating a vast empire in his time. He knew his success was above all others and built his kingdom by his own hand. But Daniel interpreted a dream Nebuchadnezzar had, saying that the king would be driven from the people. He would live like an animal until he acknowledged that God alone ruled over the nations. And indeed, the king appears to have gone mad for a time, until he decided that God was the one true king.' Edward's head dropped forward. 'The monk told me the same fate would overtake me if I did not acknowledge God as my creator and provider. He cursed me with madness because I do not believe God is supreme. And now, here I am, insane by all accounts. You see what he did?'

His face lifted again, and a depth of pain was written in those brown eyes. Whether it was true or not, Edward believed he was under a curse. Serena made a mental note to read the story of Daniel and Nebuchadnezzar as soon as she had a spare moment. She needed to learn more about this situation. Could a monk really have cursed Edward with madness? It seemed incredulous.

'I ... I don't know what to say, Edward.' Truer words, she had never spoken. If she agreed with him, would she help him sink further in delusion? But if she argued that he had misunderstood somehow, would he feel betrayed?

Edward must have studied her face as these shifting thoughts swept through her, for he shook his head and closed his eyes. His voice came out deeper, more guttural. 'Please don't pity me. I cannot bear it.'

On impulse, she reached out and touched his hand. 'No. That's not ... I was not ... This—what you have told me—gives me much to ponder. I need time to contemplate. Yes, perhaps that's what I should do.' Serena rose quickly. If it had been awkward in his presence before, right now was ten times worse.

'You don't believe me.' It was a statement, not a question.

Serena's heart constricted, as though a vice tightened around it. She didn't want to hurt him and make things worse.

But she didn't want to encourage him in fantasy either, and this curse talk might be exactly that. 'Edward, please, just give me time. Right now, I don't know what to think.'

His face fell in disappointment. 'I thought you loved me.'

The vice around her heart tightened. Serena couldn't breathe. 'I do.' Her voice squeaked.

Edward looked up again. 'Not enough to accept me, curse and all.'

Dear God, how was she supposed to respond to that? She couldn't deny it, but neither could she agree. Serena opened her mouth, but found nothing to say that would make this moment any better. 'I'm sorry, Edward.'

Before he could respond, she made a hasty retreat, not pausing until she was locked in her room to be alone with her troubled thoughts.

26

Although Serena paced back and forth in her room enough to wear a rut into the rug, no amount of reasoning could help straighten her mind. What she needed was to talk the matter over with someone, but with whom? Who in this house would be most likely to give her honest answers?

Serena blew out a deep breath and leaned against the wardrobe. Perhaps the blame was not so misplaced after all. Since she'd come to Aleron, Edward's equilibrium *had* been unbalanced. When she'd arrived he'd been in a sour mood, then slipped into a mania of euphoria and excitement, and now the depths of despair. He called it a curse, but the family claimed he was 'brain sick'. The question was, had Edward been relatively stable before she came? Not if Mrs Jones was to be believed. But Mr Simon held an opposing opinion. Who was right?

Before Serena had fully formed the idea, she'd flung open the door and headed for the gardens, ignoring the chilly wind that howled through the countryside. She needed to speak candidly with Mr Simon and understand the truth of his revulsion once and for all. Serena found him in a corner of the garden, on hands and knees, weeding one of the flower beds.

Still churning with unresolved emotion, Serena placed her hands on her hips, her skirts whipping around her legs. 'What is it precisely you hold against me, Mr Simon?'

He hadn't even sensed her approach judging by the way he started, colour rushing to his neck. He stammered, as he rocked back onto his haunches and straightened, dirt smeared on clothes and hands. Even his face was smudged with black soil.

'You know exactly what the problem is, Miss Bellingham. I've not tried to hide my thoughts on the matter.' Mr Simon gritted his teeth, even as he wiped black muck from his hands onto a rag from his trouser pocket.

'Except that your accusations are completely unfounded.' Serena swung her arms out, impatient for truth.

'I doubt it.' He folded his arms, resolute.

'How do you suppose I came to be here, Mr Simon?'

A mirthless laugh escaped his lips. 'You somehow wormed into Edward's affections and manipulated him into an invitation here on the pretence of work.'

Serena pressed her lips together so tight they must have gone white, but it was preferable to screaming at the belligerent man. 'How wrong you are.' She bit out the words.

'You deny that Uncle Eddie is beguiled?' Mr Simon's mouth twisted with cynical amusement.

'How Mr King feels now is irrelevant. I—'

'Ha! You admit it then?'

'Admit what?

'That he is enamoured of you?'

'I am not admitting anything. He *forced* me to come here!' Serena finished the sentence he'd cut off earlier.

A blank stare replaced the bitter expression he wore seconds earlier. 'Forced?'

She hissed a frustrated sigh. 'My father presumed to help himself to shelter and food from the dining table one day when the weather was poor. Papa then dared to pocket one of Mr King's miniature roses when your uncle found him. He threatened to have Papa incarcerated, and I was left with no choice but offer to work off his debt, lest my sisters and I starve. And thus, you find me.'

Weakened by the vehemence of her outburst, Serena slumped onto the damp grass, heedless of the mud that might seep through her dress. She watched as thoughts and emotions flashed across Mr Simon's face.

'Even if that is true, you cannot deny you have bewitched him.'

'I beg pardon?' Serena gazed up at him in disbelief.

'Once you saw how vulnerable Uncle Eddie was, you resolved to turn his head. You only want his money. Confess. The same thieving blood that runs through your father's veins, flows through yours.'

From where did this absurd, twisted, poison stem? 'How dare you insult me, sir? How dare you?' Heat burned in her face and neck as she stood to look him in the eye, rigid with anger.

'I dare because someone has to tell you what you are.' Mr Simon stepped closer, stretching to his full height. A device to intimidate, no doubt, even though he smelled strongly of clay.

'And what am I?' Serena's eyes narrowed to slits, and she clenched her fists around the folds of her dress.

Mr Simon leaned in close and lowered his voice to a dangerous whisper. 'A manipulative, scheming, thieving witch.'

The shock of his words sucked the air from her lungs. No one, *ever*, had spoken to her thus. It stung, more than she thought possible. They had never been on friendly terms after all. 'I cannot conceive of why you paint me so low. My motives are innocent. I was here against my will from the beginning and I resent that you make it otherwise. Never have I met a more callous, unfeeling young man. I only pray God will have mercy on you.'

Serena turned to walk away, deflated, but faced him again when another notion struck her. 'You know, I do not even understand why Mr King always speaks so highly of you. You obviously fooled him well.'

'Pardon?'

'What do you mean, "pardon"?'

'What … what did Eddie say about me?'

Serena released an impatient breath. 'Only that you were clever and talented and a loyal nephew. The loyal part I suppose I can understand, but …'

This time Mr Simon sank to the grass, the fight gone out of him. 'Uncle Eddie is my hero. I've only ever aspired to emulate him. He's smart. And fervent about, well, about *everything*. He's been granted good looks, and he's so, *so* talented. I've always tried to match him, making things with wood, you know? I've tried to be the champion when he needs help. His approval is all I ever wanted.' His voice grew husky and his eyes became distant in reflection.

Mr Simon's gaze focused again and landed on her, hardening. 'But then you came along and suddenly, you are all he talks about, thinks about, and does anything for. It's like the rest of us no longer exist.'

Realisation washed over Serena. 'You're jealous.'

'Jealous?' He seemed just as shocked. 'Yes, I suppose I am, and why shouldn't I be? I'm his flesh and blood and you are just an imposition in our home, even if you are more beautiful than any woman we've laid eyes on.'

Serena pressed a hand over her mouth in surprise. Did her ears deceive her? Mr Simon considered her beautiful? He was not just jealous of his uncle, but jealous over her as well? Mr Simon's face drained of colour. Clearly, he hadn't meant to blurt that out. It ruined his show of defensiveness. But this admission made sense. It made sense of everything in his behaviour. Uncle Eddie had everything Mr Simon wanted, and he couldn't even get an acknowledgment.

Amusement threatened to overtake Serena's offended senses, and she kept her fingers over her mouth to hide the smile. 'Well, you really need not be jealous of me, Mr Simon. Please believe me when I tell you I never intended for things to get so out of hand. I am as puzzled by Mr King's interest in me as you are. And I sincerely did not come here to cause any trouble. May we please call a truce?' She thrust out a hand, hoping he wouldn't leave it there, hanging in mid-air.

He grunted after a long moment. 'Very well.' He shook with her, albeit reluctantly, leaving her hand smudged with clay, as if she'd been the one weeding.

Once again, Serena turned to leave but had second thoughts. Perhaps she might put this fragile truce to the test.

'Tell me truthfully, was Mr King really more sound before I arrived?'

Mr Simon shrugged, pulling a blade of grass and squinting up at her. 'Only for a time. He's had these episodes previously.'

'Has it always been triggered by a girl?'

Another shrug. 'By a girl? No. There seems no particular reason for it. But Mother has tried her hardest to keep him sensible, lest people learn of it.'

Serena tapped a finger on her chin. 'I wonder. Do you believe in this curse of which he speaks?' She joined him on the lawn.

'There is no curse.'

'You don't believe him, or you know this for certain?'

'He's twisted the truth in his mind over time.'

'So, something did happen then?'

'Uncle Eddie met a priest of some sort, not sure what church, and spent time with him. The priest told him he was too proud and needed to "lean not on his own understanding." The priest warned Uncle Eddie, if I remember correctly, that pride comes before a fall. The priest invited Uncle Eddie to surrender to God's will, but knowing my uncle, I'm guessing he refused.'

'Did the priest mention King Nebuchadnezzar?'

'King who? No, I've never heard of him.'

'King Nebuchadnezzar was a king in the Bible who went insane after he boasted his own glory and refused to acknowledge God. I read the Scriptures over and over this morning after Mr King told me of the story.'

Mr Simon's face became grave. 'I see. Uncle Eddie has read many religious texts over the years. It makes sense he would know of it. But I do not think he learned the story from the priest.'

Serena reached out a hand and touched him on the forearm, feeling specks of dirt on his sleeve. 'You have helped me very much, Mr Simon. Who could imagine we would find accord? Perhaps we might even be friends?'

He looked at her with solemn eyes and nodded. 'What shall we do about Uncle Eddie?'

'I'm uncertain, but you can trust me in this—I am determined to do what I can to help. I have grown to admire your uncle. Very much.'

Serena, feeling unready to return to the house, walked instead to the small bay at the edge of the property. Though the air still held a chill, the wind had died down a little. The coolness refreshed her. Perhaps it would cleanse her mind of all the doubt and confusion. She stood on the shore and gazed at the lapping waves. Funny how the one person whom she thought was her greatest opposition, might in fact turn out to be her greatest ally. Once Mr Simon got past his own emotion, he'd been open and honest, and she now had a clearer picture of the truth than she had in all these weeks.

Now, how to proceed with that truth?

Was there a way to convince Edward he was not cursed? If the Jones family failed to make him see reason, what made her assume she would succeed? They all seemed to believe she impacted Edward, that she held an influence over him.

Serena didn't want to let them down. They all suffered grief for their dear Edward. They fought hard for his protection. And now they were placing their hope in her. The pressure was great. Perhaps too great. There was no guarantee of success. Especially when she could not fathom how to go ahead. After all, she had no training or experience in these matters.

A seagull hovered over the waves, using the stiff breeze to keep itself suspended above the water, watching for small fish to swim near the surface. How did these birds know where to find food? They had a built-in instinct for it. The way God created them.

And God created her with inbuilt instincts, too. What did those tell her? With a sigh, she acknowledged she was at a complete loss. As if she were the little fish in the big wide ocean, with a huge bird hovering over to snap her up for lunch. Out of her depth. Alone. Undone.

The only place she could turn was the very creator who designed her path and led her here to Aleron in the first place. It didn't matter that it was through the vehicle of Papa's indiscretion.

For years she had been quietly angry at her father and sisters, trying not to blame them for her predicament. She'd convinced herself that they needed her, that they couldn't survive without her. But in truth, they survived more than capably, and Providence was their supplier, not her.

And then, when she came to Aleron and grew closer to Edward, Serena had wondered at fate. But it was not fate or Papa's doing that brought her here. God was the director of paths and designer of futures. He must have a hand in it, and therefore, He must have an answer. Edward's family believed she had the power to save him and bring healing, but only God provided the healing and answers.

Serena needed to stop trying to help Edward herself, and instead get on her knees and ask for help; open the Bible more and seek his Word. She exhaled a deep breath of decision and turned to head back to do exactly that.

As she lifted her eyes to the trees that lined the beach, she stopped in her tracks. Edward stood in the shadows of a mighty gum, watching. Only pausing momentarily, Serena straightened her shoulders and lifted her chin, determined to be cheerful.

'Edward.' She stretched out both hands to him in an open greeting. 'What brings you here?'

He did not respond, but continued to look at her, face sullen and listless.

Awkward, she rubbed her hands against her thighs and turned a full circle to take in the view once more. The wind made the leaves rustle and hiss as it blew them about. 'The cold air is invigorating, don't you agree?'

His chest rose and fell as a deep sigh escaped him. 'Perhaps

I shall go for a swim.'

Serena feigned a titter, although his demeanour was not in the least funny. 'No, Edward. It's far too cold in the water. You'll catch your death.'

'As if you care.' The flat statement hit her as though he had slapped her, and his eyes narrowed.

'Of—of course I care. Why else should I advise you against swimming?'

His eyes narrowed even further. 'Humph.' He brushed past her and headed for the water.

'No, Edward. Please.' She ran after him, her heart a lump in her throat.

'Why?' He spun around, eyes flashing. 'Why not, Serena?'

'Like I said, it's too cold.' The words stammered from her lips. He was frightening her now. 'And you are fully clothed. The cold and water will weigh you down. You'll drown.'

'So?' He glared at her. 'Wouldn't that be better for everyone?' He continued toward the water's edge.

'No! Stop!' She lunged at him and grabbed his sleeve to hold him back. 'It would not be better.'

'Yes, it would.' Edward swivelled and gripped her by the shoulders. Gripped her hard enough she winced. She could feel where each of his fingers dug into her skin. 'I'm cursed! Don't you see it, Serena? I'm *cursed*.'

'You are not cursed, Edward. You think you are, but you're not.' God in heaven, how could she make him see?

His lip curled in disgust and he hissed. 'No, that's right. It's not a curse. It's a sickness. *Edward is a lunatic. An unhinged madman.* That's how you all consider me, isn't it?' He thrust her away from him and she stumbled, almost falling to the sand.

'No! Edward. Please.' Sobs came up from deep within,

choking her with grief.

'I'll never be good enough for you. *Poor Eddie. He's queer in the attic.* That's all you'll ever see.'

'No.' Serena shook her head, crying. 'We love you.'

'We love you.' He mimicked, his eyes glazed, mouth twisted in mockery. 'To hell with all of you!'

His roar shook her to the core, and she trembled as he backed away, his eyes wild with rage, arms flinging out.

'I'm sick to death of your coddling and false compassion. Leave me alone. Get out of my house. I never want to see you again.'

Sobbing, shaking, terrified of what Edward was becoming, Serena was unable to move. *Please, God, help me.*

'Go!'

If she obeyed, if she walked away, what would he do? Would he try to drown himself? There was no way to know. He was out of his mind.

'Go!'

His screams were only increasing in intensity. His torment felt like a knife in her stomach. How he suffered. *God please look after Edward. Keep him safe. He is in your hands now.*

Slowly, Serena turned around and walked off the sand into the trees, where she lifted her skirts and ran. Ran from Edward. Ran for help. Ran until she no longer heard his wild yelling behind her. She ran until she could no longer breathe, exertion mixed with grief choking her at every step, the taste of salty tears on her tongue. Until she was beyond the gates of Aleron and safely on her way home.

27

Wednesday, 8th June, 1842

There is no reason to go on. I drove her away. Once I started, I could not stop myself. It is as if I have become another man. Not even that. A beast.

Xavier found me asleep on the sand. A few brief moments of respite from this eternal torture. A torment which only increased once I realised what I had done.

I've ruined everything.

Judith, Xavier, Simon, all look at me with such dull eyes. They must hate me. I have disappointed them again. More than ever this time.

I am worthless.

There is no point to my existence in this world.

All I do is hurt people.

And disappoint them.

And burden them.

They would be better off without me. Without my curse.

28

'Thank goodness you came so quickly.' Julianne threw open the door to greet Serena with wide eyes.

Puzzled, Serena arched a brow. 'You were expecting me?'

'We sent for you.' A small frown creased her forehead. 'Only an hour or so ago.'

Awareness of the worry in her sister's eyes struck her with anxiety. 'Why did you send for me? I must have missed your courier. What has happened?'

'It's Papa. He ... he collapsed.' Julianne's bottom lip trembled. 'The doctor says he is gravely ill.'

Serena searched her face for any sign of doubt. 'Take me to him.'

'The fever is too high.' Julianne filled her in as Serena rushed to Papa's room. 'We don't know what to do.' Her voice cracked on the last few words as the truth of her admission assaulted her. 'What shall we do, Serena? How will we go on without him?'

Serena whirled on her sister and gripped her arm. 'Papa will not die, Julianne. Go and heat the kettle on the stove and prepare tea for us. Settle yourself.'

With a deep, shaky breath, Julianne nodded and headed to the kitchen, wiping at her tear-stained face.

Serena stood outside the sickroom for a moment to compose herself. Her nerves fluttered, and a lump had grown in her throat. Papa's condition couldn't be as serious as that, surely. She wiped her damp hands on her skirt and pushed the door open.

An atmosphere of fear hung in the bedroom. Rachel sat beside the bed, holding Papa's hand, without expression, shadows beneath her eyes. How long since she had slept or eaten? Serena's eyes shifted to the shape of her father lying still, his skin pale as death, and his breath shallow and raspy.

'Oh, Papa.' Serena leaned over the bed and brushed a hand over his head. It was so hot. And dry. She lifted her eyes to her sister. 'How long has he been sick?'

Rachel shrugged, miserable. 'A few days. But he is much worse today.'

'Julianne mentioned that the doctor has been. What did he say?'

'Only that we should do our best to keep him cool, and that he'd come back and check on Papa tomorrow.' Rachel's face crumpled. 'His face was so grim, Serena, I don't think he held much hope for Papa.'

'Nonsense.' The word came out harsher than intended, but she needed to halt the running fear her sisters were allowing. Serena looked Rachel in the eye. 'You are tired and worrying too much. I want you to refresh yourself. Find nourishment, even if all you manage is a piece of fruit or a slice of bread. We will be of no help to Papa if we starve and exhaust ourselves. I'll stay here until you return.'

Rachel's eyes widened, but she did not argue. With a deep sigh, she let go of Papa's hand and rose from her position. 'Please call me if there are any changes.'

'Of course, my love.' That went without saying.

Once her sister left the room, Serena reached to collect

a cloth from the bowl of water next to the bed. Wringing it out, she dabbed at her father's brow. Why did she have to leave from one heart-breaking environment only to come home to another? No, that was just selfish thinking. Serena pushed the thought deep down. Her focus needed to be on her family now. Edward had cast her out. There was no choice but to leave his care with his family, and of course, with God.

And so, the hours crept by, the three sisters rotating turns to eat and rest. Although, Serena rarely left the bedroom for long. Papa was her responsibility. Instead, she often dozed while sitting in the chair by his bed, or spent time praying for him and for Edward. It was too much for her sisters to bear, seeing Papa thrashing or mumbling in delirium. Often it sent them into fits of tears and so Serena would send them away.

This sudden illness of Papa's brought back painful memories of when Mama had passed. She had been sick with the dropsy for several years, but in the end, her heart failed completely. Just as now, the family had held vigil beside her bed, knowing they were sharing their last moments with her. Somewhere in the early hours of one morning, before the birds had started their morning call, Mama had stirred and opened her eyes. Strength came to her hands as she returned the clasp of their hold. 'My dear, dear girls.' Mama's voice was as cracked and dry as her lips.

Serena had reached for a glass of water, and with one hand behind Mama's head, raised her a little to sip.

'Thank you, my love.'

She had knelt beside the bed, and Papa did the same. He placed one hand on Mama's shoulder, and with the other, caressed the hair at her temples. 'My darling. It is good to see you.'

Mama had attempted a feeble smile, but then a hacking

cough shook her body, taking her energy again. Her eyes closed.

Serena and her sisters poured out their love while they had the chance. The girls spoke words of endearment and encouragement. Serena could not have been more proud of her family in the way they handled that tragic, but special time. Papa had continued to stroke her face and added his affection often. Mama occasionally nodded or mumbled her thanks, letting them know she heard everything.

'Serena, my girl.' Mama had drawn her attention with the barest of whispers.

She had leaned down so her ear was near her mother's mouth. 'Yes, Mama?'

'Take care of them. You are strong. You can do it.' Her hand had fluttered up to find Serena's cheek.

'Yes, Mama,' Serena swallowed, grief making a lump in her throat. Tears welled and dripped onto her mother's pillow.

'Good girl.'

Mama's eyes flicked open and sought Papa. 'My dearest. Thank you for loving me all these years, even in my weakness. Don't weep for me too long. You have a life to live. I'll not expect you to mourn forever. Be happy, my love.' She sighed and sunk back into the pillow. 'Be happy.'

Within moments they knew she was gone. One burden had lifted to be replaced with another. They suffered watching her deteriorate, but now they suffered from her loss and the sense of floating adrift, with no anchor on which to hold. The storm of grief tossed them to and fro, until they found their feet again. And for Papa, finding strength and hope had taken many years. Serena had been the one to care for her family, in the best way she could, as young as she had been.

And now, the real possibility of living through that again

threatened to overwhelm Serena. When her sisters were out of earshot, she succumbed to her own fear of losing Papa and what that would mean, and quietly sobbed into a pillow. She must not allow Julianne and Rachel to see how worried she was.

Mercifully, in the early hours of the morning, Papa's fever broke. The fact brought relief, but he would still have much recovery ahead of him. He slept deeply and for extended periods of time, with little energy to converse when he did wake.

'You're here,' he murmured when he was lucid enough to recognise her.

'Yes, Papa. Always.' Serena smiled affectionately at him.

He swallowed, with obvious difficulty. His throat must have been so dry. 'But, I thought …'

'Hush.' She held a cup to his lips, which he sipped gratefully. Serena held back a sigh of regret and disappointment, and forced another smile. 'As it turns out, they didn't need me as much as they thought.'

Papa seemed to accept this and soon dropped back to sleep.

Later that day, a knock reverberated through the house. Assuming it was the doctor come to check on Papa, Serena sent Julianne to the door. But when she returned to the bedroom, she shook her head. 'Just a parcel from Aleron House, returned with the courier I sent yesterday.'

'Oh,' Serena nodded. 'I suppose I left everything behind when I rushed out of there.'

'Why did you leave in such a hurry if you weren't running to our side?'

She fidgeted with the lace trim on the bed quilt, and keeping her eyes lowered, shrugged her shoulders. 'I cannot say, Julianne. Something happened, and I had to leave at a moment's notice, but please do not ask more of me.'

She lifted her head to find her sisters watching her. Clearly, they wanted more information. She could see the questions flashing across their faces. 'It matters not, anyway. What matters is us, our family, and seeing Papa well again.'

All eyes returned to her father. For now, she had successfully diverted their attention away from Edward King and Aleron House.

Papa's recovery was slow, and while he convalesced, Serena kept herself busy keeping house. As the weeks passed, it became clear that ongoing complications from the fever were here to stay. He often complained of pain in his knees and hands. He often became short of breath and succumbed to fits of coughing. Eventually the doctor pronounced that Papa suffered from the rheumatism. There was no guarantee he would ever fully recover and Serena worried over how he would continue to provide for the family. They needed her now more than ever.

Serena tried to hide her fears as they spent many hours reminiscing over days gone by when they lived in the big house and Mama was still with them. So many happy memories, like buried treasure.

Serena released a wistful sigh. Those days when she believed her dreams were a future reality, not just the fantastical imaginings of a child. And those dreams came crashing down when Mama died and then Papa despaired for so long, resulting in so much loss. But, she shouldn't dwell on the past. She must focus on the present. A handsome, broody face popped into her mind. Especially not on possibilities with Edward. Only now mattered.

With another sigh, Serena gathered empty teacups from

around Papa's chair in the parlour, and the half-empty pot of tea, long gone cold. It was time to clean dishes, and perhaps wash the linen, if the weather permitted. She shivered as she peered out the window. A fine mist of rain fell from heavy clouds. Perhaps she might hang a few small items in front of the stove and the fireplace.

As Serena placed a tea cup on the tray, her eyes alighted on a discarded parcel in the corner. Oh, she had forgotten about that. The package the courier brought back from Aleron weeks ago. She had never thought to unpack her belongings amidst the trials with Papa. After taking the tray to the kitchen, she took the parcel to her bedroom, and placed it on the bed to open it. It was a large bundle, larger than she remembered come to think of it, and why they hadn't put her things in her bag and sent that, she wasn't sure. Serena untied the strings and pulled the brown paper away from the contents. She caught a folded letter as it slid from the pile of garments. Opening the folds, she at once recognised Edward's hand, and recognised the scent of tobacco and cinnamon that must have been on his fingers. Her heart fluttered and her breath quickened. What had he to say to her?

> My dearest Serena,
> I wish to apologise most sincerely for the way I spoke to you last. My behaviour was reprehensible and unforgivable. You did not deserve to be sent away in such a harsh fashion. If I could justify myself, I would beg your forgiveness and ask you to return, but I shall not. I cannot. You have only ever shown me kindness, and I have repaid you with contempt and insult.
> So, all I shall do is offer this gift and release you from any obligation. You shall never hear from me again

and your father can be at peace. I will not inform the
police of his trespass. I hold you in too high esteem to
put any further burden on you than I already have.
Please accept this as a token of my earnest remorse and
believe me when I say I love you with all my heart. I do
solemnly wish things had ended better between us. One
thing I ask of you, Serena—try to remember me with
fondness, not as the beast you believe me to be.
With all my heart,

Edward King.

A beast? She'd never thought of him as a beast. As a poor, sick man, yes, but not as a monster. Serena swallowed back new tears. He'd let her go. Released her. Not that she really wanted that. Or did she? The conflicting emotions in her heart made it difficult to even know. She loved him and wanted to be near him, but, she wanted to escape at times, too. Wanted to lose the threat of her father's incarceration plaguing her mind. Wanted that freedom to choose to be near him. Well, now the choice was available to her. But it was too late.

Just before she refolded the letter, she noted a post script.

P.S. If any adjustments to the garments are required,
take them to Mr Broughton. I have covered any cost
in advance.

As realisation dawned, Serena put the note aside and shifted her own things to see his gift. She lifted the dress, shaking out the folds. This was the evening dress Edward commissioned for her. So much had happened since, she had forgotten that day. The blue silk stood out against her plain surroundings like a whitewashed building on a green hill. She would never have the occasion to wear something so grand now, but the gift still touched her. She pressed the fabric to her heart, closing her eyes against the pain that swelled.

'Where did you get that?'

Serena had not heard Julianne approach the doorway.

'Mr King had it made for me.'

Julianne came closer and took the dress, examining it in the light by the window. 'Exquisite embroidery.'

Serena shifted her gaze back to the package on her bed. There was more. The cape rested among her plain dresses. She brushed her hands over the soft beige velvet, warmth flooding her whole body, and not just from the pleasant texture of the fabric. 'A pelisse as well.' She lifted the mantle to hold it up for her sister, but something hard fell from between the folds and landed with a clunk on the floor.

The sisters looked toward the floor with curiosity. Serena handed the velvet mantle to Rachel and leaned down to gather the mysterious item from the shadows beneath the hem of her skirts. As soon as her hand touched the hard surface, she knew what it was. Her hand trembled as she brought it into the light. A small frame. She swallowed and turned it over in her hand. 'It is the miniature rose.' She lifted her gaze to her sisters. 'The one Papa tried to take.'

29

He'd given her the precious rose. More than the dress and pelisse, more than Edward's words of endearment, more than his kisses, the rose meant much to Serena. The miniature painting, the reason she had been at Aleron in the first place, the symbol of everything that had passed between them, was in her hands. It now belonged to her. Edward loved her! It wasn't and had never been a mild flirtation, a symptom of his illness. He actually loved her enough to let go of something precious. Indeed, he'd even released her and her father of their debt.

Serena pressed the tiny painting to her chest as tears of wonder slid down her cheeks. Wonder mixed with sadness for something that could never be. If only she'd known, understood, before she'd left.

'Why, what is wrong, Serena?' Rachel's wide eyes turned to her.

Serena attempted a soft laugh, brushing the moisture from her face. 'Nothing, dear. Mr King's gifts have touched me. That is all.' She would not concern them with her own troubles at this moment. One day, when she had healed, she would tell them. But not now. 'I must show Papa.' Serena brushed past her sisters, still holding the dress and pelisse and hurried to the parlour.

'See, Papa.' She held out the miniature. 'Mr King has seen fit to give me the rose after all.'

Her father took the painting, turning the small frame in his hands and releasing a long, slow breath. 'Well, I'll be. I never thought he had a generous side.'

'That's where you're wrong, Papa. He has always been generous. But he didn't appreciate the presumption upon his kindness.'

Papa studied her for a time. 'Well, he had an unusual way of showing it.'

'I'll not argue with you on that score. But Mr King is not the ogre we judged him to be. Far from it in fact.'

Again, he watched her. This time, however, his only response was a 'humph.'

It wasn't until later in the evening, while the girls tidied up the kitchen and washed dishes, that he brought their conversation back to Aleron.

'You care for him, don't you?'

'Who, Papa?' Serena feigned ignorance as she tucked his blankets about him for the night. But she well knew to whom he referred.

'Edward King.'

'Mr King?' She shook her head and tried to appear astonished at the suggestion. 'Why ever should I?' Despite her denials, Serena knew the heat in her face betrayed her. She avoided his gaze and pretended to smooth her skirt, picking at an imaginary crumb.

Papa rubbed his chin. 'You could do worse, I suppose.'

'There is no supposing, Papa.' Serena pressed her lips together. 'Even if I were to hold him in affection, the fact is that I was sent away and released. Do you think if Mr King cared for me, he would have dismissed me?' Even though that is exactly what he did. He'd released her. If she ever returned to Aleron, it would be by choice, not by a request from him or a demand from the family.

'I guess not,' he shrugged. 'If that is true, then I am sorry.'

'Oh, do not be sorry for me, Papa.' Serena forced a brave smile. 'You have enough to worry about without me adding to it. And I don't want you to worry about me. Or the girls. We are old enough to find employment and look after you if needed.'

'That may be true, but you are also old enough to marry and look after your own families, except for Rachel perhaps.' He rubbed his face again.

Serena leaned forward to pat him on the knee. 'But Julianne is the only one who has even met a man, so stop counting troubles before they've beset you. Right now, we are here and we are together.'

'You're a good girl, Serena.' He covered her hand with his and gave it a squeeze. 'It is still a shame that Mr King did not find you desirable as a wife.'

Oh, but he did, Papa. He did. She bit on her lip. Dare she admit to the truth?

'Papa?' She gulped.

'Yes, lass?'

'Wh...what if he did? Want me as a wife, I mean?'

Papa stared hard at her for a long moment, then his shoulders relaxed. 'So, I was right. Was I also correct in the assumption that you care for Mr King, too?'

She chewed her lip again. 'Perhaps.'

'Did he ask for your hand?'

'Well ... yes. I know he didn't come and ask for your permission first. It was very spontaneous, but yes, he proposed.'

'And you said no?'

Serena flung her hands in the air. 'How could I say yes? I

was not sure of his sincerity.'

'But now you are?' He eyed her.

'Yes, I believe he was indeed sincere.' Her voice sounded small in her ears. 'But, Papa, he is, by all accounts, mentally unsound. I couldn't possibly marry him.'

'I see.' Papa's face was grim.

'What do you mean, "I see"?'

Papa fingered the edge of the blanket for several long moments. 'Would you really deny a man love because of an illness?'

Serena opened her mouth, but had no real response to offer.

'Did you stop loving your mother and walk away when she suffered dropsy all those years?'

Serena stared hard at her father. 'No Papa. I would never have abandoned her.'

'Will you stop loving and caring for me, now I have the rheumatism? Do you want to leave me?'

She twisted her fingers together. 'No. Of course not.'

'But you would do that to Mr King? Perhaps you do not love him after all.' Papa closed his eyes then, signalling the end of the conversation and moments later, deep breaths lifted his chest. He was asleep.

But it wasn't me who left. Edward had told her to leave. It was different.

But it wasn't. She hadn't exactly fought him on the issue, or stayed despite his words. Papa was right. She had deserted Edward in his hour of need. Serena had heard the wedding vows that couples spoke often enough. In sickness and in health. Did sickness only mean physical and passing illnesses? No. A proper commitment meant one stayed through the worst of circumstances. True love was unconditional, unbiased and all-encompassing.

Serena dropped her head into her hands. *I've been such a fool.* She sat and pondered her father's words for a long time before rising from the chair beside him. With a brief touch of her hand to Papa's smooth cheek, she turned and took the painting to her room. She stowed the garments in her trunk with a tender smile, then placed the precious miniature next to her bed where she could see it always. Letting out a cleansing breath, she whispered, 'I shall do as you ask, Edward. I shall always remember you with fondness.' She planted a kiss on the tiny frame and straightened, a crease forming between her brows.

The similarity between what she had just done and what her whole family had done years ago with Mama struck her. No, it couldn't be. Edward did not express that kind of goodbye, surely. Or did he? Too many mournful thoughts fuelled her imagination. It was merely a considerate goodbye so her memories of him wouldn't be tainted and sour. That's all.

But, as Serena busied herself over the next few days, the thought niggled. Whether walking to the noisy market, hanging washing in the sunshine, kneading the dough, or making beds, the doubt refused to leave her alone. What if Edward planned to end his life? Should she make a trip to Aleron to check on him? But she would look foolish if she were wrong. Quite foolish. It was probably a silly worry, anyway. Surely it was.

But what if it wasn't?

What if her gut feeling was correct? After all, he had almost leapt from that cliff weeks ago, and threatened to walk into the ocean. At the cliffs he had been in a different frame of mind. Elated. Not despairing as of late. In desperation, would he do something similar? *Dear God, please don't let him do something terrible.*

No matter how much Serena talked to herself, tried to convince herself otherwise, her conviction grew each day. And the more it grew, the more she prayed she was wrong.

'What has you frowning so much?' Rachel quizzed her one afternoon.

Serena glanced up at her. 'Frowning?' She shrugged. 'Why, I'm just cross over the stain in this sheet.'

'No, that's not it,' her sister argued with a knowing grimace.

Serena put the sheet she'd been about to fold back in the basket. 'I cannot stop thinking about Mr King. I think something is wrong.'

'Why do you think so?'

'I don't really know. Something in his letter. I'm not sure. I have this feeling that all is not right and I cannot shake it.'

Rachel picked up one end of the sheet and gestured for Serena to take the other end. 'Perhaps you should go and see.'

Serena pulled the end of the sheet taut. 'I don't want to appear a silly worrier.'

'Well, don't.'

'Don't what? Don't go?'

'No. Don't appear a silly worrier.' Rachel pulled against her and then they folded the ends together.

'Ha. Easy for you to say. Isn't worry your middle name?' Serena pulled a little harder than needed and made her sister lose balance.

They fell into each other, giggling.

'Seriously, though, go there on the pretence of a friendly visit. Take a basket of goodies with you or something. Make subtle inquiries. If you are wrong, you shall soon find out.'

Serena opened her mouth to protest once again, but let out a long sigh instead. 'Perhaps you're right. Maybe I should go, just to put my mind at rest. Tomorrow morning.'

She reached out and gave her sister's hair a gentle tug. 'Thank you.'

'You can pay me later.' Rachel winked.

'You may lick the spoon if you come and help me bake the currant cake. It was your idea after all.' Serena put the folded sheet down and gave Rachel a friendly shove toward the kitchen.

Mid-morning the next day, Serena stood at the door to Aleron House. At first, her knocks went unanswered, but just as Serena was ready to give up, the door opened a crack. A shadow peeked through the gap and then slowly opened the door. Mr Xavier stood there in silence, face grave, then turned and walked back into the house leaving the door wide. Was that an invitation to enter? Serena could only assume it was, but Mr Xavier's attitude only doubled her fears. Something was very wrong.

She followed the sound of retreating footsteps to the parlour—that room where Edward had left her on that fateful night. The flash of memory of him catching her prostrate on the floor almost made her smile. Instead, she cleared her throat. A gravity that allowed no humour filled the room. The entire family sat, silent and solemn. All of them, except Edward.

As Serena glanced from one to the other—their bereft faces, lack of eye contact or greeting—the weight of their grief descended upon her. She sank onto the nearest chair and let the wicker basket slide from her hand. Her worst fear must have come true. There could be no other explanation. A fist-like grip clenched around her heart as dread reached a peak.

'Is he ... Is he ...?' Serena couldn't say it, that word that brought finality to everything.

Mrs Jones came to life then, with a deep gasp, as though she'd been holding her breath for a long while. 'No. He isn't. We caught him in time.'

'Caught him? I don't understand.'

Mr Jones shook his head and sighed. None of the others spoke.

'May I see Edward?' she ventured.

Another deep sigh from across the room. Serena looked over at Mr Simon.

'He's not here.'

'Not ...?' Not here, as in absent from the house, or not here, as in they'd locked him in the cellar again?

Mr Xavier must have read her mind. 'We are not hiding the truth from you this time, Miss Bellingham. Uncle Ed... He is ...'

At the shake of his mother's head, Mr Xavier halted, though he swallowed hard. Whatever he intended to say must have been dreadful.

'I'm not sure it's right for you to know more than he's alive and looked after.'

Serena's gaze swerved to Mrs Jones, who studied her fingernails. Her lips trembled although she pressed them together to hide it. What was so terrible that they appeared so stricken?

'Once perhaps, we thought you might be of use. To help Ed recover.' Mr Jones spoke this time, his voice hoarse, face ashen. 'It's too late now.' His focus shifted to the floor as though weighed down with shame.

'Too late?' Serena's voice hollowed as their unanimous grief infected her. The room suddenly felt airless, as though she might suffocate. And she could barely draw two thoughts together as loud buzzing filled her head. A black cloud seeped in from all sides.

'Breathe, Miss Bellingham.'

A warm hand on her back brought Serena back to her senses, and she gasped for air. She looked into the face of Mr Simon kneeling before her, compassion in his eyes, a welcome change from him.

'That's better. Can you stand? I think you need a walk in the garden.'

What was this strange treatment? Certainly, they had called a truce and been on better terms, but this was downright caring. Serena found her feet though her legs wobbled. Mr Simon poured a glass of water from a jug on the sideboard and she drank it with a grateful nod.

'Yes, do take her out for air, Simon.' Mrs Jones agreed, her face a weary mask. 'I will have tea made for when you return.'

Serena glanced at the basket on the floor and gestured with her hand. 'I brought something for tea.' Although the timing for baked goods was not appropriate. She shrugged haplessly as Mr Simon led her from the room and outdoors.

They walked in silence for a few minutes and Serena tried to quiet the thousand questions in her mind. She breathed deeply of the eucalypt and grassy aromas.

It was Mr Simon who spoke first.

'I have learnt enough respect for you, Miss Bellingham, to know you deserve the full truth. But, please bear in mind this tale is an ugly one. If you do not wish to hear, tell me now.'

Serena stopped walking at the gravity in his voice and studied his face. Pain lined his features, and perhaps regret. Mr Simon did not exaggerate. She drew in a deep breath. Did she really want to know? She might regret hearing the truth. But then again, what if she could help? Releasing her breath, she nodded. 'Tell me.'

Even with permission, he took several moments to begin. Mr Simon turned and continued walking, but then stopped again, staring at the enormous Moreton Bay Fig tree, hands deep in his pockets. 'This is where we found Uncle Ed.' He shuddered. With a thrust of his chin he indicated the tree. 'He ... he tried ... to hang himself.'

Her premonition had been correct, but it still came as a shock to Serena. Her legs lost strength, and she sank onto the damp grass. If only the blackness would overtake her and leave her in blissful ignorance. She covered her face with her hands and groaned. 'I knew it.'

Mr Simon was quiet and still for a while but then sat beside her. 'What do you mean, you knew?'

Serena lifted her gaze to his, although his face was blurry through the tears pooling in her eyes. 'For days, I've had a sense of foreboding. As though Edward might do something desperate. But I kept telling myself I was being silly. He wrote me a letter, you see, and it felt like goodbye. Forever goodbye. You understand?'

Mr Simon stared at her for what seemed an age, but then nodded.

'You said you found him in time. So, what happened?'

'It's my fault he got that far.' His voice cracked, haunted by the memory. 'I mean, I work out here. And I didn't see him.'

'I'm sure you cannot be held responsible—'

'Xavier found him.' Mr Simon cut her off, thrusting his chin toward the fig again. 'Up there. Tied one end of a rope to that big bough and the other around his neck.' He swallowed and turned his face to the ground, kicking at the sods. 'He was about to jump when Xavier caught up to him. I heard Xavier trying to convince Uncle Eddie to come down. I climbed up while my brother kept him talking.'

'What did Mr King say? Did he give a reason?' Serena's stomach clenched at the thought of what these men had suffered.

Mr Simon shrugged, a helpless expression. 'The same old ramblings about the curse and how everyone would be better off without him. How nobody understands or cares and that he's a burden on all of us.'

Serena reached out and touched his forearm. There were no words to bring comfort. But she understood. Oh, she understood.

'Persuading him was hard, but we eventually got him down.' Mr Simon pressed his lips together then rubbed his hands over his face.

Serena waited for him to continue, but he had closed the door on the conversation.

'So, where is Mr King now?'

Mr Simon's face hardened, his eyes burning into hers. 'You don't want to know.'

He turned his back and started to trudge back to the house.

Serena scrambled to her feet, lifted her skirt and ran after him. 'Why don't I? Tell me where he is. You've told me everything else. Why stop now?'

The young man halted in front of her, nearly causing her to collide with him in her pursuit. Mr Simon tilted his head back and closed his eyes. The air whistled in his nose as he drew in a deep breath. 'We saw Caleb Moncrief running from the gardens. No doubt he'd been watching Uncle Ed. He saw everything.' Mr Simon faced her again and gave an intense gaze.

That could only mean ...

'They called on the magistrate. Before we had a chance to settle my uncle, they came and took him away to Bedlam Point.'

'The Asylum?'

'Tarban Creek Lunatic Asylum. Yes.'

30

Edward was in the lunatic asylum and it was her fault! It must be her fault. If she'd never met him, none of this would have happened. He was fine before she arrived at Aleron, before he became attached to her, before she fell for him. He would have been fine if he remained with his family and no one else.

If only Papa never came to Aleron House. If only she'd come back earlier. If only she'd said yes to Edward's proposal *to begin with*. If only she were here when he climbed the tree. *If only, if only, if only* ... Serena's mind screamed for a solution.

Serena dropped to her knees right there in the grass, careless of whether Mr Simon remained or not, and prayed like she'd never prayed before. Silent whispers beneath her breath. Desperate whispers. Pleading whispers. Tears ran unchecked down her cheeks as she recalled stories from the Scriptures where the Messiah had healed. She prayed them as reminders to herself and perhaps to God of what He could do.

After long moments, Serena sensed movement beside her as Mr Simon knelt and joined her. Together they lifted their voices in supplication for God's intervention in Edward's life. When at last she opened her eyes, a new sense of peace washed over her. A peace that went beyond her comprehension.

'He will be all right. It's going to be fine.' How she knew this, she couldn't say, but there it was—a confidence deep in her soul. She breathed in and felt the chill air deep inside her lungs, like fresh life.

Simon stared at her, his face still grim, but he nodded. Then he jerked his chin toward the house. 'Here comes Mother.'

Serena turned as the woman strode up to them.

'Are you ready for some tea?'

Serena looked at her, considering for a moment. 'Actually, I should like to go to Mr King's room. May I do that?'

Mrs Jones shrugged. 'I don't see why not. Take care though, as it's still a mess.'

Serena pushed to her feet and brushed off her damp dress. With a nod and a small smile, she headed back to the house. Why she wanted to be in his room, she couldn't say. With deliberate, slow steps, she climbed the stairs, each one a reminder of those nights rambling through the house with Edward, dancing in the ball room. He was so dear to her, she couldn't imagine life without him in it, no matter how absurdly he behaved. She loved him, she knew that now.

The kind of love that Papa had pressed her about. If Edward remained brain sick for the rest of his life, she would stay by his side. She would encourage him as best she could and support him through the worst of it. Not because he needed her, and not because she thought she might save him, but because she loved him.

Edward's room was, indeed, still in chaos—clothes strewn haphazardly, dirty dishes, discarded and crumpled pieces of paper. Edward had lived under torment for too long. Serena sighed. What was she doing here? What was she looking for?

She made her way to the small room which held his art. An unfinished mural covered part of one wall, and she immediately recognised herself as the central focus of the painting. It was beautiful. Her chin wobbled as tears threatened. It overwhelmed her that he esteemed her enough to paint her on his wall.

She dabbed at the moisture in her eyes, and turned to move into his bedroom, where she pulled the drapes back to let in light. As she stood there at the window, she noticed that blasted fig tree filling the view. How many hours had he lain looking at that tree? Had he imagined himself hanging from that tree so many times that he eventually tried it? 'Oh, Edward.'

On a side table rested a jug and bowl for morning ablutions. Serena picked up a small vial and put it to her nose. Lavender oil. The familiar scent he used. With a sigh, she placed the jar back.

Serena sat on the edge of his bed. One day soon, she intended to share this room with him. She would have the fig removed and do everything in her power to help Edward remain stable. But first, she needed to get him out of the asylum. Since the magistrate sent him there, she supposed it wouldn't be an easy thing to have him released again. What if his family, and herself, wrote letters to the magistrate, defending his character? Surely, they would listen to several voices against the one testimony of Caleb Moncrief.

Oh! Serena balled her hands into fists at the thought of the man. He needed to be taught a lesson or two.

She shook her head. She didn't have time to dwell on Moncrief now. There must be a way to have Edward returned to his family. Serena stood and moved to his desk. There would surely be paper and ink to begin her own letter to the Magistrate. Sure enough, she found the writing materials, and sat to begin her testimony. Then her eyes alighted on his snuff box, and her throat convulsed. Edward carried his snuff everywhere. She flicked it open and smelled the contents—tobacco, vanilla and cinnamon—bringing back memories of being close to him.

There were several layers of paper on the desk which she needed to move aside to work. As she did so, she uncovered the journal she had stumbled upon once before. On that occasion, she had resisted the curiosity that begged her to read. This time, she did not hesitate. Something within those pages might be of help.

Opening the journal, she began at the beginning and read the journey of his mind. Moments of euphoria, moments of utter despair and moments that were lucid and down-to-earth. His ideas and inspirations, his troubles and doubts. It was all there. Edward hid nothing from the private pages of his journal.

His love for her was as real as hers was for him. Exaggerated at times, yes, but still real. Several of those embellished passages brought waves of heat to Serena's neck and cheeks, and warmth to her heart. Poems and sonnets—she could live with that without a doubt.

The harder part to live with would be the down times, the words of despair and defeat. And the words of confusion and delusion. She still needed to convince Edward that he wasn't under a curse. She found and read the journal entry of his meeting with the priest, which read as harmless while it was fresh in his mind. It must have been later that the memory morphed into something quite different.

As she read, the frequent mention of his sister revealed a pattern. A pattern that deeply concerned Serena. Even if several of the passages were delusional or exaggerated, there was still enough to cast serious doubt over her behaviour. A behaviour that seemed at odds with that which she presented to everyone else. Certainly, she feared the reputation that madness would bring to the family. But had that fear transcended normal protective behaviours, and made her act underhandedly? Serena sat back and tried to recount her own exchanges with Mrs Jones and frowned more deeply. Surely not. It couldn't be.

After more than an hour of reading, Serena turned to the last entry. The date on the page read Monday, 11th July 1842. Several weeks after that fateful day on the beach, possibly the day he climbed the tree. The ink smudged on the page. Serena ran her hand over the flawless script. How desperate must a person be to want to end their life?

The giant fig calls me, its branches like bony fingers beckon. Through the rain that blurs my eyes, I can still see them. I can hear the wind howling my name. There is nothing left. She is gone. I have let her go. She does not deserve to be burdened with me. I have given her the only things that matter, and there is an end. I cannot go on. Life…

What is life?

Not this.

Not this.

God, take this curse, or take me.

I am done.

Xavier, Simon, Serena, goodbye.

Be happy.

I love you.

Forgive me.

Edward.

Sobs broke forth from Serena as she finished reading. *Dear God, be with him, keep him safe.*

Serena stormed down the staircase. Now that she'd finished the journal and considered the things Edward wrote about his sister, her alarm turned to anger. How dare she? And to her own brother, no less. That woman had some answering to do. She found Judith sitting in the parlour, at first glance serene, then quickly transforming into a picture of grief.

How had Serena never noticed these swift changes in Mrs Jones's demeanour? If only she was more observant. Perhaps then none of this would have happened. Serena willed herself to calm, Edward's illness did not stem from his sister's scheming ways. If she became hysterical and over-reacted now, it would not help.

'The one person who should support Edward above all, and instead the whole time you devise ways to undermine him and control him.'

Surprise lit Mrs Jones's features, and again a look of disbelief quickly displaced it, and even a feigned expression of hurt. If it weren't so serious, Serena could almost laugh.

'What ridiculous idea has gotten into your head now, Miss Bellingham?'

Serena narrowed her eyes at the woman. 'Edward keeps a journal, did you know?'

Once again, for the briefest moment, Mrs Jones looked stunned, but she covered it deftly with a shrug and a nod. 'Of course I know.'

Lies. Blatant lies.

'I have learnt much this afternoon, Mrs Jones. Edward banned you from entering his rooms, unhappy with your treatment of him. I think if you knew of this journal, and what it contains, you would not so readily have allowed me to go there.'

A scornful laugh erupted from the woman's throat. 'I cannot conceive of what you—how did you say it—learnt.' A hard glint flashed in her eyes. 'But whatever it is, I am surprised that you, an intelligent girl by all accounts, accept the rantings of a deranged mind as fact.'

Serena's eyes widened. This, she had not expected. 'Deranged mind? What happened to the caring sister?'

'Oh, I care. I care about my family and what the public will think of them if society discovers Edward's sickness. We have tried to hide it for so many years. It's exhausting. Perhaps it is best he is kept away from society's prying eyes in the asylum.'

Serena stared at Mrs Jones. There seemed to be an element of defeat in her words, resignation. Did she really believe this outcome was for the best?

'According to Edward, you've pestered him to give you control of his estate for years. And now you have apparently succeeded.'

Mrs Jones gripped her hands together and grimaced. 'When my father died, we lost *everything*. And our family's name was slurred because of my father's illness. My husband is not able to provide for us due to his injury in battle, apart from a small government pension he received. Edward was the only one of us with income, but his name lost recognition because of Papa. We came to Australia to start again. Can you imagine how I felt when Edward showed signs of the same malady? I could not go through it all again. This family, we've lived in this house with him, to support *him*. We've done everything for *him*. But it is as though he is blind to our sacrifice and to our plight. He wastes his funds as though they will last forever.'

Serena recalled when Edward had wanted to lavish her

with a whole new wardrobe, and when he had bought those pastries. Is this what Mrs Jones meant by wasting? She opened her mouth to argue but a broken voice came from behind her, stopping her words.

'Did you never trust I could provide for you, Judith?' Mr Jones had obviously overheard their conversation. 'I may not have full use of my arm, but I am yet able to earn. But I suppose that is not enough for you.'

As Serena turned around to face him, she met a gaze filled with sadness and disappointment. Just behind him stood their two sons, equally astonished by this revelation.

'What is happening?' Simon pushed past them to stand before his mother. 'What are you saying?'

Mrs Jones averted her gaze, wringing her hands once again. 'What I am saying, Simon, is we were on the brink of losing everything again. Your uncle was ready to settle his wealth on this girl'—she gestured toward Serena—'leaving us with nothing. He is *my* brother. We are the ones who've made the sacrifices for *him*. But he wants to marry her. And what do we get for all our trouble? Empty pockets and a name stained with madness. That is what I am saying.'

The exaggerated reasoning from this woman's mouth astonished Serena, and by the looks of her husband and sons, they were also stunned.

'You go too far, Judith. It was you who insisted none of us work outside of this house, that we needed to protect and support Ed. We might have set ourselves up quite nicely in town. We still could. The boys are yet young enough to make something of themselves.'

'There's no need for that.' Mrs Jones shook her head emphatically. 'Eddie has given me control of his assets now, and he is being looked after. All will be well.'

Mr Jones shook his head in bewilderment. 'All is not well. How can you say that? I… I am shocked to hear you speak so. You put all of your faith in your brother's property? What then, am I to you?' He turned his back on her and strode to the mantel, where he stared down into the blazing fire.

Silence reigned for several long seconds, and then Mr Simon spoke.

'None of this solves how we get Uncle Eddie out of the asylum.'

Serena jerked her chin toward Mrs Jones. '*She* thinks he is better off in the asylum. Hidden away from the shameful stares and comments that society might throw her way.'

All heads turned to Mrs Jones once again. The poor family. Serena's anger melted a little.

Mrs Jones's face crumpled. 'I cannot endure it anymore. For six years I have fought this. Fought his illness, fought to keep it secret. I'm so tired. At least this way, we no longer need worry that he will do something indiscreet or take desperate measures with his life. And the boys' reputations may remain safe for a while, at least.'

She dropped her head into her hands and sobbed quietly.

'Why do you fret over your sons? They are fine, upstanding young men.' Serena didn't grasp the depth of concern the woman showed.

'Don't you see?' Mrs Jones pleaded through trembling lips and tear-filled eyes. 'Once everyone knows Edward is mad, they will assume that my sons are mad too. After all, my father had the same mania, which killed him. Who can say neither of them will contract it?' She turned sorrowful eyes to each of them. 'The rumours and gossip will begin with Edward, and soon they will whisper about our father and then they will suspect the boys. It's better if we leave Eddie in the asylum where the doctors can treat him.'

Mr Jones turned and stared at her as though she were a stranger. 'You know very well that patients rarely ever return home from Tarban Creek. You would condemn your brother for the slight chance our sons carry the same condition?'

'It's for the best.' Mrs Jones's voice rasped.

Clearly, she believed in what she was saying, but her family was not convinced. And neither was Serena.

In fact—

'Were you involved in him being sent to the asylum?'

Mrs Jones jerked up straight, as though she'd been poked in the rib cage. 'Why would you ask such a thing?'

Serena shrugged, but narrowed her eyes. 'It seems fortuitous for you, that soon after you had Edward's signature handing over control, the magistrate learnt of his illness.'

'What you are suggesting is preposterous.' But she looked as guilty as a child whose face is smeared with the very crumbs of the cake they denied eating. She glanced around at each member of her family, then pointed at Serena. 'It is this *chit* who was set to ruin Edward, not I.'

'Me?' Serena was livid. Mrs Jones thought to divert the attention from herself. But she had acted subversively the whole time while making out she empathised with Serena's situation. 'You've deceived me, led me to believe that Edward is a libertine. That he has made advances on several young women. But nothing in his journal indicates any other woman in his life beyond a brief acquaintance. And further, according to his words, you have tried to convince him that I am no more than a fortune hunter, in league with my father of course.'

The disappointment in Mr Jones face deepened. 'Is this true, Elizabeth?'

'I am not convinced she cares for him.' Mrs Jones pressed her lips together, avoiding her husband's gaze.

'It should be enough that *he* cares for *her*,' Mr Xavier said. 'That was enough for me to stand down.'

Serena turned to face him and saw colour flood into his cheeks. So, she had been right. He had been interested in her at first.

'I apologise if that embarrasses you, Miss Bellingham.' He inclined his head towards her.

Serena nodded in turn, unable to express her thoughts while her emotions jumbled and churned so much. She looked at Mrs Jones. 'I would still like to know if you were involved in Mr King's admittance to the asylum.'

'Yes. Answer her, Mother,' Mr Simon stepped closer to her, so he loomed over her.

'Yes, do, please enlighten us further,' Mr Jones agreed, his body stiff.

Mr Xavier put a hand on her shoulder. 'Did you have a hand in it, Mother?'

Mrs Jones drew in a deep breath and let it out slowly. Then she gave a light shrug. 'I did perhaps send a message to Mr Moncrief.'

Moncrief! Again.

The wheels were turning in Serena's head as pieces of information connected in her mind. 'Caleb Moncrief? Let's talk about him for a moment.'

31

'What is there to say?'

Why Mrs Jones persisted in feigning innocence, Serena did not understand.

'Edward and Mr Moncrief were friends once. What happened?'

'Moncrief turned on him when he discovered Uncle Ed was sick.' Mr Simon was on the defensive once again.

Serena eyed Mrs Jones, who had dropped her gaze to her lap. 'Are you certain that's what happened?'

'What else could have happened?' Mr Xavier seemed perplexed. Mr Jones shook his head and turned back to the hearth.

'From Edward's journal, I take it they were close before his illness.' Serena addressed Mr Xavier and Mr Simon, although she kept her eyes on Mrs Jones to watch her responses.

Mr Xavier shrugged. 'Those two used to cut up quite a lark. Out all hours of the night, haring around the countryside. They were rather inseparable, to be honest.'

'Yes, Moncrief was here almost daily. But he turned sour so quickly.' His brows knitted together. 'I can't remember precisely why.'

Mrs Jones remained motionless, apart from kneading her fingers.

'I have an inkling,' Serena said. 'I wonder if you, Mrs Jones, poisoned his mind against Edward, much as you tried to do with me.'

The woman's head shot up. 'What possible reason would I have for doing that?'

'I'm not sure, but I'll wager you have one.'

'Are you going to allow this impertinent miss to continue accusing me?' Mrs Jones addressed her husband's back.

Mr Jones did not move from where he leaned against the mantel, but Serena continued.

'Never mind. I shall find out the truth from Mr Moncrief myself.'

Serena turned to leave, but not before she recognised the drain of colour from Mrs Jones's face. Mr Moncrief's version of events would be rather intriguing, she had no doubt. As she turned to pull the big door closed behind her, a hand reached out to hold it open.

'Miss Bellingham.' Mr Xavier halted her. 'Please forgive us. This admission of Mother's is rather a shock to us. We never realised ...' he swallowed. 'This will take time for us to comprehend.'

Serena offered him a compassionate smile. 'I don't blame you, Mr Xavier. Your mother's secret ambitions are at fault here. I do hope you can make peace with her. And I hope Edward will also when we get him out of that asylum.'

'How shall we accomplish that? You heard what Father said.'

'I did, but there must be a way. Why don't we start with petitioning the Magistrate? While I meet Mr Moncrief, why don't you write a letter, defending your uncle's character?'

Mr Xavier swallowed and nodded. 'All right. I will.'

With that they parted ways, and almost an hour later, Serena burst into her home and sought her father.

'Papa! I need your help. I must go and speak with a gentleman at the newspaper office. The same one as Julianne gave my story to. Will you come with me?'

Her father looked alarmed on seeing Serena's animated expression.

'What has happened, pet?' He asked as he rose slowly from his chair.

'Mr King has been taken to Bedlam Point.'

'What?'

'It is a long story, but I promise to tell you on the way. Will you come?'

'Of course, my dear. But we must hail a cab. I fear my knees are too swollen to walk far.'

Papa gathered his coat and they were soon on their way, heads close together as they rode, while Serena recounted the morning's revelations to him.

Barely noticing the passing of time, they soon arrived at the *Sydney Morning Herald* office where Serena asked for Mr Caleb Moncrief.

'Please have a seat, Miss...?'

'Bellingham. And this is Mr Bellingham, my father.'

'Miss Bellingham. I shall see if Mr Moncrief is receiving visitors.' The gentleman at the front desk made his way along a narrow and somewhat shadowy hallway, leaving Serena and her father to gaze at their surroundings. Several framed copies of the newspaper hung on the wall, along with a portrait of the founder. The smell of the printing press drifted to them from the back rooms, along with the sounds of men working.

Moments later, the gentleman returned with a nod. 'Right

this way, Mr Bellingham, Miss Bellingham.'

Still fuelled by the outrage that had stirred within her since she'd read Edward's journal, Serena experienced no nervousness whatsoever. Very unlike her usual self. The man paused outside an office door and knocked for her. 'Here you are.'

Serena straightened her skirts and gathered her thoughts. Upon hearing the 'yes' from within the office, Papa opened the door.

Mr Moncrief stood as they entered. 'Mr Bellingham. Miss Bellingham. To what do I owe this pleasure?' He seemed nervous in his greeting, but offered a polite bow.

Sitting in one of the two chairs opposite his desk, while Papa sat beside her, Serena got right to the point. 'We're here to discuss Mr Edward King.'

'I see.' A slight frown appeared on his brow as he reclaimed his seat.

'A shameful thing has been done to him.'

A sigh left his lips. 'Agreed.' He picked up a pen and tapped it repeatedly on the desk in agitation.

'Agreed?' Thrown by this unexpected comment, Serena gaped at him. 'But you are involved in this debacle.'

Mr Moncrief put the pen down, stood up and moved to close the door of the small office. Serena had to crane her neck around to see him. He turned to face her, leaning against the door. 'Not as involved as you might assume.' He pushed away from the door, opening his hands before him and returning to his seat. 'Or, should I say, involved in a different way than you might assume.'

She did not know what to say. Puzzlement disoriented her. She had planned to come in and give Mr Moncrief the lecture of his life, but now, she wasn't sure. 'You did print that story about him, courtesy of my very own sister. Perhaps you should explain yourself.'

'I will. But I must go back to the beginning if you will bear with me.'

Serena glanced at her father, whose face remained expressionless, then looked back at the man behind the desk. She studied him. Mr Moncrief seemed genuine, so she nodded.

'Edward and I became great friends soon after he landed in Sydney. We were both nineteen then, but I had grown up in Sydney, so I helped him get used to his new home. We got along very well most of the time.'

'Most of the time?'

'I will presume you know what I mean when I say his, er, intelligence, frustrated me at times.'

Serena's lips twitched. She did know and inclined her head in acknowledgement.

Mr Moncrief smiled at that. 'I thought as much. You have experienced the same. But I always got over it. Ed's other virtues outweighed his faults. Always.'

The tightness in Serena's shoulders eased. This man cared for Edward. Had she been wrong about him from the beginning? Just as she had been wrong about Mrs Jones. And even Edward himself. 'So, what happened?'

Mr Moncrief clasped his hands together, leaning forward in his chair. 'When he was twenty-two, I noticed strange things in the way he acted at times. I had learnt from him the story of his father's demise. I wanted to search for a way to help Ed, but his sister refused me. Mrs Jones wanted to keep his illness hidden and found her own ways to conceal and control it. Over time, I suspect she told him terrible lies about me. I know she told *me* things about *him* that weren't true. At least, they didn't sound true of Ed's nature.'

'What kind of things?'

'Such as Ed didn't want to associate with me anymore. That he had come to his senses, whatever that means. I never really accepted that he had cut me off like that.'

'And that's why you came to Aleron that day?'

Mr Moncrief nodded. 'I did that now and then, on the off chance I might catch him outside, or hoping things had changed within the walls. It's been three years since I last spoke to Ed. He hasn't tried to contact me, which is why I think Mrs Jones has turned him against me.'

'But you published that damning article after one of my daughters contacted you,' Papa interrupted. 'Why would you do that?'

Mr Moncrief rubbed his stained hands over his face. 'I am ashamed of myself. At the time, I thought I was doing the right thing. I thought that perhaps if I revealed the truth, it would break the hold Mrs Jones has over him, that Ed could get the help he needs. I was a fool. Now I've made things much worse.'

Serena swallowed. What a mess. He most definitely had made things much worse.

'And then you called on the Magistrate.'

At that, Mr Moncrief sat up straight. 'No.' He shook his head with vehemence. 'I had nothing to do with that.'

'But you were there. You saw him.'

'Yes. No. Not precisely.'

'Mrs Jones said she sent you a message.'

'No. She didn't. I can only assume she sent it to the Magistrate.'

It made sense, sadly. Serena nodded. 'The tragedy with her father made her overly fearful, and now it's all become too much, I'm afraid. Did you know his sister managed to have him sign over control of his funds?'

Mr Moncrief's face paled. 'She didn't! Now that takes the cake. I would wager she sent a message to the Magistrate in my name after she heard I was there that day, to cover her own tracks and make it seem my fault.

'You see, I went to Aleron in an attempt to see Ed again. When I got there, I noticed from the gate what was happening at the fig tree. They had just encouraged him down. I couldn't believe what I'd witnessed, so I crept closer. When Simon Jones saw me, he hurled threats at me, so I ran. But I had learnt enough to know that Ed needs our help more than ever. I have read of new ways to treat people with brain sickness that are more compassionate than current practices. I have searched for any doctors of that kind in Australia, but I have had no luck. He may need to return to England, or even the Americas to find better help.'

It was much to process, but Serena believed him. Caleb Moncrief was the best friend Edward had, even if he didn't know it. But what to do with this new change of facts. Serena ran her fingers over the bumpy nails that fixed the leather to her chair, considering her options. More than anything, she just wanted to see Edward free of the asylum. The rest could be dealt with later. 'So, you agree that we need to get him out of Tarban Creek?'

'Absolutely.' His nod was firm.

'Would you care to join us right now?'

'To go to the asylum?'

'Yes. I'm ready to break him out if I have to.' Remembering her father's rheumatism, she turned to him. 'That is, if you are well enough, Papa.'

Papa chuckled. 'I'm always ready for an adventure. Don't mind me. I'll manage.'

Serena turned to face Mr Moncrief again. 'So?'

Mr Moncrief's mouth curved in an appreciative smile. 'Let's go.'

By the time they pulled up at the entrance to the Tarban Creek Asylum for the Insane, the afternoon had waned. Serena's apprehension had returned, particularly after Mr Moncrief had warned her of what to expect at the hospital.

'The treatment of patients is inhumane to say the least,' he had told her and Papa while deftly guiding his pair of bays around a corner.

'Have you been there?'

'No. I have heard stories, that's all. Since realising that Edward is mentally ill, I took it upon myself to find out everything I can. That's how I learnt of the new treatments available for these patients. I believe they wanted that to happen here, but the medical staff are just not advanced enough in their knowledge, and so, the old ways persist.'

'The old ways?'

Mr Moncrief pressed his lips together in a thin line. 'Just prepare yourself for unpleasant sights and sounds.'

As they entered the two-storied stone building, Serena reflected that Edward would find the simplistic shape rather dull architecturally, and smiled to herself. She had learnt from him, after all. She allowed Mr Moncrief to place the enquiry and used the few moments of waiting to inspect her surroundings, while gripping hard onto Papa's arm. A hallway ran in both directions, the length of the building, with a staircase leading to the upper floor ahead of them. The stairway also led downwards, to a basement she presumed. The rooms nearest them seemed to be offices, or perhaps consulting rooms. Serena could see none of the patients, but the odd cry in the distance met her ears. Involuntarily, she shivered. The sounds a troubled mind could make were eerie indeed.

'Right this way.' The voice of one of the staff broke her from her thoughts. He led them downstairs.

Mr Moncrief whispered to them as they walked. 'They're bringing him to us. They don't want to offend the lady's sensibilities, or break with propriety.' He rolled his eyes. 'More likely they don't want us to see how their patients suffer.'

Not that their path avoided them that distress, anyway. As soon as they descended the bottom step, the smell made Serena want to retch. She covered her nose and mouth as a mixture of stale vomit, unwashed bodies and urine assaulted her. The basement was airless and dim, and here the cries, weeping and growling of various patients were unmistakable, and Serena dug her fingers deeper into her father's arm. He reached over with his other hand and patted hers, giving her minor comfort, although the fetid air soon stirred him into a fit of coughing.

As they made their way through a gloomy hallway past the wards in the male division, Mr Moncrief kept up his spiel of information. 'This place should house up to sixty patients, but is already overcrowded.'

'How many are here?' Serena spoke from behind her handkerchief.

'I think around one hundred.'

She wondered how many patients they crammed into these small rooms. And what accommodations they had. Were they provided with any comforts, or just a bed? What were they fed?

Serena chewed on her lip, uncertain. What condition would Edward be in?

The medic led them into an empty room, a few lamps giving minimal light to their surroundings. Serena hugged herself, even though the chill was only part of what made her cold. She let out a long, slow breath.

A few minutes later another medic wheeled Edward into the room, barely clothed and slumped in a chair, his head hanging low.

Serena gasped. 'Edward!'

Even Papa uttered an oath under his breath.

Serena hurried and knelt at Edward's side, lifting his chin to look into his sunken, empty eyes. 'Oh. Dear God, what have they done to you?'

Edward blinked and slowly focused. 'Serena. You came.' His voice sounded like a rasp on dry wood. Noticing Papa standing close by, he blinked again. 'Mr Bellingham.' Then his eyes flickered to over her right shoulder. 'Caleb?'

'Yes. I'm here too.'

Without warning, Edward started to sob. 'I thought...I thought...'

'Hush,' Mr Moncrief put a hand on his shoulder. 'I'm here. That's all that matters.'

Serena swallowed the ball of emotion rising in her throat. Why hadn't she realised the truth about Moncrief earlier?

'I just want it to be over,' Edward groaned. 'I just want it to be over.'

Mr Moncrief straightened and addressed the medic who stood by. 'What treatments have you given to Mr King?'

The medic cleared his throat. 'Well, er, on admission, we administered a purgative as we do with all patients. He has been prescribed shock treatment—cold showers—to help bring him out of this state of mind. However, he has refused to eat, forcing the need for restraint so we can feed him via tube. And we've given him laudanum, of course.'

Tears sprang to Serena's eyes as she noted the bruises around Edward's wrists, and even across his chest. Hair matted with bile stuck to his cheeks and neck. How could they leave him in such a state? He probably felt as though he'd suffered torture. An ache swelled in Serena's chest. 'We must get him out of here, Papa, Mr Moncrief.'

'I daresay,' agreed Papa, and the young man nodded, concern clearly etched on his face.

'I want it to be over.' Edward continued sobbing.

Serena lifted his chin once again, so she could look straight into his eyes.

'I don't think so, darling. You haven't married me yet.'

Edward blinked and focused on her, although his eyelids drooped and dark rings surrounded them. 'What?'

'You said you wanted to marry me.' She dabbed at his tear-stained cheeks with her handkerchief.

'But you said no.' His eyes searched hers.

'I'm sorry, my love, I didn't know my own mind then.'

'But I am cursed.'

'No, Edward.' Serena blinked back her own tears. 'You are only unwell. And I don't see how that should keep us apart. My mother had the dropsy, and my father suffers from rheumatism, and I still love them. Why shouldn't I love you?'

His lips trembled again. 'You love me?'

'I think it began that night when we toured the house together. Do you remember?' She lifted his cold hand and pressed it to her lips, her tears running over her cheeks and onto his fingers.

'How could I forget?'

A throat-clearing echoed in the room, as Papa drew her attention back to their situation, and lack of privacy.

Serena pulled away from Edward, straightening and mopping at her face. 'We need to take him home.'

Mr Moncrief turned to the medic. 'You heard the lady. This man has a wedding to prepare.'

'I beg pardon, but Mr King is in no condition to go anywhere,' the medic protested.

'Mr King is here against his own, his fiancee's and most of his family's will. In fact, I think you will find he is here under fraudulent circumstances. I suspect my signature was forged on the report to the magistrate.'

'Go before the magistrate and prove it. A patient must not be removed without him signing the authority.'

Mr Moncrief's brow darkened. 'Oh, I'll prove it. But if you do not release this man immediately, the whole of Sydney will learn of the injustices being administered in the name of medicine here.'

The medic smirked. 'Your threats do not intimidate me, sir'

'Perhaps they should.' All eyes swerved to Edward, whose lips twitched into a half smile. 'Do you know who this man is?'

The man shrugged.

'This is Mr Caleb Moncrief of the *Sydney Herald*, and yes, he has the power to cause you very much trouble.'

32

Getting Edward out of the asylum was easier once they'd unleashed the threat of notoriety. Mr Moncrief demanded trousers for his friend and removed his own coat to cover Edward's bare torso. He pushed the chair as far as he could before he and Papa half assisted, half carried Edward between them. Edward's head lolled, and his legs crumpled several times.

Before they reached the front door, Papa's strength waned and he had to let go and rest against the wall, while coughs shook his weakened frame.

'I'm sorry, Papa.' Serena laid a hand on his arm. 'This has been too much for you, hasn't it?'

Recovering his breath, Papa shook his head. 'Don't worry about me, pet. Let's get this young man to safety.'

'Too much laudanum,' Mr Moncrief grunted as he bore the brunt of Edward's weight and they continued.

Finally, they seated him in the carriage, although keeping him upright presented a challenge.

'I'm afraid you must allow Ed to lean on you, Mr Bellingham.'

But one glance at Papa's pale face told them he would have trouble keeping himself upright.

'I'll do it,' Serena offered without hesitation.

It was the only solution. Mr Moncrief needed his arms free to drive. Serena remembered the night she fell asleep against

Edward's shoulder. He had not complained about that. The least she could do was return the favour. She climbed up next to him and Mr Moncrief let him go. Edward slumped against her, hardly conscious, his head heavy on her shoulder, while Papa rode in the front with Mr Moncrief. The pungent smell of bile met her nose, but she forced herself to ignore it. 'What will we do with him?' Serena worried her lip.

'If the situation at Aleron is as you said, I don't think it wise to take him home as yet. We'll take him to my place.'

'I'm not sure that is suitable, Mr Moncrief. How will you care for him when you must work?'

'She's right,' Edward murmured, coming around a little. 'Better take me home.'

'All is well, old man.' Mr Moncrief grinned over his shoulder. 'I got myself leg-shackled two years ago. I wanted you to stand up with me, but I could not get past Mrs Jones.' His eyes flickered with disappointment, but then he shifted his gaze to Serena. 'I think you and my wife will get along rather well, Miss Bellingham. And she is more than capable of nursing Ed.'

An oath spluttered from Edward's lips and he raised his head a little. 'My sister. She never mentioned it.'

'Not surprising.' Mr Moncrief shrugged. 'She told me you never wanted to see me again.'

Edward groaned. 'I should have known. She told me you wanted to ruin me once you knew about the curse. And I never questioned her.' He groaned again. 'What a fool I have been. I wish I had been there on your wedding day. Congratulations.'

'We also'—and this time he winked—'have a recent addition.'

Edward swore again, then erupted in a fit of coughing, and Serena tried to soothe him.

'Surely, we will be an imposition then, Mr Moncrief. Although I offer felicitations.' Serena didn't want to sound ungrateful.

'If you think that, then you underestimate my Francine.' Mr Moncrief raised his eyebrows. He seemed to enjoy meting out surprises on his old friend.

'Boy or girl?' Edward rasped.

'I have a son, his name is Edmond, and you can be his token uncle, all right, old man?'

At last, Edward's mouth curved slightly. 'It would be my pleasure.'

At Mr Moncrief's home, Serena was left to her own devices for a time as Mr Moncrief set about bathing Edward and putting him into bed, while Papa napped on the sofa in their parlour. Mrs Moncrief was more than accommodating with a welcome that was enthusiastic to say the least, and bustled about fetching water and clothing. Later, Mrs Moncrief confided to Serena that she had worried over her husband's estrangement from Edward, even though she'd never met the latter. She'd perceived that the broken friendship grieved her husband greatly and prayed for its restoration. It thrilled the rosy-cheeked new mother to harbour Edward under her roof for as long as needed.

The couple's home was modest, but comfortable, and little Edmond crawled around after his mother in plump gorgeousness. When at last Serena tore her eyes away from the beautiful, blue-eyed child with his gurgling laughter, she noted that several paintings decorated their walls. Some contained depictions of roses and Serena stepped closer to inspect them. As suspected, they bore Edward's mark.

It was such a shame she had never endeavoured to speak to Mr Moncrief all these months, just taking Mrs Jones's word as truth. How different circumstances might have been if she'd taken the time to listen.

When Mr Moncrief emerged from Edward's room, closing the door behind him, she sighed. 'All of this might have been avoided.'

Mr Moncrief shook his head and smiled. 'There's no sense in berating yourself. You weren't to know. What's done is done. We need to look to the future now.'

'Yes, I suppose you're right.'

Her father stirred and glanced at the clock on the parlour wall. 'The hour is growing late. I probably should take you home, pet.'

Home. Serena hadn't thought of her sisters all day. Now that Papa mentioned it, she did feel rather tired. And hungry. But she didn't want to leave Edward. 'I need to see him. There are so many things...'

Mr Moncrief put a hand on her shoulder. 'I understand. But, they gave him too much laudanum, and he's barely eaten in days. It sounds like the tubes they forced down have damaged his throat, too. Ed won't be well enough to talk properly for a couple of days. I daresay he'll sleep for much of that time. Let my wife give you both supper and then you may go home to rest. I shan't keep you from seeing Ed when you return.'

Serena knew Mr Moncrief spoke wisdom, even though she didn't want to hear it. If it hadn't been improper, she would have curled up on the floor next to Edward's bed until he was well again. She let her head drop forward and scuffed a shoe on the floor, but then nodded her consent. This would be the longest few days of her life.

At home, after telling her sisters all that had transpired, Julianne handed Serena a message from Mr Xavier Jones.

'When did this arrive?'

'A couple hours ago, by courier,' Julianne answered.

Serena tore the seal open and read.

> *Miss Bellingham,*
>
> *I and my brother, Father and Mr Becker have written accounts to support Uncle Edward's character. I will present these to the magistrate first thing in the morning.*
>
> *Please reply with news of your efforts today. I am eager to learn of Moncrief and his involvement. Have you been to see Uncle Ed? I yearn to know how he progresses. You may reply by return courier at our expense.*
>
> *Sincerely,*
>
> *Xavier Jones.*

Poor Mr Xavier. He must feel the affront of what his mother had inflicted upon Edward. Serena excused herself from her family, promising to return anon, and went to her room to write back to Mr Xavier. Although exhausted after a long and emotional day, she filled several pages with her account since leaving Aleron House, explaining the surprising news of Mr Moncrief's friendship with Edward. She finished with the information that Edward convalesced at Mr Moncrief's home if Mr Xavier wanted to call on him. Hopefully, Mr Moncrief would have the grace to permit him entry.

As Mr Moncrief suggested, Serena waited two days before returning to his house—two days that passed with interminable slowness. Although she busied herself constantly—even scrubbing the walls—the time dragged.

When at last the time came to go, Serena pulled out the gown that Edward had purchased for her, taking time to dress in the beautiful blue silk. Although it was an evening gown, it was the best garment she owned, and she wanted Edward to see her in the gift. Julianne and Rachel helped her fasten the dress, fussing to make sure it sat right. Julianne then styled her hair into a high knot with several golden curls tumbling down her shoulders. She finished off with a dab of musk behind her ears.

'You look like you're off to a ball, not to a man's sick bed,' Rachel giggled.

Julianne offered a knowing smile. 'But you've never been in love, so you wouldn't understand.' She cuffed Rachel gently on the cheek. Turning to Serena, she leaned in and kissed her. 'Mr King will adore you.'

Serena squeezed her hand before pulling the soft velvet pelisse tight around her shoulders. Her heart was in her throat as nerves danced a jig in her stomach. She stopped in the parlour on her way to the door where Papa sat reading the newspaper. He gasped softly when he saw her.

'How lovely you look, my sweet.' He rose with a grimace of pain.

'Don't get up, Papa. I can see myself out.'

Acquiescent, he lowered himself back down. 'Come here and kiss me then.'

Serena smiled and leaned to brush her lips on his cheek. 'I'm hoping to return properly betrothed, Papa.'

He looked at her, head to one side.

'Edward—Mr King—would probably like to ask your permission first, but he is not up to the task. May I ask on his behalf for your blessing?'

Papa's shoulders shook in silent laughter. 'Of course. Tell

him that I give my whole-hearted approval of this match.'

'Thank you, Papa.' She kissed his cheek a second time.

Half an hour later, she knocked tentatively on Mr Moncrief's door, the jig in her stomach having become a whirlwind. Serena didn't have to wait long before Mrs Moncrief answered the door with little Edmond on her hip, and gave her entry, bidding her wait in the parlour.

Mr Moncrief soon joined her with a welcoming smile on his face.

'How is Mr King?' Serena asked as soon as the pleasantries were exchanged.

'As I suspected, he slept most of the time, and was not enormously sensible in the moments he was awake. He often weeps. He kept repeating the words, "he heard me," and I'm sure I don't know what that's about. But, he seems much calmer this morning and has, in fact, been asking for you.'

'He has?' Serena's heart fluttered so powerfully she felt light-headed for a moment.

'Yes. We have had quite the catch up this morning.' Mr Moncrief could not hide his contentment.

'Does he understand what has happened?'

Mr Moncrief nodded. 'For the most part, I think so.'

'May I see him now?' Serena needed to get this over with so she could breathe normally again.

'Of course. I shall send him to you.'

'Oh.' Serena had expected to sit by the invalid's bed. Edward had been so weak when they had taken him from the asylum.

Her heart was still thumping in her throat and neck minutes later when footsteps sounded outside the room and Edward stepped in. Serena stood to her feet, wanting to run and throw her arms around him. Instead she pressed her hands hard against her stomach, fighting the urge to cry or giggle or faint. She drew in a shaky breath as far as possible and let it out slowly.

'Serena.' He stretched his hands out toward her. 'How beautiful you look. Broughton is an exceptional dressmaker, is he not?'

She stepped forward and put her hands in his, blinking traitorous tears away. Edward looked so much better. His eyes were still ringed with shadow, but there was a faint light in them now. What to say? Where to start?

'Did I imagine it, or did an angel meet me in that purgatory and agree to marry me?' The hope in his eyes was unmistakable.

A wobbly laugh burst from her. 'I would never claim to be an angel, but you did not imagine the rest.'

'Oh, but you are.' The gravity in his voice was unwavering. 'My angel. I love you so, Serena.'

'And I love you, my darling Edward.'

He put a stop to anything else she might say by pulling her into his arms and pressing his warm lips firmly on her mouth. Was it possible that his kiss could turn her upside down so? And yet she was spinning, falling, into a dream of bliss. A dream from which she never wanted to wake.

Eventually, he drew back, and gazed into her eyes. 'Sit with me.' Edward drew her to a small sofa where they sat together, still holding hands, the warmth from his clasp reaching her heart. 'I need to ask you again, if you are certain you want to marry someone who is cursed as I am.'

A bubble of frustration rose within Serena. Why could he not let this go? 'It is not a curse, Edward. You have an illness, and yes, I will marry you with that illness. I suspect your sister has encouraged you to believe the curse was real. But it's not. Mr

Moncrief and your own diary can attest to that. Did you never read back over your journal?'

Edward's brows lowered. 'Do you mean to say you've read my journal?'

Serena opened and closed her mouth, sudden guilt assaulting her. He must feel violated. She squeezed Edward's hand, apologetic. 'Only because I wanted to understand. And if I hadn't, we would never have uncovered your sister's duplicity.'

He let go of her hand and stood, pacing away from her, at war with his own feelings. 'I never read back over it. It was private. My deepest thoughts. Things I could not express to others for fear they would condemn me as a lunatic.' Edward ran a hand through his hair. 'Although that ended up happening, anyway.'

Serena moved to him and placed her hands on his cool cheeks. 'You need not fear that from me. I have read it all and I still promise to join my life with yours.'

Edward turned and looked at her, studying her face. 'You really love me, despite the curse.'

'Yes, but—'

'But there is no curse.' Mr Moncrief stood in the doorway, hands thrust in his pockets. When they both started, he explained. 'I'm sorry. I was coming to see if you would like tea, but overheard this tripe about a curse, Ed.'

'It's not tripe.'

'It is indeed.' Mr Moncrief entered the room and sat. 'You and I spoke the day after you met with the monk, don't you remember?'

Edward shook his head, but looked in doubt.

'You spent hours having theological and philosophical debates with him. In the end, he told you that you were too

251

closed-minded and lost in your own pride. I suspect he got fed up with your high-minded, I'm-smarter-than-everybody-else attitude and gave you the cold, hard truth.'

'And what truth is that?' Edward pressed his lips into a grim line.

'*That pride goeth before destruction, and a haughty spirit before a fall*. It's a verse from Proverbs, and *not a curse*. The monk told you that you needed to stop fighting the truth and acknowledge God as the giver of your gifts.'

Edward remained silent.

'The earliest entries in your journal that mention this say the same thing. No mention of a curse,' Serena added.

Edward looked like he wanted to argue, but defeat—or perhaps resignation—dulled his fight. He released a long sigh. 'It's a funny thing. Since I've met you, Serena, I have been thinking about God more. You have such confidence in what you believe, and you live according to it. It made me question everything I had assumed. I know I argued with you like a pompous fool.' He drew in a deep breath and swallowed hard. 'Just before ... just before I tried to ... end it, I challenged God to save me if he could. I was done fighting. When Simon and Xavier stopped me at the tree, I thought little of it. But when you two came to Bedlam Point, I knew it. He heard me.' Edward looked at them both, with tears brimming in his eyes. 'He heard me.'

Serena and Mr Moncrief exchanged a knowing glance.

'So, no more talk of a curse then, old man. Are we agreed?'

'There is no curse?'

'None at all,' Serena assured him with a gentle touch to his forearm.

Edward sank onto the nearest chair. 'I'm free?'

'In more ways than one.' Mr Moncrief winked.

'It seems so simple. Too simple.' Edward shook his head.

'We all make life more complicated than it needs to be sometimes. I am guilty of the same.'

'Me, too,' agreed Serena, sitting beside Edward. 'I had myself in a turmoil thinking my family couldn't survive without me. It was all vanity—thinking more of myself than I ought.'

Edward turned to her and clasped her hands. 'And I took you from them in my selfishness. Will they ever forgive me?'

'It is already done,' Serena giggled. 'Papa has even given his consent to our marriage.'

'Speaking of which,' Mr Moncrief slapped his thighs and stood. 'I'm sure you two have some planning to do. Shall I fetch some tea?'

'Tea would be wonderful.'

With a nod, the young man departed and Serena had Edward to herself again.

Serena bit on her lip as she looked into his eyes. 'I never dreamt I would have the happiness of planning my wedding. But, here we are.'

'Yes, we are. However, I must speak to you about something.' Edward drew her to her feet and clasped her hands.

'What is it?' Serena searched his eyes.

'That last day on the beach,' he ducked his head momentarily, scuffing at an imaginary lump on the floor. 'I am not that man. I am not a fiend. Can you ever forgive me?' He raised his face again, and held her gaze with his plea written in its depths.

Serena reached up and stroked a strand of his hair away from his brow, as all the love she possessed pooled in her eyes.

'I know you are not a fiend. You are the man I love. A man who is exuberant and loyal and generous and very gifted.'

'And you are the sweetest, most unselfish, loving woman I could be blessed to have as my wife. With just the right amount of impertinence.' He gave her a sly wink.

Serena almost snorted. 'Beast.'

'Perhaps. But only a little,' he murmured as he lowered his lips to hers in a kiss that promised many more to come.

33

Sunday 25th September, 1842

Yesterday, my bride stood beside me at the altar and we exchanged our vows. She indeed looked like the angel I often call her.

Through her, I found my healing. I stood, for the first time in many years, as a whole man, fully present in my mind. All along, Providence had his hand upon me, as I have discovered just as the Psalmist did.

'So foolish was I, and ignorant: I was as a beast before thee. Nevertheless I am continually with thee: thou hast holden me by my right hand.'

Serena and I married in the church, then celebrated in a gazebo with whitewashed columns and arches, which I built for her on the shore.

Our families surrounded us, offering their love and congratulations. Judith was subdued, but she has turned a corner and has now accepted that Serena and I are pledged to one another. She is slowly coming to accept I am not the source of her ruin, nor am I the source of her security. And I in turn have slowly learnt to forgive her. Serena and Caleb have shown me that holding bitterness against her will achieve nothing.

Caleb stood beside me yesterday, grinning like a school lad. I am eternally grateful for his friendship to me these years, even when I was no friend to him. It was a day I shall hold dearly for the rest of my life.

This morning, my wife and I will to go to church and then we shall leave for our wedding tour. We shall be gone a long while. To the Holy Land where Serena can see the places of the Bible and I shall see the incredible architecture of a millenia ago.

Enough, she is awaking, her golden smile drawing me away from these pages, and I would not resist her for the world. She is, and will ever be, my angel.

AUTHOR'S NOTE

Thank you for reading *Unhinged*, and I do hope you have enjoyed Edward and Serena's journey. Mental Health is such a widespread struggle in our society today, but it still holds a stigma of shame, even with the better understanding and treatments available in our day and age.

For the purposes of a Beauty and the Beast story, I have 'magically' allowed Edward to become whole. Sadly, for many people who struggle with mental health issues, the battle is an ongoing, lifelong one.

I do not wish to trivialise mental illness, even though I do believe that God can heal. The best approach seems to be to seek medical help, counselling and combine that with a spiritual journey of faith.

If you, or someone around you suffers with mental health problems, such as depression or anxiety, the best first step is to seek help. This can be from your GP or a mental health support agency such as Beyond Blue- www.beyondblue.org.au.